George Eliot's Home, Foleshill Road, Coventry.
ESSAYS

ESSAYS AND LEAVES
FROM A NOTE BOOK

BY

GEORGE ELIOT

ILLUSTRATED

LITTLE, BROWN, AND COMPANY
BOSTON

CONTENTS.

PREFACE.

WISHES have often been expressed that the articles known to have been written by George Eliot in the "Westminster Review" before she had become famous under that pseudonym, should be republished. Those wishes are now gratified—as far, at any rate, as it is possible to gratify them. For it was not George Eliot's desire that the whole of those articles should be rescued from oblivion. And in order that there might be no doubt on the subject, she made some time before her death a collection of such of her fugitive writings as she considered deserving of a permanent form; carefully revised them for the press; and left them, in the order in which they here appear, with written injunctions that no other pieces written by her, of date prior to 1857, should be republished.

It will thus be seen that the present collection of Essays has the weight of her sanction, and has had, moreover, the advantage of such corrections and alterations as a revision long subsequent to the period of writing may have suggested to her.

The opportunity afforded by this republication seemed a suitable one for giving to the world some "notes," as George Eliot simply called them, which belong to a much later period, and which have not been previously published. The exact date of their writing cannot be fixed with any certainty, but it must have been some time between the appearance of "Middlemarch" and that of "Theophrastus Such." They were probably written without any distinct view to publication— some of them for the satisfaction of her own mind; others perhaps as memoranda, and with an idea of working them out more fully at some later time. It may be of interest to know that, besides the "notes" here given, the note-book contains four which appeared in "Theophrastus Such," three of them practically as they there stand; and it is not impossible that some of those in the present volume might also have been so utilized had they not happened to fall outside the general scope of the work. The marginal titles are George Eliot's own, but for the general title, "Leaves from a Note-Book," I am responsible.

I need only add that, in publishing these notes, I have the complete concurrence of my friend Mr. Cross.

CHARLES LEE LEWES.

HIGHGATE, *December* 1883.

ESSAYS.

WORLDLINESS AND OTHER-WORLDLINESS: THE POET YOUNG.

THE study of men, as they have appeared in different ages, and under various social conditions, may be considered as the natural history of the race. Let us, then, for a moment imagine ourselves, as students of this natural history, "dredging" the first half of the eighteenth century in search of specimens. About the year 1730 we have hauled up a remarkable individual of the species *divine*—a surprising name, considering the nature of the animal before us; but we are used to unsuitable names in natural history. Let us examine this individual at our leisure. He is on the verge of fifty, and has recently undergone his metamorphosis into the clerical form. Rather a paradoxical specimen, if you observe him narrowly: a sort of cross between a sycophant and a psalmist; a poet whose imagination is alternately fired by the "Last Day" and by a creation of peers, who fluctuates between rhapsodic applause of King George and rhapsodic applause of Jehovah. After spending "a foolish youth, the sport of peers and poets," after being a hanger-on of the profligate Duke of Wharton, after aiming in vain at a parliamentary career, and angling for pensions and preferment with fulsome dedications and fustian odes, he is a little disgusted with his imperfect success, and has determined to retire from the general mendicancy business to a particular branch; in other words, he has determined on that renunciation of the world implied in "taking orders," with the prospect of a good living and an advantageous matrimonial connection. And he personifies the nicest

balance of temporalities and spiritualities. He is equally impressed with the momentousness of death and of burial fees;
he languishes at once for immortal life and for "livings"; he
has a fervid attachment to patrons in general, but on the whole
prefers the Almighty. He will teach, with something more
than official conviction, the nothingness of earthly things; and
he will feel something more than private disgust if his meritorious efforts in directing men's attention to another world are
not rewarded by substantial preferment in this. His secular
man believes in cambric bands and silk stockings as characteristic attire for "an ornament of religion and virtue"; hopes
courtiers will never forget to copy Sir Robert Walpole; and
writes begging-letters to the King's mistress. His spiritual
man recognizes no motives more familiar than Golgotha and
"the skies"; it walks in graveyards, or it soars among the
stars. His religion exhausts itself in ejaculations and rebukes,
and knows no medium between the ecstatic and the sententious.
If it were not for the prospect of immortality, he considers,
it would be wise and agreeable to be indecent, or to murder
one's father; and, heaven apart, it would be extremely irrational in any man not to be a knave. Man, he thinks, is a compound of the angel and the brute: the brute is to be humbled
by being reminded of its "relation to the stalls," and frightened
into moderation by the contemplation of death-beds and skulls;
the angel is to be developed by vituperating this world and ex-
alting the next; and by this double process you get the Christian—"the highest style of man." With all this, our new-
made divine is an unmistakable poet. To a clay compounded
chiefly of the worldling and the rhetorician, there is added a
real spark of Promethean fire. He will one day clothe his
apostrophes and objurgations, his astronomical religion and his
charnel-house morality, in lasting verse, which will stand, like
a Juggernaut made of gold and jewels, at once magnificent and
repulsive: for this divine is Edward Young, the future author
of the "Night Thoughts."

Judging from Young's works, one might imagine that the
preacher had been organized in him by hereditary transmission through a long line of clerical forefathers,—that the dia-
monds of the "Night Thoughts" had been slowly condensed

from the charcoal of ancestral sermons. Yet it was not so. His grandfather, apparently, wrote himself *gentleman*, not *clerk;* and there is no evidence that preaching had run in the family blood before it took that turn in the person of the poet's father, who was quadruply clerical, being at once rector, prebendary, court chaplain, and dean. Young was born at his father's rectory of Upham, in 1681. In due time the boy went to Winchester College, and subsequently, though not till he was twenty-two, to Oxford, where, for his father's sake, he was befriended by the wardens of two colleges, and in 1708, three years after his father's death, nominated by Archbishop Tenison to a law fellowship at All Souls. Of Young's life at Oxford in these years, hardly anything is known. His biographer, Croft, has nothing to tell us but the vague report that, when "Young found himself independent and his own master at All Souls, he was not the ornament to religion and morality that he afterward became," and the perhaps apocryphal anecdote, that Tindal, the atheist, confessed himself embarrassed by the originality of Young's arguments. Both the report and the anecdote, however, are borne out by indirect evidence. As to the latter, Young has left us sufficient proof that he was fond of arguing on the theological side, and that he had his own way of treating old subjects. As to the former, we learn that Pope, after saying other things which we know to be true of Young, added, that he passed "a foolish youth, the sport of peers and poets"; and, from all the indications we possess of his career till he was nearly fifty, we are inclined to think that Pope's statement only errs by defect, and that he should rather have said, "a foolish youth and *middle age.*" It is not likely that Young was a very hard student, for he impressed Johnson, who saw him in his old age, as "not a great scholar," and as surprisingly ignorant of what Johnson thought "quite common maxims" in literature; and there is no evidence that he filled either his leisure or his purse by taking pupils. His career as an author did not begin till he was nearly thirty, even dating from the publication of a portion of the "Last Day," in the *Tatler;* so that he could hardly have been absorbed in composition. But where the fully developed insect is parasitic, we believe the larva is usually parasitic also, and we shall probably not be far wrong in supposing that Young at Oxford, as elsewhere, spent a good deal of his time in hanging about possible and actual patrons, and accommodating himself to their habits with considerable flexibility of conscience and of tongue; being none the less ready, upon occasion, to present himself as the champion of theology, and to rhapsodize at convenient moments in the company of the skies or of skulls. That brilliant profligate, the Duke of Wharton, to whom Young afterward clung as his chief patron, was at this time a mere boy; and, though it is probable that their intimacy had already begun, since the Duke's father and mother were friends of the old Dean, that intimacy ought not to aggravate any unfavorable inference as to Young's Oxford life. It is less likely that he fell into any exceptional vice, than that he differed from the men around him chiefly in his episodes of theological advocacy and rhapsodic solemnity. He probably sowed his wild oats after the coarse fashion of his times, for he has left us sufficient evidence that his moral sense was not delicate; but his companions, who were occupied in sowing their own oats, perhaps took it as a matter of course that he should be a rake, and were only struck with the exceptional circumstance that he was a pious and moralizing rake.

There is some irony in the fact that the two first poetical productions of Young, published in the same year, were his "Epistle to Lord Lansdowne," celebrating the recent creation of peers—Lord Lansdowne's creation in particular; and the "Last Day." Other poets, besides Young, found the device for obtaining a Tory majority by turning twelve insignificant commoners into insignificant lords, an irresistible stimulus to verse; but no other poet showed so versatile an enthusiasm— so nearly equal an ardor for the honor of the new baron and the honor of the Deity. But the twofold nature of the sycophant and the psalmist is not more strikingly shown in the contrasted themes of the two poems, than in the transitions from bombast about monarchs, to bombast about the resurrection, in the "Last Day" itself. The dedication of this poem to Queen Anne, Young afterward suppressed, for he was always ashamed of having flattered a dead patron. In this dedication, Croft tells us, "he gives her Majesty praise indeed for her victories, but says that the author is more pleased to see her rise from this lower world, soaring above the clouds, passing the first and second heavens, and leaving the fixed stars behind her; nor will he lose her there, he says, but keep her still in view through the boundless spaces on the other side of creation, in her journey toward eternal bliss, till he behold the heaven of heavens open, and angels receiving and conveying her still onward from the stretch of his imagination, which tires in her pursuit, and falls back again to earth."

The self-criticism which prompted the suppression of the dedication, did not, however, lead him to improve either the rhyme or the reason of the unfortunate couplet,—

> "When other Bourbons reign in other lands,
> And, if men's sins forbid not, other Annes."

In the "Epistle to Lord Lansdowne," Young indicates his taste for the drama; and there is evidence that his tragedy of "Busiris" was "in the theatre" as early as this very year, 1713, though it was not brought on the stage till nearly six years later; so that Young was now very decidedly bent on authorship, for which his degree of B.C.L., taken in this year, was doubtless a magical equipment. Another poem, "The Force of Religion; or, Vanquished Love," founded on the execution of Lady Jane Grey and her husband, quickly followed, showing fertility in feeble and tasteless verse; and on the Queen's death, in 1714, Young lost no time in making a poetical lament for a departed patron a vehicle for extravagant laudation of the new monarch. No further literary production of his appeared until 1716, when a Latin oration which he delivered on the foundation of the Codrington Library at All Souls, gave him a new opportunity for displaying his alacrity in inflated panegyric.

In 1717 it is probable that Young accompanied the Duke of Wharton to Ireland, though so slender are the materials for his biography, that the chief basis for this supposition is a passage in his "Conjectures on Original Composition," written when he was nearly eighty, in which he intimates that he had once been in that country. But there are many facts surviv-

ing to indicate that for the next eight or nine years Young
was a sort of *attaché* of Wharton's.   In 1719, according to
legal records, the Duke granted him an annuity, in consideration of his having relinquished the office of tutor to Lord Bur-
leigh, with a life annuity of £100 a year, on his Grace's as-
surances that he would provide for him in a much more ample
manner.   And again, from the same evidence, it appears that
in 1721 Young received from Wharton a bond for £600, in
compensation of expenses incurred in standing for Parliament
at the Duke's desire, and as an earnest of greater services
which his Grace had promised him on his refraining from the
spiritual and temporal advantages of taking orders with a certainty of two livings in the gift of his college.   It is clear,
therefore, that lay advancement, as long as there was any
chance of it, had more attractions for Young than clerical
preferment; and that at this time he accepted the Duke of
Wharton as the pilot of his career.

A more creditable relation of Young's was his friendship
with Tickell, with whom he was in the habit of interchanging
criticisms, and to whom in 1719—the same year, let us note,
in which he took his doctor's degree—he addressed his "Lines
on the Death of Addison."   Close upon these followed his
"Paraphrase of Part of the Book of Job," with a dedication
to Parker, recently made Lord Chancellor, showing that the
possession of Wharton's patronage did not prevent Young from
fishing in other waters.   He knew nothing of Parker, but that
did not prevent him from magnifying the new Chancellor's
merits; on the other hand, he *did* know Wharton, but this
again did not prevent him from prefixing to his tragedy, "The
Revenge," which appeared in 1721, a dedication attributing
to the Duke all virtues, as well as all accomplishments.   In
the concluding sentence of this dedication, Young naïvely
indicates that a considerable ingredient in his gratitude was
a lively sense of anticipated favors.   "My present fortune
is his bounty, and my future his care; which I will venture
to say will always be remembered to his honor; since he, I
know, intended his generosity as an encouragement to merit,
though, through his very pardonable partiality to one who
bears him so sincere a duty and respect, I happen to receive

the benefit of it." Young was economical with his ideas and images; he was rarely satisfied with using a clever thing once, and this bit of ingenious humility was afterward made to do duty in the "Instalment," a poem addressed to Walpole:—

> "Be this thy partial smile, from censure free,
> 'Twas meant for merit, though it fell on me."

It was probably "The Revenge" that Young was writing when, as we learn from Spence's "Anecdotes," the Duke of Wharton gave him a skull with a candle fixed in it, as the most appropriate lamp by which to write tragedy. According to Young's dedication, the Duke was "accessory" to the scenes of this tragedy in a more important way, "not only by suggesting the most beautiful incident in them, but by making all possible provision for the success of the whole." A statement which is credible, not indeed on the ground of Young's dedicatory assertion, but from the known ability of the Duke, who, as Pope tells us, possessed

> "Each gift of Nature and of Art,
> And wanted nothing but an honest heart."

The year 1722 seems to have been the period of a visit to Mr. Dodington, at Eastbury, in Dorsetshire—the "pure Dorsetian downs" celebrated by Thomson,—in which Young made the acquaintance of Voltaire; for in the subsequent dedication of his "Sea Piece" to "Mr. Voltaire," he recalls their meeting on Dorset Downs; and it was in this year that Christopher Pitt, a gentleman-poet of those days, addressed an "Epistle to Dr. Edward Young, at Eastbury, in Dorsetshire," which has at least the merit of this biographical couplet,—

> "While with your Dodington retired you sit,
> Charm'd with his flowing Burgundy and wit."

Dodington, apparently, was charmed in his turn, for he told Dr. Warton that Young was "far superior to the French poet in the variety and novelty of his *bonmots* and repartees." Unfortunately, the only specimen of Young's wit on this occasion that has been preserved to us is the epigram represented as an

extempore retort (spoken aside, surely) to Voltaire's criticism
of Milton's episode of Sin and Death :—

> "Thou art so witty, profligate, and thin,
>   At once we think thee Milton, Death, and Sin";

an epigram which, in the absence of "flowing Burgundy,"
does not strike us as remarkably brilliant.   Let us give Young
the benefit of the doubt thrown on the genuineness of this epigram by his own poetical dedication, in which he represents
himself as having "soothed" Voltaire's "rage" against Milton
"with gentle rhymes"; though in other respects that dedication is anything but favorable to a high estimate of Young's
wit.   Other evidence apart, we should not be eager for the
after-dinner conversation of the man who wrote,—

> "Thine is the Drama, how renown'd !
>   Thine Epic's loftier trump to sound ;—
>   *But let Arion's sea-strung harp be mine :*
>   *But where's his dolphin ? Know'st thou where ?*
>   *May that be found in thee, Voltaire !* "

The "Satires" appeared in 1725 and 1726, each, of course,
with its laudatory dedication and its compliments insinuated
amongst the rhymes.   The seventh and last is dedicated to
Sir Robert Walpole, is very short, and contains nothing in
particular except lunatic flattery of George I. and his prime
minister, attributing that monarch's late escape from a storm
at sea to the miraculous influence of his grand and virtuous
soul—for George, he says, rivals the angels :—

> "George, who in foes can soft affections raise,
>   And charm envenomed satire into praise.
>   Nor human rage alone his pow'r perceives,
>   But the mad winds and the tumultuous waves.
>   Ev'n storms (Death's fiercest ministers !) forbear,
>   And in their own wild empire learn to spare.
>   Thus, Nature's self, supporting Man's decree,
>   Styles Britain's sovereign, sovereign of the sea."

As for Walpole, what *he* felt at this tremendous crisis—

> "No powers of language, but his own, can tell,—
>   His own, which Nature and the Graces form,
>   At will, to raise, or hush, the civil storm."

It is a coincidence worth noticing, that this seventh Satire was published in 1726, and that the warrant of George I., granting Young a pension of £200 a year from Lady-day 1725, is dated May 3, 1726. The gratitude exhibited in this Satire may have been chiefly prospective, but the "Instalment" —a poem inspired by the thrilling event of Walpole's installation as Knight of the Garter—was clearly written with the double ardor of a man who has got a pension, and hopes for something more. His emotion about Walpole is precisely at the same pitch as his subsequent emotion about the Second Advent. In the "Instalment" he says:—

> "With invocations some their hearts inflame ;
> *I need no muse, a Walpole is my theme.*"

And of God coming to judgment, he says, in the "Night Thoughts":—

> "I find my inspiration in my theme ;
> *The grandeur of my subject is my muse.*"

Nothing can be feebler than this "Instalment," except in the strength of impudence with which the writer professes to scorn the prostitution of fair fame, the "profanation of celestial fire."

Herbert Croft tells us that Young made more than three thousand pounds by his "Satires,"—a surprising statement, taken in connection with the reasonable doubt he throws on the story related in Spence's "Anecdotes," that the Duke of Wharton gave Young £2,000 for this work. Young, however, seems to have been tolerably fortunate in the pecuniary results of his publications; and with his literary profits, his annuity from Wharton, his fellowship, and his pension, not to mention other bounties which may be inferred from the high merits he discovers in many men of wealth and position, we may fairly suppose that he now laid the foundation of the considerable fortune he left at his death.

It is probable that the Duke of Wharton's final departure for the Continent and disgrace at Court in 1726, and the consequent cessation of Young's reliance on his patronage, tended not only to heighten the temperature of his poetical enthu-

siasm for Sir Robert Walpole, but also to turn his thoughts
toward the Church again, as the second-best means of rising
in the world.   On the accession of George II., Young found
the same transcendent merits in him as in his predecessor,
and celebrated them in a style of poetry previously unat-
tempted by him—the Pindaric ode, a poetic form which helped
him to surpass himself in furious bombast.   "Ocean, an Ode:
concluding with a Wish," was the title of this piece.   He
afterward pruned it, and cut off, amongst other things, the
concluding Wish, expressing the yearning for humble retire-
ment, which, of course, had prompted him to the effusion; but
we may judge of the rejected stanzas by the quality of those
he has allowed to remain.   For example, calling on Britain's
dead mariners to rise and meet their "country's full-blown
glory" in the person of the new King, he says:—

> "What powerful charm
> Can Death disarm?
> Your long, your iron slumbers break?
> *By Jove, by Fame,*
> *By George's name*
> Awake! awake! awake! awake!"

Soon after this notable production, which was written with
the ripe folly of forty-seven, Young took orders, and was presently appointed chaplain to the King.   "The Brothers," his
third and last tragedy, which was already in rehearsal, he now
withdrew from the stage, and sought reputation in a way
more accordant with the decorum of his new profession, by
turning prose-writer.   But after publishing "A True Estimate of Human Life," with a dedication to the Queen, as one
of the "most shining representatives" of God on earth, and
a sermon, entitled "An Apology for Princes; or, the Reverence due to Government," preached before the House of Commons, his Pindaric ambition again seized him, and he matched
his former ode by another, called "Imperium Pelagi; a Naval
Lyric, written in Imitation of Pindar's spirit, occasioned by
his Majesty's Return from Hanover, 1729, and the succeeding
Peace."   Since he afterward suppressed this second ode, we
must suppose that it was rather worse than the first.   Next
came his two "Epistles to Pope, concerning the Authors of the

Age," remarkable for nothing but the audacity of affectation with which the most servile of poets professes to despise servility.

In 1730, Young was presented by his college with the rectory of Welwyn, in Hertfordshire; and in the following year, when he was just fifty, he married Lady Elizabeth Lee, a widow with two children, who seems to have been in favor with Queen Caroline, and who probably had an income—two attractions which doubtless enhanced the power of her other charms. Pastoral duties and domesticity probably cured Young of some bad habits; but, unhappily, they did not cure him either of flattery or of fustian. Three more odes followed, quite as bad as those of his bachelorhood, except that in the third he announced the wise resolution of never writing another. It must have been about this time, since Young was now "turned of fifty," that he wrote the letter to Mrs. Howard (afterward Lady Suffolk), George II.'s mistress, which proves that he used other engines, besides the Pindaric, in "besieging Court favor." The letter is too characteristic to be omitted :—

" Monday Morning.

"MADAM,—I know his majesty's goodness to his servants, and his love of justice in general, so well, that I am confident, if his majesty knew my case, I should not have any cause to despair of his gracious favor to me.

"Abilities.	Want.	
Good Manners.	Sufferings	} for his
Service.	and	majesty.
Age.	Zeal	}

These, madam, are the proper points of consideration in the person that humbly hopes his majesty's favor.

"As to *Abilities,* all I can presume to say is, I have done the best I could to improve them.

"As to *Good Manners,* I desire no favor, if any just objection lies against them.

"As for *Service,* I have been near seven years in his majesty's, and never omitted any duty in it, which few can say.

"As for *Age,* I am turned of fifty.

"As for *Want,* I have no manner of preferment.

"As for *Sufferings,* I have lost £300 per ann. by being in his majesty's service; as I have shown in a *Representation* which his majesty has been so good as to read and consider.

2

"As for *Zeal*, I have written nothing without showing my duty to their majesties, and some pieces are dedicated to them.

"This, madam, is the short and true state of my case. They that make their court to the ministers, and not their majesties, succeed better. If my case deserves some consideration, and you can serve me in it, I humbly hope and believe you will: I shall, therefore, trouble you no farther; but beg leave to subscribe myself, with truest respect and gratitude, yours, &c.   EDWARD YOUNG.

"*P.S.*—I have some hope that my Lord Townshend is my friend; if therefore soon and before he leaves the court, you had an opportunity of mentioning me, with that favor you have been so good to show, I think it would not fail of success; and, if not, I shall owe you more than any." —*Suffolk Letters*, vol. i. p. 285.

Young's wife died in 1741, leaving him one son, born in 1733. That he had attached himself strongly to her two daughters by her former marriage, there is better evidence in the report, mentioned by Mrs. Montagu, of his practical kindness and liberality to the younger, than in his lamentations over the elder as the "Narcissa" of the "Night Thoughts." "Narcissa" had died in 1735, shortly after marriage to Mr. Temple, the son of Lord Palmerston; and Mr. Temple himself, after a second marriage, died in 1740, a year before Lady Elizabeth Young. These, then, are the three deaths supposed to have inspired "The Complaint," which forms the three first books of the "Night Thoughts":—

> "Insatiate archer, could not one suffice?
> Thy shaft flew thrice; and thrice my peace was slain;
> And thrice, ere thrice yon moon had filled her horn."

Since we find Young departing from the truth of dates, in order to heighten the effect of his calamity, or at least of his climax, we need not be surprised that he allowed his imagination great freedom in other matters besides chronology, and that the character of "Philander" can, by no process, be made to fit Mr. Temple. The supposition that the much-lectured "Lorenzo" of the "Night Thoughts" was Young's own son, is hardly rendered more absurd by the fact that the poem was written when that son was a boy, than by the obvious artificiality of the characters Young introduces as targets for his arguments and rebukes. Among all the trivial efforts of conjectural criticism, there can hardly be one more futile than the attempt to discover the original of those pitiable lay-figures, the "Lorenzos" and "Altamonts" of Young's didactic prose and poetry. His muse never stood face to face with a genuine, living human being; she would have been as much startled by such an encounter as a stage necromancer whose incantations and blue fire had actually conjured up a demon.

The "Night Thoughts" appeared between 1741 and 1745. Although he declares in them that he has chosen God for his "patron" henceforth, this is not at all to the prejudice of some half-dozen lords, duchesses, and right honorables, who have the privilege of sharing finely turned compliments with their co-patron. The line which closed the Second Night in the earlier editions—

"Wits spare not Heaven, O Wilmington!—nor thee"—

is an intense specimen of that perilous juxtaposition of ideas by which Young, in his incessant search after point and novelty, unconsciously converts his compliments into sarcasms; and his apostrophe to the moon as more likely to be favorable to his song if he calls her "fair Portland of the skies," is worthy even of his Pindaric ravings. His ostentatious renunciation of worldly schemes, and especially of his twenty-years' siege of Court favor, are in the tone of one who retains some hope, in the midst of his querulousness.

He descended from the astronomical rhapsodies of his Ninth Night, published in 1745, to more terrestrial strains in his "Reflections on the Public Situation of the Kingdom," dedicated to the Duke of Newcastle; but in this critical year we get a glimpse of him through a more prosaic and less refracting medium. He spent a part of the year at Tunbridge Wells; and Mrs. Montagu, who was there too, gives a very lively picture of the "divine Doctor" in her letters to the Duchess of Portland, on whom Young had bestowed the superlative bombast to which we have just referred. We shall borrow the quotations from Dr. Doran, in spite of their length, because, to our mind, they present the most agreeable portrait we possess of Young:—

"'I have great joy in Dr. Young, whom I disturbed in a reverie. At first he started, then bowed, then fell back into a surprise; then began a speech, relapsed into his astonishment two or three times, forgot what he had been saying; began a new subject, and so went on. I told him your grace desired he would write longer letters; to which he cried "Ha!" most emphatically, and I leave you to interpret what it meant. He has made a friendship with one person here, whom I believe you would not imagine to have been made for his bosom friend. You would, perhaps, suppose it was a bishop or dean, a prebend, a pious preacher, a clergyman of exemplary life, or, if a layman, of most virtuous conversation, one that had paraphrased St. Matthew, or wrote comments on St. Paul. . . . You would not guess that this associate of the doctor's was —old Cibber! Certainly, in their religious, moral, and civil character, there is no relation; but in their dramatic capacity there is some.'— Mrs. Montagu was not aware that Cibber, whom Young had named not disparagingly in his Satires, was the brother of his old schoolfellow; but to return to our hero. 'The waters,' says Mrs. Montagu, ' have raised his spirits to a fine pitch, as your grace will imagine, when I tell you how sublime an answer he made to a very vulgar question. I asked him how long he stayed at the Wells: he said, As long as my rival stayed;— as long as the sun did.' Among the visitors at the Wells were Lady Sunderland (wife of Sir Robert Sutton) and her sister, Mrs. Tichborne. 'He did an admirable thing to Lady Sunderland: on her mentioning Sir Robert Sutton, he asked her where Sir Robert's lady was; on which we all laughed very heartily, and I brought him off, half ashamed, to my lodgings, where, during breakfast, he assured me he had asked after Lady Sunderland, because he had a great honor for her; and that, having a respect for her sister, he designed to have inquired after her, if we had not put it out of his head by laughing at him. You must know, Mrs. Tichborne sat next to Lady Sunderland. It would have been admirable to have had him finish his compliment in that manner.' . . . 'His expressions all bear the stamp of novelty, and his thoughts of sterling sense. He practises a kind of philosophical abstinence. . . . He carried Mrs. Rolt and myself to Tunbridge, five miles from hence, where we were to see some fine old ruins. . . . First rode the doctor on a tall steed, decently caparisoned in dark gray; next, ambled Mrs. Rolt on a hackney horse; . . . then followed your humble servant on a milk-white palfrey. I rode on in safety, and at leisure to observe the company, especially the two figures that brought up the rear. The first was my servant, valiantly armed with two uncharged pistols; the last was the doctor's man, whose uncombed hair so resembled the mane of the horse he rode, one could not help imagining they were of kin, and wishing, for the honor of the family, that they had had one comb betwixt them. On his head was a velvet cap, much resembling a black saucepan, and on his side hung a little basket.—At last we arrived at the King's Head, where the loyalty of the doctor induced him to alight; and then, knight-errant-like, he took his damsels from off their palfreys, and courteously handed us into the inn.' . . . The party returned to the Wells; and 'the silver Cynthia held up her lamp in the heavens' the while. 'The night silenced all but our divine doctor, who sometimes uttered things fit to be spoken in a season when all nature seems to be hushed and hearkening. I followed, gathering wisdom as I went, till I found, by my horse's stumbling, that I was in a bad road, and that the blind was leading the blind. So I placed my servant between the doctor and myself; which he not perceiving, went on in a most philosophical strain, to the great admiration of my poor clown of a servant, who, not being wrought up to any pitch of enthusiasm, nor making any answer to all the fine things he heard, the doctor, wondering I was dumb, and grieving I was so stupid, looked round and declared his surprise.'"

Young's oddity and absence of mind are gathered from other sources besides these stories of Mrs. Montagu's, and gave rise to the report that he was the original of Fielding's "Parson Adams"; but this Croft denies, and mentions another Young, who really sat for the portrait, and who, we imagine, had both more Greek and more genuine simplicity than the poet. His love of chatting with Colley Cibber was an indication that the old predilection for the stage survived, in spite of his emphatic contempt for "all joys but joys that never can expire"; and the production of "The Brothers" at Drury Lane in 1753, after a suppression of fifteen years, was perhaps not entirely due to the expressed desire to give the proceeds to the Society for the Propagation of the Gospel. The author's profits were not more than £400—in those days a disappointing sum, and Young, as we learn from his friend Richardson, did not make this the limit of his donation, but gave a thousand guineas to the Society. "I had some talk with him," says Richardson, in one of his letters, "about this great action. 'I always,' said he, 'intended to do something handsome for the Society. Had I deferred it to my demise, I should have given away my son's money. All the world are inclined to pleasure; could I have given myself a greater by disposing of the sum to a different use, I should have done it.'"

His next work was "The Centaur not Fabulous; in Six Letters to a Friend, on the Life in Vogue," which reads very much like the most objurgatory parts of the "Night Thoughts" reduced to prose. It is preceded by a preface which, though addressed to a lady, is in its denunciations of vice as grossly indecent and almost as flippant as the epilogues written by "friends," which he allowed to be reprinted after his tragedies

in the latest edition of his works.   We like much better than
"The Centaur," "Conjectures on Original Composition," written in 1759, for the sake, he says, of communicating to the
world the well-known anecdote about Addison's death-bed,
and, with the exception of his poem on Resignation, the last
thing he ever published.

The estrangement from his son, which must have imbittered
the later years of his life, appears to have begun not many years
after the mother's death.   On the marriage of her second
daughter, who had previously presided over Young's household, a Mrs. Hallows, understood to be a woman of discreet
age, and the daughter (or widow) of a clergyman who was
an old friend of Young's, became housekeeper at Welwyn.
Opinions about ladies are apt to differ.   "Mrs. Hallows was
a woman of piety, improved by reading," says one witness.
"She was a very coarse woman," says Dr. Johnson; and we
shall presently find some indirect evidence that her temper
was perhaps not quite so much improved as her piety.   Servants, it seems, were not fond of remaining long in the house
with her; a satirical curate, named Kidgell, hints at "drops
of juniper" taken as a cordial (but perhaps he was spiteful,
and a teetotaler); and Young's son is said to have told his
father that "an old man should not resign himself to the management of anybody."   The result was, that the son was ban-
ished from home for the rest of his father's lifetime, though
Young seems never to have thought of disinheriting him.

Our latest glimpses of the aged poet are derived from certain letters of Mr. Jones, his curate—letters preserved in the
British Museum, and, happily, made accessible to common mortals in Nichols's "Anecdotes."   Mr. Jones was a man of some
literary activity and ambition,—a collector of interesting documents, and one of those concerned in the "Free and Candid
Disquisitions," the design of which was "to point out such
things in our ecclesiastical establishment as want to be re-
viewed and amended."   On these and kindred subjects he corresponded with Dr. Birch, occasionally troubling him with
queries and manuscripts.   We have a respect for Mr. Jones.
Unlike most persons who trouble others with queries or manuscripts, he mitigates the infliction by such gifts as "a fat

pullet," wishing he "had anything better to send; but this depauperizing vicarage (of Alconbury) too often checks the freedom and forwardness of my mind." Another day comes a "pound canister of tea"; another, a "young fatted goose." Mr. Jones's first letter from Welwyn is dated June, 1759, not quite six years before Young's death. In June, 1762, he expresses a wish to go to London "this summer. But," he continues,—

"My time and pains are almost continually taken up here, and . . . I have been (I now find) a considerable loser, upon the whole, by continuing here so long. The consideration of this, and the inconveniences I sustained, and do still experience from my late illness, obliged me at last to acquaint the Doctor (Young) with my case, and to assure him that I plainly perceived the duty and confinement here to be too much for me; for which reason I must (I said) beg to be at liberty to resign my charge at Michaelmas. I began to give him these notices in February, when I was very ill: and now I perceive, by what he told me the other day, that he is in some difficulty : for which reason he is at last (he says) resolved to advertise, *and even (which is much wondered at) to raise the salary considerably higher.* (What he allowed my predecessors was £20 per annum, and now he proposes £50, as he tells me.) I never asked him to raise it for me, though I well knew it was not equal to the duty ; nor did I say a word about myself when he lately suggested to me his intentions upon this subject."

In a postscript to this letter he says :—

"I may mention to you farther, as a friend that may be trusted, that, in all likelihood, the poor old gentleman will not find it a very easy matter, unless by dint of money, *and force upon himself,* to procure a man that he can like for his next curate, *nor one that will stay with him so long as I have done.* Then, his great age will recur to people's thoughts; and if he has any foibles, either in temper or conduct, they will be sure not to be forgotten on this occasion by those who know him ; and those who do not will probably be on their guard. On these and the like considerations, it is by no means an eligible office to be seeking out for a curate for him, as he has several times wished me to do ; and would, if he knew that I am now writing to you, wish your assistance also. But my best friends here, *who well foresee the probable consequences,* and wish me well, earnestly dissuade me from complying; and I will decline the office with as much decency as I can: but high salary will, I suppose, fetch in somebody or other, soon."

In the following July, he writes :—

"The old gentleman here (I may venture to tell you freely) seems to me to be in a pretty odd way of late,—moping, dejected, self-willed, and as if surrounded with some perplexing circumstances. Though I visit him pretty frequently for short intervals, I say very little to his affairs, not choosing to be a party concerned, especially in cases of so critical and tender a nature. There is much mystery in almost all his temporal affairs, as well as in many of his speculative theories. Whoever lives in this neighborhood to see his exit, will probably see and hear some very strange things. Time will show ;—I am afraid, not greatly to his credit. There is thought to be *an irremovable obstruction to his happiness within his walls, as well as another without them;* but the former is the more powerful, and like to continue so. He has this day been trying anew to engage me to stay with him. No lucrative views can tempt me to sacrifice my liberty or my health, to such measures as are proposed here. *Nor do I like to have to do with persons whose word and honor cannot be depended on.* So much for this very odd and unhappy topic."

In August, Mr. Jones's tone is slightly modified. Earnest entreaties, not lucrative considerations, have induced him to cheer the Doctor's dejected heart by remaining at Welwyn some time longer. The Doctor is, "in various respects, a very unhappy man," and few know so much of these "respects" as Mr. Jones. In September, he recurs to the subject:—

"My ancient gentleman here is still full of trouble: which moves my concern, though it moves only the secret laughter of many, and some untoward surmises in disfavor of him and his household. The loss of a very large sum of money (about £200) is talked of; whereof this vill and neighborhood is full. Some disbelieve; others say, '*It is no wonder, where about eighteen or more servants are sometimes taken and dismissed in the course of a year.*' The gentleman himself is allowed by all to be far more harmless and easy in his family than some one else who hath too much the lead in it. This, among others, was one reason for my late motion to quit."

No other mention of Young's affairs occurs until April 2, 1765, when he says that Dr. Young is very ill, attended by two physicians.

"Having mentioned this young gentleman (Dr. Young's son), I would acquaint you next, that he came hither this morning, having been sent for, as I am told, by the direction of Mrs. Hallows. Indeed, she intimated to me as much herself. And if this be so, I must say that it is one of the most prudent acts she ever did, or could have done in such a case as this; as it may prove a means of preventing much confusion after the death of the Doctor. I have had some little discourse with the son: he seems much affected, and I believe really is so. He earnestly wishes his father might be pleased to ask after him; for you must know he has not yet done this, nor is, in my opinion, like to do it. And it has been said farther, that upon a late application made to him on the behalf of his son, he desired that no more might be said to him about it. How true this may be, I cannot as yet be certain; all I shall say is, it seems not improbable. . . . I heartily wish the ancient man's heart may prove tender toward his son; though, knowing him so well, I can scarce hope to hear such desirable news."

Eleven days later, he writes:—

"I have now the pleasure to acquaint you, that the late Dr. Young, though he had for many years kept his son at a distance from him, yet has now at last left him all his possessions, after the payment of certain legacies; so that the young gentleman (who bears a fair character, and behaves well, as far as I can hear or see) will, I hope, soon enjoy and make a prudent use of a handsome fortune. The father, on his death-bed, and since my return from London, was applied to in the tenderest manner, by one of his physicians, and by another person, to admit the son into his presence, to make submission, entreat forgiveness, and obtain his blessing. As to an interview with his son, he intimated that he chose to decline it, as his spirits were then low, and his nerves weak. With regard to the next particular, he said, 'I heartily forgive him'; and upon mention of this last, he gently lifted up his hand, and letting it gently fall, pronounced these words, 'God bless him!' . . . I know it will give you pleasure to be farther informed, that he was pleased to make respectful mention of me in his will; expressing his satisfaction in my care of his parish, bequeathing to me a handsome legacy, and appointing me to be one of his executors."

So far Mr. Jones, in his confidential correspondence with a "friend who may be trusted." In a letter communicated apparently by him to the "Gentleman's Magazine" seventeen years later—namely, in 1782—on the appearance of Croft's biography of Young, we find him speaking of "the ancient gentleman" in a tone of reverential eulogy, quite at variance with the free comments we have just quoted. But the Rev. John Jones was probably of opinion, with Mrs. Montagu, whose contemporary and retrospective letters are also set in a different key, that "the interests of religion were connected with the character of a man so distinguished for piety as Dr. Young." At all events, a subsequent quasi official statement weighs nothing as evidence against contemporary, spontaneous, and confidential hints.

To Mrs. Hallows, Young left a legacy of £1,000, with the

request that she would destroy all his manuscripts.   This final request, from some unknown cause, was not complied with, and among the papers he left behind him was the following letter from Archbishop Secker, which probably marks the date of his latest effort after preferment:—

"DEANERY OF ST. PAUL'S, July 8, 1758.

"GOOD DR. YOUNG,—I have long wondered that more suitable notice of your great merit hath not been taken by persons in power.   But how to remedy the omission I see not.   No encouragement hath ever been given me to mention things of this nature to his Majesty.   And therefore, in all likelihood, the only consequence of doing it would be weakening the little influence which else I may possibly have on some other occasions.   *Your fortune and your reputation set you above the need of advancement; and your sentiments above that concern for it on your own account,* which, on that of the public, is sincerely felt by

"Your loving Brother,

"THO. CANT."

The loving brother's irony is severe!

Perhaps the least questionable testimony to the better side of Young's character is that of Bishop Hildesley, who, as the vicar of a parish near Welwyn, had been Young's neighbor for upward of twenty years.   The affection of the clergy for each other, we have observed, is, like that of the fair sex, not at all of a blind and infatuated kind; and we may therefore the rather believe them when they give each other any extra-official praise.   Bishop Hildesley, then, writing of Young to Richardson, says:—

"The impertinence of my frequent visits to him was amply rewarded; forasmuch as, I can truly say, he never received me but with agreeable open complacency; and I never left him but with profitable pleasure and improvement.   He was one or other, the most modest, the most patient of contradiction, and the most informing and entertaining I ever conversed with—at least, of any man who had so just pretensions to pertinacity and reserve."

Mr. Langton, however, who was also a frequent visitor of Young's, informed Boswell—

"That there was an air of benevolence in his manner; but that he could obtain from him less information than he had hoped to receive from one who had lived so much in intercourse with the brightest men of what had been called the Augustan age of England; and that he showed a degree of eager curiosity concerning the common occurrences that were then passing, which appeared somewhat remarkable in a man of such intellectual stores, of such an advanced age, and who had retired from life with declared disappointment in his expectations."

The same substance, we know, will exhibit different qualities under different tests; and, after all, imperfect reports of individual impressions, whether immediate or traditional, are a very frail basis on which to build our opinion of a man. One's character may be very indifferently mirrored in the mind of the most intimate neighbor; it all depends on the quality of that gentleman's reflecting surface.

But, discarding any inferences from such uncertain evidence, the outline of Young's character is too distinctly traceable in the well-attested facts of his life, and yet more in the self-betrayal that runs through all his works, for us to fear that our general estimate of him may be false. For, while no poet seems less easy and spontaneous than Young, no poet discloses himself more completely. Men's minds have no hiding-place out of themselves—their affectations do but betray another phase of their nature. And if, in the present view of Young, we seem to be more intent on laying bare unfavorable facts than on shrouding them in charitable speeches, it is not because we have any irreverential pleasure in turning men's characters the seamy side without, but because we see no great advantage in considering a man as he was *not*. Young's biographers and critics have usually set out from the position that he was a great religious teacher, and that his poetry is morally sublime; and they have toned down his failings into harmony with their conception of the divine and the poet. For our own part, we set out from precisely the opposite conviction—namely, that the religious and moral spirit of Young's poetry is low and false; and we think it of some importance to show that the "Night Thoughts" are the reflex of a mind in which the higher human sympathies were inactive. This judgment is entirely opposed to our youthful predilections and enthusiasm. The sweet garden-breath of early enjoyment lingers about many a page of the "Night Thoughts," and even of the "Last Day," giving an extrinsic charm to passages of stilted rhetoric and false sentiment; but the sober and repeated reading of maturer years has convinced us that it would hardly be possible to find a more typical instance than Young's poetry, of the mistake which substitutes interested obedience for sympathetic emotion, and baptizes egoism as religion.

Pope said of Young, that he had "much of a sublime genius without common sense." The deficiency Pope meant to indicate was, we imagine, moral rather than intellectual: it was the want of that fine sense of what is fitting in speech and action, which is often eminently possessed by men and women whose intellect is of a very common order, but who have the sincerity and dignity which can never coexist with the selfish preoccupations of vanity or interest. This was the "common sense" in which Young was conspicuously deficient; and it was partly owing to this deficiency that his genius, waiting to be determined by the highest prizes, fluttered uncertainly from effort to effort, until, when he was more than sixty, it suddenly spread its broad wing, and soared so as to arrest the gaze of other generations besides his own. For he had no versatility of faculty to mislead him. The "Night Thoughts" only differ from his previous works in the degree and not in the kind of power they manifest. Whether he writes prose or poetry, rhyme or blank verse, dramas, satires, odes, or meditations, we see everywhere the same Young—the same narrow circle of thoughts, the same love of abstractions, the same telescopic view of human things, the same appetency toward antithetic apothegm and rhapsodic climax. The passages that arrest us in his tragedies are those in which he anticipates some fine passage in the "Night Thoughts," and where his characters are only transparent shadows through which we see the bewigged *embonpoint* of the didactic poet, excogitating epigrams or ecstatic soliloquies by the light of a candle fixed in a skull. Thus, in "The Revenge," Alonzo, in the conflict of jealousy and love that at once urges and forbids him to murder his wife, says:—

"This vast and solid earth, that blazing sun,
Those skies, through which it rolls, must all have end.
What then is man? The smallest part of nothing.
Day buries day; month, month; and year the year!
Our life is but a chain of many deaths.

Can then Death's self be feared?   Our life much rather:
Life is the desert, life the solitude;
Death joins us to the great majority:
'Tis to be born to Plato and to Cæsar;
'Tis to be great forever;
'Tis pleasure, 'tis ambition, then, to die."

His prose writings all read like the "Night Thoughts," either diluted into prose, or not yet crystallized into poetry. For example, in his "Thoughts for Age," he says:—

"Though we stand on its awful brink, such our leaden bias to the world, we turn our faces the wrong way; we are still looking on our old acquaintance, *Time;* though now so wasted and reduced, that we can see little more of him than his wings and his scythe: our age enlarges his wings to our imagination; and our fear of death, his scythe; as Time himself grows less.   His consumption is deep; his annihilation is at hand."

This is a dilution of the magnificent image:—

"Time in advance behind him hides his wings,
  And seems to creep decrepit with his age.
  Behold him when past by! What then is seen
  But his broad pinions, swifter than the winds?"

Again:—

"A requesting Omnipotence?   What can stun and confound thy reason more?   What more can ravish and exalt thy heart? It cannot but ravish and exalt; it cannot but gloriously disturb and perplex thee, to take in all *that* thought suggests.   Thou child of the dust! thou speck of misery and sin! how abject thy weakness! how great is thy power! Thou crawler on earth, and possible (I was about to say) controller of the skies! weigh, and weigh well, the wondrous truths I have in view: which cannot be weighed too much; which the more they are weighed, amaze the more; which to have supposed, before they were revealed, would have been as great madness, and to have presumed on as great sin, as it is now madness and sin not to believe."

Even in his Pindaric odes, in which he made the most violent effort against nature, he is still neither more nor less than the Young of the "Last Day," emptied and swept of his genius, and possessed by seven demons of fustian and bad rhyme.   Even here, his "Ercles' vein" alternates with his moral platitudes, and we have the perpetual text of the "Night Thoughts":—

"Gold pleasure buys;
  But pleasure dies,
For soon the gross fruition cloys;
  Though raptures court,
  The sense is short;
But virtue kindles living joys;—

"Joys felt alone!
  Joys asked of none!
Which Time's and Fortune's arrows miss·
  Joys that subsist,
  Though fates resist,
An unprecarious, endless bliss!

"Unhappy they!
  And falsely gay!
Who bask forever in success;
  A constant feast
  Quite palls the taste,
And long enjoyment is distress."

In the "Last Day," again, which is the earliest thing he wrote, we have an anticipation of all his greatest faults and merits. Conspicuous among the faults is that attempt to exalt our conceptions of Deity by vulgar images and comparisons, which is so offensive in the later "Night Thoughts." In a burst of prayer and homage to God, called forth by the contemplation of Christ coming to judgment, he asks, Who brings the change of the seasons? and answers—

"Not the great Ottoman, or greater Czar;
  Not Europe's arbitress of peace and war!"

Conceive the soul, in its most solemn moments, assuring God that it does not place His power below that of Louis Napoleon or Queen Victoria!

But in the midst of uneasy rhymes, inappropriate imagery, vaulting sublimity that o'erleaps itself, and vulgar emotions, we have in this poem an occasional flash of genius, a touch of simple grandeur, which promises as much as Young ever achieved. Describing the oncoming of the dissolution of all things, he says:—

> "No sun in radiant glory shines on high;
> *No light but from the terrors of the sky.*"

And again, speaking of great armies:—

> "Whose rear lay wrapt in night, while breaking dawn
> Rous'd the broad front, and call'd the battle on."

And this wail of the lost souls is fine:—

> "And this for sin?
> Could I offend if I had never been?
> But still increas'd the senseless, happy mass,
> Flow'd in the stream, *or shiver'd in the grass?*
> Father of mercies! why from silent earth
> Didst Thou awake and curse me into birth?
> Tear me from quiet, ravish me from night,
> And make a thankless present of Thy light?
> Push into being a reverse of Thee,
> And *animate a clod with misery?*"

. But it is seldom in Young's rhymed poems that the effect of a felicitous thought or image is not counteracted by our sense of the constraint he suffered from the necessities of rhyme,— that "Gothic demon," as he afterward called it, "which modern poetry tasting, became mortal." In relation to his own power, no one will question the truth of his dictum, that "blank verse is verse unfallen, uncurst; verse reclaimed, re-enthroned in the true language of the gods; who never thundered nor suffered their Homer to thunder in rhyme." His want of mastery in rhyme is especially a drawback on the effect of his Satires; for epigrams and witticisms are peculiarly susceptible to the intrusion of a superfluous word, or to an inversion which implies constraint. Here, even more than elsewhere, the art that conceals art is an absolute requisite, and to have a witticism presented to us in limping or cumbrous rhythm is as counteractive to any electrifying effect as to see the tentative grimaces by which a comedian prepares a grotesque countenance. We discern the process, instead of being startled by the result.

This is one reason why the Satires, read *seriatim*, have a flatness to us, which, when we afterward read picked passages, we are inclined to disbelieve in, and to attribute to some deficiency in our own mood.   But there are deeper reasons for that dissatisfaction.   Young is not a satirist of a high order. His satire has neither the terrible vigor, the lacerating energy of genuine indignation, nor the humor which owns loving fellowship with the poor human nature it laughs at; nor yet the personal bitterness which, as in Pope's characters of Sporus and Atticus, insures those living touches by virtue of which the individual and particular in Art becomes the universal and immortal.   Young could never describe a real complex human being; but what he *could* do with eminent success, was to describe with neat and finished point obvious *types* of manners rather than of character,—to write cold and clever epigrams on personified vices and absurdities.   There is no more emotion in his satire than if he were turning witty verses on a waxen image of Cupid, or a lady's glove.   He has none of those felicitous epithets, none of those pregnant lines, by which Pope's Satires have enriched the ordinary speech of educated men.   Young's wit will be found in almost every instance to consist in that antithetic combination of ideas which, of all the forms of wit, is most within reach of clever effort. In his gravest arguments, as well as in his lightest satire, one might imagine that he had set himself to work out the problem, how much antithesis might be got out of a given subject.   And there he completely succeeds.   His neatest portraits are all wrought on this plan.   Narcissus, for example, who—

> "Omits no duty; nor can Envy say
> He miss'd, these many years, the Church or Play
> He makes no noise in Parliament, 'tis true;
> But pays his debts, and visit when 'tis due;
> His character and gloves are ever clean,
> And then he can out-bow the bowing Dean;
> A smile eternal on his lip he wears,
> Which equally the wise and worthless shares.
> In gay fatigues, this most undaunted chief,
> Patient of idleness beyond belief,
> Most charitably lends the town his face
> For ornament in every public place;
> As sure as cards he to th' assembly comes,
> And is the furniture of drawing-rooms:
> When Ombre calls, his hand and heart are free,
> And, joined to two, he fails not—to make three:

Narcissus is the glory of his race;
For who does nothing with a better grace?
To deck my list by nature were designed
Such shining expletives of human kind,
Who want, while through blank life they dream along,
Sense to be right and passion to be wrong."

It is but seldom that we find a touch of that easy slyness which gives an additional zest to surprise; but here is an instance:—

"See Tityrus, with merriment possest,
Is burst with laughter ere he hears the jest.
What need he stay? for when the joke is o'er,
His *teeth* will be no whiter than before."

Like Pope, whom he imitated, he sets out with a psychological mistake as the basis of his satire, attributing all forms of folly to one passion—the love of fame, or vanity,—a much grosser mistake, indeed, than Pope's exaggeration of the extent to which the "ruling passion" determines conduct in the individual. Not that Young is consistent in his mistake. He sometimes implies no more than what is the truth—that the love of fame is the cause, not of all follies, but of many.

Young's satires on women are superior to Pope's, which is only saying that they are superior to Pope's greatest failure. We can more frequently pick out a couplet as successful than an entire sketch. Of the too emphatic Syrena, he says:—

"Her judgment just, her sentence is too strong;
Because she's right, she's ever in the wrong."

Of the diplomatic Julia:—

"For her own breakfast she'll project a scheme,
Nor take her tea without a stratagem."

Of Lyce, the old painted coquette:—

"In vain the cock has summoned sprites away;
She walks at noon and blasts the bloom of day."

Of the nymph who, "gratis, clears religious mysteries":—

"'Tis hard, too, she who makes no use but chat
Of her religion, should be barr'd in that."

The description of the literary *belle*, Daphne, well prefaces that of Stella, admired by Johnson :—

> "With legs toss'd high, on her sophee she sits,
> Vouchsafing audience to contending wits:
> Of each performance she's the final test;
> One act read o'er, she prophesies the rest;
> And then, pronouncing with decisive air,
> Fully convinces all the town—*she's fair*.
> Had lovely Daphne Hecatessa's face,
> How would her elegance of taste decrease!
> Some ladies' judgment in their features lies,
> And all their genius sparkles in their eyes.
> But hold, she cries, lampooner! have a care:
> Must I want common sense because I'm fair?
> O no; see Stella: her eyes shine as bright
> As if her tongue was never in the right;
> And yet what real learning, judgment, fire!
> She seems inspir'd, and can herself inspire.
> How then (if malice ruled not all the fair)
> *Could Daphne publish, and could she forbear ?* "

After all, when we have gone through Young's seven Satires, we seem to have made but an indifferent meal. They are a sort of fricassee, with little solid meat in them, and yet the flavor is not always piquant. It is curious to find him, when he pauses a moment from his satiric sketching, recurring to his old platitudes :—

> "Can gold calm passion, or make reason shine?
> Can we dig peace or wisdom from the mine?
> Wisdom to gold prefer" ;

platitudes which he seems inevitably to fall into, for the same reason that some men are constantly asserting their contempt for criticism—because he felt the opposite so keenly.

The outburst of genius in the earlier books of the "Night Thoughts" is the more remarkable, that in the interval between them and the Satires, he had produced nothing but his Pindaric odes, in which he fell far below the level of his previous works. Two sources of this sudden strength were the freedom of blank verse and the presence of a genuine emotion. Most persons, in speaking of the "Night Thoughts," have in their minds only the two or three first Nights, the majority of readers rarely getting beyond these, unless, as Wilson says, they "have but few books, are poor, and live in the country." And in these earlier Nights there is enough genuine sublimity and genuine sadness to bribe us into too favorable a judgment of them as a whole. Young had only a very few things to say or sing—such as that life is vain, that death is imminent, that man is immortal, that virtue is wisdom, that friendship is sweet, and that the source of virtue is the contemplation of death and immortality,—and even in his two first Nights he had said almost all he had to say in his finest manner. Through these first outpourings of "complaint" we feel that the poet is really sad, that the bird is singing over a rifled nest; and we bear with his morbid picture of the world and of life, as the Job-like lament of a man whom "the hand of God hath touched." Death has carried away his best-beloved, and that "silent land" whither they are gone has more reality for the desolate one than this world which is empty of their love:—

> "This is the desert, this the solitude;
> How populous, how vital is the grave!"

Joy died with the loved one:—

> "The disenchanted earth
> Lost all her lustre. Where her glitt'ring towers?
> Her golden mountains, where? All darken'd down
> To naked waste; a dreary vale of tears:
> *The great magician's dead!*"

Under the pang of parting, it seems to the bereaved man as if love were only a nerve to suffer with, and he sickens at the thought of every joy of which he must one day say—"*it was.*" In its unreasoning anguish, the soul rushes to the idea of perpetuity as the one element of bliss:—

> "O ye blest scenes of permanent delight!—
> Could ye, so rich in rapture, fear an end,—
> That ghastly thought would drink up all your joy,
> And quite unparadise the realms of light."

In a man under the immediate pressure of a great sorrow, we tolerate morbid exaggerations; we are prepared to see him

turn away a weary eye from sunlight and flowers and sweet
human faces, as if this rich and glorious life had no significance but as a preliminary of death; we do not criticise his
views, we compassionate his feelings.   And so it is with
Young in these earlier Nights.   There is already some artificiality even in his grief, and feeling often slides into rhetoric,
but through it all we are thrilled with the unmistakable cry of
pain, which makes us tolerant of egoism and hyperbole :—

> "In every varied posture, place, and hour,
> How widow'd ev'ry thought of ev'ry joy !
> Thought, busy thought ! too busy for my peace !
> Through the dark postern of time long elapsed
> Led softly, by the stillness of the night,—
> Led like a murderer (and such it proves !)
> Strays (wretched rover !) o'er the pleasing past,—
> In quest of wretchedness, perversely strays ;
> And finds all desert now ; and meets the ghosts
> Of my departed joys."

But when he becomes didactic, rather than complaining,—
when he ceases to sing his sorrows, and begins to insist on his
opinions,—when that distaste for life which we pity as a
transient feeling, is thrust upon us as a theory, we become
perfectly cool and critical, and are not in the least inclined to
be indulgent to false views and selfish sentiments.

Seeing that we are about to be severe on Young's failings and
failures, we ought, if a reviewer's space were elastic, to dwell
also on his merits,—on the startling vigor of his imagery—on
the occasional grandeur of his thought—on the piquant force
of that grave satire into which his meditations continually
run.   But, since our "limits" are rigorous, we must content
ourselves with the less agreeable half of the critic's duty ; and
we may the rather do so, because it would be difficult to say
anything new of Young in the way of admiration, while we
think there are many salutary lessons remaining to be drawn
from his faults.

One of the most striking characteristics of Young is his *radical insincerity as a poetic artist*.   This, added to the thin and
artificial texture of his wit, is the true explanation of the par-
adox—that a poet who is often inopportunely witty has the
opposite vice of bombastic absurdity.   The source of all gran-

diloquence is the want of taking for a criterion the true qualities of the object described, or the emotion expressed. The
grandiloquent man is never bent on saying what he feels or
what he sees, but on producing a certain effect on his audience;
hence he may float away into utter inanity without meeting
any criterion to arrest him. Here lies the distinction between
grandiloquence and genuine fancy or bold imaginativeness.
The fantastic or the boldly imaginative poet may be as sincere
as the most realistic: he is true to his own sensibilities or inward vision, and in his wildest flights he never breaks loose
from his criterion—the truth of his own mental state. Now,
this disruption of language from genuine thought and feeling
is what we are constantly detecting in Young; and his insincerity is the more likely to betray him into absurdity, because
he habitually treats of abstractions, and not of concrete objects
or specific emotions. He descants perpetually on virtue, religion, "the good man," life, death, immortality, eternity—subjects which are apt to give a factitious grandeur to empty
wordiness. When a poet floats in the empyrean, and only
takes a bird's-eye view of the earth, some people accept the
mere fact of his soaring for sublimity, and mistake his dim
vision of earth for proximity to heaven. Thus:—

> "His hand the good man fixes on the skies,
> And bids earth roll, nor feels her idle whirl,"

may perhaps pass for sublime with some readers. But pause
a moment to realize the image, and the monstrous absurdity
of a man's grasping the skies, and hanging habitually suspended there, while he contemptuously bids the earth roll,
warns you that no genuine feeling could have suggested so unnatural a conception.

Examples of such vicious imagery, resulting from insincerity, may be found, perhaps, in almost every page of the
"Night Thoughts." But simple assertions or aspirations,
undisguised by imagery, are often equally false. No writer
whose rhetoric was checked by the slightest truthful intentions, could have said,—

> "An eye of awe and wonder let me roll,
> And roll for ever."

Abstracting the more poetical associations with the eye, this is hardly less absurd than if he had wished to stand forever with his mouth open.

Again—

> "Far beneath
> A soul immortal is a mortal joy."

Happily for human nature, we are sure no man really believes that. Which of us has the impiety not to feel that our souls are only too narrow for the joy of looking into the trusting eyes of our children, of reposing on the love of a husband or wife,—nay, of listening to the divine voice of music, or watching the calm brightness of autumn afternoons? But Young could utter this falsity without detecting it, because, when he spoke of "mortal joys," he rarely had in his mind any object to which he could attach sacredness. He was thinking of bishoprics and benefices, of smiling monarchs, patronizing prime ministers, and a "much indebted muse." Of anything between these and eternal bliss, he was but rarely and moderately conscious. Often, indeed, he sinks very much below even the bishopric, and seems to have no notion of earthly pleasure, but such as breathes gaslight and the fumes of wine. His picture of life is precisely such as you would expect from a man who has risen from his bed at two o'clock in the afternoon with a headache, and a dim remembrance that he has added to his "debts of honor":—

> "What wretched repetition cloys us here!
> What periodic potions for the sick,
> Distemper'd bodies, and distemper'd minds!"

And then he flies off to his usual antithesis:—

> "In an eternity what scenes shall strike!
> Adventures thicken, novelties surprise!"

"Earth" means lords and levees, duchesses and Dalilahs, South-Sea dreams and illegal percentage; and the only things distinctly preferable to these are, eternity and the stars. Deprive Young of this antithesis, and more than half his eloquence would be shrivelled up. Place him on a breezy common, where the furze is in its golden bloom, where children are playing, and horses are standing in the sunshine with

fondling necks, and he would have nothing to say. Here are
neither depths of guilt, nor heights of glory; and we doubt
whether in such a scene he would be able to pay his usual
compliment to the Creator:—

"Where'er I turn, what claim on all applause!"

It is true that he sometimes—not often—speaks of virtue as
capable of sweetening life, as well as of taking the sting from
death and winning heaven; and, lest we should be guilty of
any unfairness to him, we will quote the two passages which
convey this sentiment the most explicitly. In the one, he
gives Lorenzo this excellent recipe for obtaining cheerfulness:—

> "Go, fix some weighty truth;
> Chain down some passion; do some generous good;
> Teach Ignorance to see, or Grief to smile;
> Correct thy friend; befriend thy greatest foe;
> Or, with warm heart, and confidence divine,
> Spring up, and lay strong hold on Him who made thee."

The other passage is vague, but beautiful, and its music has
murmured in our minds for many years:—

> "The cuckoo seasons sing
> The same dull note to such as nothing prize
> But what those seasons from the teeming earth
> To doting sense indulge. But nobler minds,
> Which relish fruit unripen'd by the sun,
> Make their days various; various as the dyes
> On the dove's neck, which wanton in his rays.
> On minds of dove-like innocence possess'd,
> On lighten'd minds that bask in Virtue's beams,
> Nothing hangs tedious, nothing old revolves
> In that for which they long, for which they live.
> Their glorious efforts, wing'd with heavenly hopes,
> Each rising morning sees still higher rise;
> Each bounteous dawn its novelty presents
> To worth maturing, new strength, lustre, fame;
> While Nature's circle, like a chariot wheel,
> Rolling beneath their elevated aims,
> Makes their fair prospect fairer every hour;
> Advancing virtue in a line to bliss."

Even here, where he is in his most amiable mood, you see at
what a telescopic distance he stands from mother Earth and

simple human joys—"Nature's circle rolls beneath." Indeed,
we remember no mind in poetic literature that seems to have
absorbed less of the beauty and the healthy breath of the
common landscape than Young's. His images, often grand
and finely presented—witness that sublimely sudden leap of
thought,

> "Embryos we must be till we burst the shell,
> *Yon ambient azure shell*, and spring to life"—

lie almost entirely within that circle of observation which
would be familiar to a man who lived in town, hung about the
theatres, read the newspaper, and went home often by moon
and star light. There is no natural object nearer than the
moon that seems to have any strong attraction for him, and
even to the moon he chiefly appeals for patronage, and "pays
his court" to her. It is reckoned among the many deficiencies
of Lorenzo, that he "never asked the moon one question"—an
omission which Young thinks eminently unbecoming a rational
being. He describes nothing so well as a comet, and is tempted
to linger with fond detail over nothing more familiar than the
day of judgment and an imaginary journey among the stars.
Once on Saturn's ring, he feels at home, and his language
becomes quite easy:—

> "What behold I now?
> A wilderness of wonders burning round,
> Where larger suns inhabit higher spheres
> Perhaps *the villas of descending gods!*"

It is like a sudden relief from a strained posture when, in
the "Night Thoughts," we come on any allusion that carries
us to the lanes, woods, or fields. Such allusions are amaz-
ingly rare, and we could almost count them on a single hand.
That we may do him no injustice, we will quote the three
best:—

> "Like *blossom'd trees o'erturned by vernal storm*,
> Lovely in death the beauteous ruin lay."

> .   .   .   .   .   .

> "In the same brook none ever bathed him twice:
> To the same life none ever twice awoke.
> We call the brook the same—the same we think
> Our life, though still more rapid in its flow;

Nor mark the much irrevocably lapsed,
And mingled with the sea."

.　　.　　.　　.　　.　　.

"The crown of manhood is a winter joy;
An evergreen that stands the northern blast,
And blossoms in the rigor of our fate."

The adherence to abstractions, or to the personification of
abstractions, is closely allied in Young to the *want of genuine
emotion*.　He sees Virtue sitting on a mount serene, far above
the mists and storms of earth: he sees Religion coming down
from the skies, with this world in her left hand and the other
world in her right: but we never find him dwelling on virtue
or religion as it really exists—in the emotions of a man dressed
in an ordinary coat, and seated by his fireside of an evening,
with his hand resting on the head of his little daughter; in
courageous effort for unselfish ends, in the internal triumph of
justice and pity over personal resentment, in all the sublime
self-renunciation and sweet charities which are found in the
details of ordinary life.　Now, emotion links itself with particulars, and only in a faint and secondary manner with abstractions.　An orator may discourse very eloquently on injustice in general, and leave his audience cold; but let him state
a special case of oppression, and every heart will throb.　The
most untheoretic persons are aware of this relation between
true emotion and particular facts, as opposed to general terms,
and implicitly recognize it in the repulsion they feel toward
any one who professes strong feeling about abstractions,—
in the interjectional "humbug!" which immediately rises to
their lips.

If we except the passages in Philander, Narcissa, and Lucia,
there is hardly a trace of human sympathy, of self-forgetful-
ness in the joy or sorrow of a fellow-being, throughout this
long poem, which professes to treat the various phases of
man's destiny.　And even in the Narcissa Night, Young repels
us by the low moral tone of his exaggerated lament.　This
married step-daughter died at Lyons, and, being a Protestant,
was denied burial, so that her friends had to bury her in secret
—one of the many miserable results of superstition, but not a
fact to throw an educated, still less a Christian man, into a

fury of hatred and vengeance, in contemplating it after the
lapse of five years. Young, however, takes great pains to
simulate a bad feeling :—

> "Of grief
> And indignation rival bursts I pour'd,
> Half execration mingled with my pray'r ;
> Kindled at man, while I his God ador'd ;
> Sore grudg'd the savage land her sacred dust ;
> Stamp'd the cursed soil ; *and with humanity
> (Denied Narcissa) wish'd them all a grave.*"

The odiously bad taste of this last clause makes us hope that
it is simply a platitude, and not intended as a witticism, until
he removes the possibility of this favorable doubt by immediately asking, " Flows my resentment into guilt ? "

When, by an afterthought, he attempts something like sympathy, he only betrays more clearly his want of it. Thus, in
the first Night, when he turns from his private griefs to depict
earth as a hideous abode of misery for all mankind, and asks—

> "What then am I, who sorrow for myself ? "—

he falls at once into calculating the benefit of sorrowing for
others :—

> " More generous sorrow, while it sinks, exalts :
> *And conscious virtue mitigates the pang.*
> Nor virtue, more than prudence, bids me give
> Swollen thought a second channel."

This remarkable negation of sympathy is in perfect consistency
with Young's theory of ethics :—

> "Virtue is a crime,
> A crime to reason, if it costs us pain
> Unpaid."

If there is no immortality for man,—

> "Sense ! take the rein ; blind Passion, drive us on ;
> And Ignorance ! befriend us on our way. . . .
> Yes ; give the pulse full empire ; live the brute,
> Since as the brute we die. The sum of man,
> Of godlike man, to revel and to rot."

"If this life's gain invites him to the deed,
  Why not his country sold, his father slain?"

. . . . .

"Ambition, avarice, by the wise disdain'd,
  Is perfect wisdom, while mankind are fools,
  And think a turf or tombstone covers all."

. . . . .

"Die for thy country, thou romantic fool!
  Seize, seize the plank thyself, and let her sink."

. . . . .

"As in the dying parent dies the child,
  Virtue with Immortality expires.
  Who tells me he denies his soul immortal,
  Whate'er his boast, has told me he's a knave.
  His duty 'tis to love himself alone,
  Nor care though mankind perish, if he smiles."

We can imagine the man who "denies his soul immortal," replying, "It is quite possible that *you* would be a knave, and love yourself alone, if it were not for your belief in immortality; but you are not to force upon me what would result from your own utter want of moral emotion. I am just and honest, not because I expect to live in another world, but because, having felt the pain of injustice and dishonesty toward myself, I have a fellow-feeling with other men, who would suffer the same pain if I were unjust or dishonest toward them. Why should I give my neighbor short weight in this world, because there is not another world in which I should have nothing to weigh out to him? I am honest, because I don't like to inflict evil on others in this life, not because I'm afraid of evil to myself in another. The fact is, I do *not* love myself alone, whatever logical necessity there may be for that conclusion in your mind. I have a tender love for my wife, and children, and friends, and through that love I sympathize with like affections in other men. It is a pang to me to witness the suffering of a fellow-being, and I feel his suffering the more acutely because he is *mortal*—because his life is so short, and I would have it, if possible, filled with happiness and not misery. Through my union and fellowship with the men and women I *have* seen, I feel a like, though a fainter, sympathy with those I have *not* seen; and I am able so to live in imagination with the generations to come, that their good is not

alien to me, and is a stimulus to me to labor for ends which
may not benefit myself, but will benefit them. It is possible
that you might prefer to ' live the brute,' to sell your country,
or to slay your father, if you were not afraid of some disagreeable consequences from the criminal laws of another world;
but even if I could conceive no motive but by my own worldly
interest or the gratification of my animal desires, I have not
observed that beastliness, treachery, and parricide, are the
direct way to happiness and comfort on earth."

Thus far the man who " denies himself immortal" might give
a warrantable reply to Young's assumption of peculiar loftiness in maintaining that " virtue with immortality expires."
We may admit, indeed, that if the better part of virtue consists, as Young appears to think, in contempt for mortal joys,
in " meditation of our own decease," and in " applause " of
God in the style of a congratulatory address to her Majesty
—all which has small relation to the well-being of mankind on
this earth—the motive to it must be gathered from something
that lies quite outside the sphere of human sympathy. But,
for certain other elements of virtue, which are of more obvious
importance to plain people,—a delicate sense of our neighbor's
rights, an active participation in the joys and sorrows of our
fellow-men, a magnanimous acceptance of privation or suffering for ourselves when it is the condition of rescue for others
—in a word, the widening and strengthening of our sympathetic nature,—it is surely of some moment to contend, that
they have no more direct dependence on the belief in a future
state than the interchange of gases in the lungs on the plural-
ity of worlds. Nay, it is conceivable that in some minds the
deep pathos lying in the thought of human mortality—that we
are here for a little while and then vanish away, that this
earthly life is all that is given to our loved ones and to our
many suffering fellow-men—lies nearer the fountains of moral
emotion than the conception of extended existence. And
surely it ought to be a welcome fact, if the thought of *mortality*, as well as of immortality, be favorable to virtue. We can
imagine that the proprietors of a patent water-supply may
have a dread of common springs; but for those who only share
the general need there cannot be too great a security against a

lack of fresh water—or of pure morality. It should be matter
of unmixed rejoicing if this latter necessary of healthful life
has its evolution insured in the interaction of human souls as
certainly as the evolution of science or of art, with which, indeed, it is but a twin ray, melting into them with undefinable
limits.

To return to Young: We can often detect a man's deficiencies in what he admires more clearly than in what he con-
temns,—in the sentiments he presents as laudable rather than
in those he decries. And in Young's notion of what is lofty
he casts a shadow by which we can measure him without further trouble. For example, in arguing for human immortality,
he says:—

> "First, what is *true ambition?* The pursuit
> Of glory *nothing less than man can share.*
>
> . . . .
>
> The Visible and Present are for brutes,
> A slender portion, and a narrow bound!
> These Reason, with an energy divine
> O'erleaps, and claims the Future and Unseen;
> The vast Unseen, the Future fathomless!
> When the great soul buoys up to this high point,
> Leaving gross Nature's sediments below,
> Then, and then only, Adam's offspring quits
> The sage and hero of the fields and woods,
> Asserts his rank, and rises into man."

So, then, if it were certified that, as some benevolent minds
have tried to infer, our dumb fellow-creatures would share a
future existence, in which it is to be hoped we should neither
beat, starve, nor maim them, our ambition for a future life
would cease to be "lofty"! This is a notion of loftiness which
may pair off with Dr. Whewell's celebrated observation, that
Bentham's moral theory is low, because it includes justice and
mercy to brutes.

But, for a reflection of Young's moral personality on a colossal scale, we must turn to those passages where his rhetoric is
at its utmost stretch of inflation—where he addresses the
Deity, discourses of the Divine operations, or describes the last
judgment. As a compound of vulgar pomp, crawling adulation, and hard selfishness, presented under the guise of piety,

there are few things in literature to surpass the ninth Night,
entitled "Consolation," especially in the pages where he describes the last judgment—a subject to which, with naïve self-
betrayal, he applies phraseology favored by the exuberant
penny-a-liner.   Thus, when God descends, and the groans of
hell are opposed by "shouts of joy," much as cheers and groans
contend at a public meeting where the resolutions are *not*
passed unanimously, the poet completes his climax in this
way :—

> "Hence, in one peal of loud, eternal praise,
> The *charmed spectators* thunder their applause."

In the same taste, he sings :—

> "Eternity, the various sentence past,
> Assigns the sever'd throng distinct abodes,
> *Sulphureous or ambrosial.*"

Exquisite delicacy of indication!   He is too nice to be specific
as to the interior of the "sulphureous" abode; but when once
half the human race are shut up there, hear how he enjoys
turning the key on them!—

> "What ensues?
> The deed predominant, the deed of deeds !
> Which makes a hell of hell, a *heaven of heaven !*
> The goddess, with determin'd aspect, turns
> Her adamantine key's enormous size
> Through Destiny's inextricable wards,
> *Deep driving every bolt* on both their fates.
> Then, from the crystal battlements of heaven,
> Down, down she hurls it through the dark profound,
> Ten thousand, thousand fathom ; there to rust
> And ne'er unlock her resolution more.
> The deep resounds ; and Hell, through all her glooms,
> Returns, in groans, the melancholy roar."

This is one of the blessings for which Dr. Young thanks
God "most" :—

> "For all I bless Thee, most, for the severe ;
> Her death—my own at hand—*the fiery gulf,*
> *That flaming bound of wrath omnipotent !*
> *It thunders ;—but it thunders to preserve ;*
> . . . . . . its wholesome dread
> Averts the dreaded pain ; *its hideous groans*

> *Join Heaven's sweet Hallelujahs in Thy praise,*
> Great Source of good alone! How kind in all!
> In vengeance kind! Pain, Death, Gehenna, *save*" . . .

i.e., save *me*, Dr. Young, who, in return for that favor, promise to give my divine patron the monopoly of that exuberance in laudatory epithet, of which specimens may be seen at any moment in a large number of dedications and odes to kings, queens, prime ministers, and other persons of distinction. *That*, in Young's conception, is what God delights in. His crowning aim in the "drama" of the ages is to vindicate his own renown. The God of the "Night Thoughts" is simply Young himself "writ large"—a didactic poet, who "lectures" mankind in the antithetic hyperbole of mortal and immortal joys, earth and the stars, hell and heaven; and expects the tribute of inexhaustible "applause." Young has no conception of religion as anything else than egoism turned heavenward; and he does not merely imply this, he insists on it. Religion, he tells us, in argumentative passages too long to quote, is "ambition, pleasure, and the love of gain," directed toward the joys of the future life instead of the present. And his ethics correspond to his religion. He vacillates, indeed, in his ethical theory, and shifts his position in order to suit his immediate purpose in argument; but he never changes his level so as to see beyond the horizon of mere selfishness. Sometimes he insists, as we have seen, that the belief in a future life is the only basis of morality; but elsewhere he tells us—

> "In self-applause is virtue's golden prize."

Virtue, with Young, must always squint—must never look straight toward the immediate object of its emotion and effort. Thus, if a man risks perishing in the snow himself rather than forsake a weaker comrade, he must either do this because his hopes and fears are directed to another world, or because he desires to applaud himself afterward! Young, if we may believe him, would despise the action as folly unless it had these motives. Let us hope he was not so bad as he pretended to be! The tides of the divine life in man move under the thickest ice of theory.

Another indication of Young's deficiency in moral, *i.e.*, in sympathetic emotion, is his unintermitting habit of pedagogic moralizing. On its theoretic and perceptive side, Morality touches Science; on its emotional side, poetic Art. Now, the products of poetic Art are great in proportion as they result from the immediate prompting of innate power, and not from labored obedience to a theory or rule; and the presence of genius or innate prompting is directly opposed to the perpetual consciousness of a rule. The action of faculty is imperious, and supersedes the reflection *why* it should act. In the same way, in proportion as morality is emotional, it will exhibit itself in direct sympathetic feeling and action, and not as the recognition of a rule. Love does not say, " I ought to love "— it loves. Pity does not say, " It is right to be pitiful "—it pities. Justice does not say, " I am bound to be just "—it feels justly. It is only where moral emotion is comparatively weak that the contemplation of a rule or theory habitually mingles with its action; and in accordance with this, we think experience, both in literature and life, has shown that the minds which are predominantly didactic, are deficient in sympathetic emotion. A man who is perpetually thinking in monitory apothegms, who has an unintermittent flux of rebuke, can have little energy left for simple feeling. And this is the case with Young. In his highest flights of contemplation, and his most wailing soliloquies, he interrupts himself to fling an admonitory parenthesis at Lorenzo, or to hint that " folly's creed " is the reverse of his own. Before his thoughts can flow, he must fix his eye on an imaginary miscreant, who gives unlimited scope for lecturing, and recriminates just enough to keep the spring of admonition and argument going to the extent of nine books. It is curious to see how this pedagogic habit of mind runs through Young's contemplation of Nature. As the tendency to see our own sadness reflected in the external world has been called by Mr. Ruskin the " pathetic fallacy," so we may call Young's disposition to see a rebuke or a warning in every natural object, the " pedagogic fallacy." To his mind, the heavens are " forever *scolding* as they shine "; and the great function of the stars is to be a " lecture to mankind." The conception of the Deity as a didactic author is

not merely an implicit point of view with him; he works it
out in elaborate imagery, and at length makes it the occasion
of his most extraordinary achievement in the "art of sinking,"
by exclaiming—*à propos*, we need hardly say, of the nocturnal
heavens—

> "Divine Instructor! Thy first volume this
> For man's perusal! all in CAPITALS!"

It is this pedagogic tendency, this sermonizing attitude of
Young's mind, which produces the wearisome monotony of his
pauses. After the first two or three Nights, he is rarely singing, rarely pouring forth any continuous melody inspired by
the spontaneous flow of thought or feeling. He is rather occupied with argumentative insistence, with hammering in the
proofs of his propositions by disconnected verses, which he
puts down at intervals. The perpetual recurrence of the
pause at the end of the line throughout long passages, makes
them as fatiguing to the ear as a monotonous chant, which
consists of the endless repetition of one short musical phrase
For example:—

> "Past hours,
> If not by guilt, yet wound us by their flight,
> If folly bound our prospect by the grave,
> All feeling of futurity be numb'd,
> All godlike passion for eternals quench'd,
> All relish of realities expired;
> Renounced all correspondence with the skies;
> Our freedom chain'd; quite wingless our desire;
> In sense dark-prison'd all that ought to soar;
> Prone to the centre; crawling in the dust;
> Dismounted every great and glorious aim;
> Enthralled every faculty divine,
> Heart-buried in the rubbish of the world."

How different from the easy, graceful melody of Cowper's
blank verse! Indeed it is hardly possible to criticise Young,
without being reminded at every step of the contrast presented
to him by Cowper. And this contrast urges itself upon us
the more from the fact that there is, to a certain extent, a
parallelism between the "Night Thoughts" and the "Task."
In both poems, the author achieves his greatest in virtue of
the new freedom conferred by blank verse; both poems are

4

professedly didactic, and mingle much satire with their graver
meditations; both poems are the productions of men whose
estimate of this life was formed by the light of a belief in
immortality, and who were intensely attached to Christianity.
On some grounds, we might have anticipated a more morbid
view of things from Cowper than from Young.   Cowper's religion was dogmatically the more gloomy, for he was a Cal-
vinist; while Young was a "low" Arminian, believing that
Christ died for all, and that the only obstacle to any man's
salvation lay in his will, which he could change if he chose.
There was deep and unusual sadness involved in Cowper's
personal lot; while Young, apart from his ambitious and
greedy discontent, seems to have had no exceptional sorrow.

Yet see how a lovely, sympathetic nature manifests itself in
spite of creed and circumstance!   Where is the poem that sur-
passes the "Task" in the genuine love it breathes, at once
toward inanimate and animate existence—in truthfulness of
perception and sincerity of presentation—in the calm gladness
that springs from a delight in objects for their own sake, without self-reference—in divine sympathy with the lowliest pleasures, with the most short-lived capacity for pain?   Here is
no railing at the earth's "melancholy map," but the happiest
lingering over her simplest scenes with all the fond minute-
ness of attention that belongs to love; no pompous rhetoric
about the inferiority of the "brutes," but a warm plea on
their behalf against man's inconsiderateness and cruelty, and
a sense of enlarged happiness from their companionship in
enjoyment; no vague rant about human misery and human
virtue, but that close and vivid presentation of particular sorrows and privations, of particular deeds and misdeeds, which
is the direct road to the emotions.   How Cowper's exquisite
mind falls with the mild warmth of morning sunlight on the
commonest objects, at once disclosing every detail and invest-
ing every detail with beauty!   No object is too small to
prompt his song—not the sooty film on the bars, or the spout-
less teapot holding a bit of mignonette that serves to cheer
the dingy town-lodging with a "hint that Nature lives"; and
yet his song is never trivial, for he is alive to small objects,
not because his mind is narrow, but because his glance is clear

and his heart is large. Instead of trying to edify us by super-
cilious allusions to the "brutes" and the "stalls," he interests
us in that tragedy of the hen-roost when the thief has wrenched
the door—

> "Where Chanticleer amidst his harem sleeps
> *In unsuspecting pomp*"

in the patient cattle, that on the winter's morning

> "Mourn in corners where the fence
> Screens them, and seem half petrified to sleep
> *In unrecumbent sadness*"

in the little squirrel, that, surprised by him in his woodland
walk,

> "At once, swift as a bird,
> Ascends the neighboring beech; there whisks his brush,
> And perks his ears, and stamps, and cries aloud,
> With all the prettiness of feigned alarm
> And anger insignificantly fierce."

And then he passes into reflection, not with curt apothegm
and snappish reproof, but with that melodious flow of utterance which belongs to thought when it is carried in a stream
of feeling:—

> "The heart is hard in nature, and unfit
> For human fellowship, as being void
> Of sympathy, and therefore dead alike
> To love and friendship both, that is not pleased
> With sight of animals enjoying life,
> Nor feels their happiness augment his own."

His large and tender heart embraces the most every-day forms
of human life: the carter driving his team through the wintry
storm; the cottager's wife who, painfully nursing the embers
on her hearth, while her infants "sit cowering o'er the sparks,"

> "Retires, content to quake, so they be warmed";

or the villager, with her little ones, going out to pick

> "A cheap but wholesome salad from the brook":

and he compels our colder natures to follow his in its manifold
sympathies, not by exhortations, not by telling us to meditate

at midnight, to "indulge" the thought of death, or to ask ourselves how we shall "weather an eternal night," *but by presenting to us the object of his compassion truthfully and lovingly.*
And when he handles greater themes, when he takes a wider
survey, and considers the men or the deeds which have a direct influence on the welfare of communities and nations, there
is the same unselfish warmth of feeling, the same scrupulous
truthfulness.   He is never vague in his remonstrance or his
satire; but puts his finger on some particular vice or folly,
which excites his indignation or "dissolves his heart in pity,"
because of some specific injury it does to his fellow-man or to
a sacred cause.   And when he is asked why he interests himself about the sorrows and wrongs of others, hear what is the
reason he gives.   Not, like Young, that the movements of the
planets show a mutual dependence, and that

> "Thus man his sovereign duty learns in this
> Material picture of benevolence";—

or that,—

> "More generous sorrow while it sinks, exalts,
> And conscious virtue mitigates the pang."

What is Cowper's answer, when he imagines some "sage eru-
dite, profound," asking him "What's the world to you?"—

> "Much.   *I was born of woman, and drew milk*
> *As sweet as charity from human breasts.*
> I think, articulate, I laugh and weep,
> And exercise all functions of a man.
> How then should I and any man that lives
> Be strangers to each other?"

Young is astonished that men can make war on each other—
that any one can "seize his brother's throat," while

> "The Planets cry, 'Forbear.'"

Cowper weeps because—

> "There is no flesh in man's obdurate heart;
> *It does not feel for man.*"

Young applauds God as a monarch with an empire and a court

quite superior to the English, or as an author who produces
"volumes for man's perusal." Cowper sees his Father's love
in all the gentle pleasures of the home fireside, in the charms
even of the wintry landscape, and thinks—

> "Happy who walks with Him! whom what he finds
> Of flavor or of scent in fruit or flower,
> Or what he views of beautiful or grand
> In nature, from the broad majestic oak
> To the green blade that twinkles in the sun,
> *Prompts with remembrance of a present God.*"

To conclude—for we must arrest ourselves in a contrast that
would lead us beyond our bounds: Young flies for his utmost
consolation to the day of judgment, when

> "Final Ruin fiercely drives
> Her ploughshare o'er Creation";

when earth, stars, and suns are swept aside—

> "And now, all dross removed, Heaven's own pure day
> Full on the confines of our ether, flames:
> While (dreadful contrast!) far (how far!) beneath,
> Hell, bursting, belches forth her blazing seas,
> And storms sulphureous; her voracious jaws
> Expanding wide, and roaring for her prey,"—

Dr. Young, and similar "ornaments of religion and virtue,"
passing, of course, with grateful "applause" into the upper
region. Cowper finds his highest inspiration in the Millennium—in the restoration of this our beloved home of earth to
perfect holiness and bliss, when the Supreme

> "Shall visit earth in mercy; shall descend
> Propitious in His chariot paved with love;
> And what His storms have blasted and defaced
> For man's revolt, shall with a smile repair."

And into what delicious melody his song flows at the thought
of that blessedness to be enjoyed by future generations on
earth!—

> "The dwellers in the vales and on the rocks
> Shout to each other, and the mountain-tops
> From distant mountains catch the flying joy;
> Till, nation after nation taught the strain,
> Earth rolls the rapturous Hosanna round!"

The sum of our comparison is this: In Young we have the type of that deficient human sympathy, that impiety toward the present and the visible, which flies for its motives, its sanctities, and its religion, to the remote, the vague, and the unknown; in Cowper we have the type of that genuine love which cherishes things in proportion to their nearness, and feels its reverence grow in proportion to the intimacy of its knowledge.

GERMAN WIT: HEINRICH HEINE.

"Nothing," says Goethe, "is more significant of men's character than what they find laughable." The truth of this observation would perhaps have been more apparent if he had said *culture* instead of character. The last thing in which the cultivated man can have community with the vulgar is their jocularity; and we can hardly exhibit more strikingly the wide gulf which separates him from them than by comparing the object which shakes the diaphragm of a coal-heaver with the highly complex pleasure derived from a real witticism. That any high order of wit is exceedingly complex, and demands a ripe and strong mental development, has one evidence in the fact that we do not find it in boys at all in proportion to their manifestation of other powers. Clever boys generally aspire to the heroic and poetic rather than the comic, and the crudest of all their efforts are their jokes. Many a witty man will remember how, in his school-days, a practical joke, more or less Rabelaisian, was for him the *ne plus ultra* of the ludicrous. It seems to have been the same with the boyhood of mankind. The fun of early races was, we fancy, of the after-dinner kind —loud-throated laughter over the wine-cup, taken too little account of in sober moments to enter as an element into their Art, and differing as much from the laughter of a Chamfort or a Sheridan as the gastronomic enjoyment of an ancient Briton, whose dinner had no other "removes" than from acorns to beechmast and back again to acorns, differed from the subtle pleasures of the palate experienced by his turtle-eating descendant. It was their lot to live seriously through stages which to later generations were to become comedy, as those amiable-looking pre-Adamite amphibia which Professor Owen has restored for us in effigy at Sydenham doubtless took seriously the grotesque physiognomies of their kindred. Heavy

experience in their case, as in every other, was the base from
which the salt of future wit was to be made.

Humor is of earlier growth than Wit, and it is in accordance
with this earlier growth that it has more affinity with the
poetic tendencies, while Wit is more nearly allied to the
ratiocinative intellect. Humor draws its materials from situations and characteristics; Wit seizes on unexpected and complex relations. Humor is chiefly representative and descrip-
tive; it is diffuse, and flows along without any other law than
its own fantastic will; or it flits about like a will-o'-the-wisp,
amazing us by its whimsical transitions. Wit is brief and
sudden, and sharply defined as a crystal: it does not make
pictures, it is not fantastic; but it detects an unsuspected
analogy, or suggests a startling or confounding inference.
Every one who has had the opportunity of making the comparison will remember that the effect produced on him by
some witticisms is closely akin to the effect produced on him
by subtle reasoning which lays open a fallacy or absurdity;
and there are persons whose delight in such reasoning always
manifests itself in laughter. This affinity of Wit with ratio-
cination is the more obvious in proportion as the species of wit
is higher and deals less with words and with superficialities
than with the essential qualities of things. Some of Johnson's most admirable witticisms consist in the suggestion of
an analogy which immediately exposes the absurdity of an
action or proposition; and it is only their ingenuity, conden-
sation, and instantaneousness which lift them from reasoning
into Wit—they are *reasoning raised to a higher power.* On
the other hand, Humor, in its higher forms, and in proportion
as it associates itself with the sympathetic emotions, continually passes into poetry: nearly all great modern humorists
may be called prose poets.

Some confusion as to the nature of humor has been created
by the fact, that those who have written most eloquently on it
have dwelt almost exclusively on its higher forms, and have
defined humor in general as the *sympathetic* presentation of
incongruous elements in human nature and life—a definition
which only applies to its later development. A great deal of
humor may coexist with a great deal of barbarism, as we see

in the middle ages; but the strongest flavor of the humor in such cases will come, not from sympathy, but more probably from triumphant egoism or intolerance; at best it will be the love of the ludicrous exhibiting itself in illustrations of successful cunning and of the *lex talionis*, as in "Reineke Fuchs," or shaking off in a holiday mood the yoke of a too exacting faith, as in the old Mysteries. Again, it is impossible to deny a high degree of humor to many practical jokes, but no sympathetic nature can enjoy them. Strange as the genealogy may seem, the original parentage of that wonderful and delicious mixture of fun, fancy, philosophy, and feeling which constitutes modern humor, was probably the cruel mockery of a savage at the writhings of a suffering enemy—such is the tendency of things toward the better and more beautiful! Probably the reason why high culture demands more complete harmony with its moral sympathies in humor than in wit, is that humor is in its nature more prolix—that it has not the direct and irresistible force of wit. Wit is an electric shock, which takes us by violence quite independently of our predominant mental disposition; but humor approaches us more deliberately and leaves us masters of ourselves. Hence it is that, while coarse and cruel humor has almost disappeared from contemporary literature, coarse and cruel wit abounds. Even refined men cannot help laughing at a coarse *bon-mot* or a lacerating personality, if the "shock" of the witticism is a powerful one; while mere fun will have no power over them if it jar on their moral taste. Hence, too, it is that, while wit is perennial, humor is liable to become superannuated.

As is usual with definitions and classifications, however, this distinction between wit and humor does not exactly represent the actual fact. Like all other species, Wit and Humor overlap and blend with each other. There are *bon-mots*, like many of Charles Lamb's, which are a sort of facetious hybrids, we hardly know whether to call them witty or humorous; there are rather lengthy descriptions or narratives which, like Voltaire's "Micromégas," would be humorous if they were not so sparkling and antithetic, so pregnant with suggestion and satire, that we are obliged to call them witty. We rarely find wit untempered by humor, or humor without a spice of wit; and sometimes we find them both united in the highest degree in the same mind, as in Shakespeare and Molière. A happy conjunction this, for wit is apt to be cold, and thin-lipped, and Mephistophelean in men who have no relish for humor, whose lungs do never crow like Chanticleer at fun and drollery; and broad-faced rollicking humor needs the refining influence of wit. Indeed it may be said that there is no really fine writing in which wit has not an implicit, if not an explicit action. The wit may never rise to the surface, it may never flame out into a witticism; but it helps to give brightness and transparency, it warns off from flights and exaggerations which verge on the ridiculous—in every *genre* of writing it preserves a man from sinking into the *genre ennuyeux*. And it is eminently needed for this office in humorous writing; for, as humor has no limits imposed on it by its material, no law but its own exuberance, it is apt to become preposterous and wearisome unless checked by wit, which is the enemy of all monotony, of all lengthiness, of all exaggeration.

Perhaps the nearest approach Nature has given us to a complete analysis, in which wit is as thoroughly exhausted of humor as possible, and humor as bare as possible of wit, is in the typical Frenchman and the typical German. Voltaire, the intensest example of pure wit, fails in most of his fictions from his lack of humor. "Micromégas" is a perfect tale, because, as it deals chiefly with philosophic ideas and does not touch the marrow of human feeling and life, the writer's wit and wisdom were all-sufficient for his purpose. Not so with "Candide." Here Voltaire had to give pictures of life as well as to convey philosophic truth and satire, and here we feel the want of humor. The sense of the ludicrous is continually defeated by disgust, and the scenes, instead of presenting us with an amusing or agreeable picture, are only the frame for a witticism. On the other hand, German humor generally shows no sense of measure, no instinctive tact; it is either floundering and clumsy as the antics of a leviathan, or laborious and interminable as a Lapland day, in which one loses all hope that the stars and quiet will ever come. For this reason Jean Paul, the greatest of German humorists, is unendurable to many readers, and frequently tiresome to all. Here, as elsewhere, the German shows the absence of that delicate perception, that sensibility to gradation, which is the essence of tact and taste and the necessary concomitant of wit. All his subtlety is reserved for the region of metaphysics. For *Identität*, in the abstract, no one can have an acuter vision; but in the concrete he is satisfied with a very loose approximation. He has the finest nose for *Empirismus* in philosophical doctrine, but the presence of more or less tobacco-smoke in the air he breathes is imperceptible to him. To the typical German—*Vetter Michel*—it is indifferent whether his door-lock will catch; whether his teacup be more or less than an inch thick; whether or not his book have every other leaf unstitched; whether his neighbor's conversation be more or less of a shout; whether he pronounces *b* or *p*, *t* or *d*; whether or not his adored one's teeth be few and far between. He has the same sort of insensibility to gradations in time. A German comedy is like a German sentence: you see no reason in its structure why it should ever come to an end, and you accept the conclusion as an arrangement of Providence rather than of the author. We have heard Germans use the word *Langeweile*, the equivalent for *ennui*, and we have secretly wondered *what* it can be that produces *ennui* in a German. Not the longest of long tragedies, for we have known him to pronounce that *höchst fesselnd*; not the heaviest of heavy books, for he delights in that as *gründlich*; not the slowest of journeys in a *Post-wagen*, for the slower the horses the more cigars he can smoke before he reaches his journey's end. German *ennui* must be something as superlative as Barclay's treble X, which, we suppose, implies an extremely unknown quantity of stupefaction.

It is easy to see that this national deficiency in nicety of perception must have its effect on the national appreciation and exhibition of Humor. You find in Germany ardent admirers of Shakespeare, who tell you that what they think most admirable in him is his *Wortspiel*, his verbal quibbles; and it is a remarkable fact that, among the five great races concerned in modern civilization, the German race is the only one which, up to the present century, had contributed nothing classic to the common stock of European wit and humor; unless " Reineke Fuchs " can be fairly claimed as a peculiarly Teutonic product.

Italy was the birthplace of Pantomime and the immortal Pul-
cinello; Spain had produced Cervantes; France had produced
Rabelais and Molière, and classic wits innumerable; England
had yielded Shakespeare and a host of humorists.   But Germany had borne no great comic dramatist, no great satirist,
and she has not yet repaired the omission; she had not even
produced any humorist of a high order.   Among her great
writers, Lessing is the one who is the most specifically witty.
We feel the implicit influence of wit—the "flavor of mind"
—throughout his writings; and it is often concentrated into
pungent satire, as every reader of the "Hamburgische Drama-
turgie" remembers.   Still, Lessing's name has not become
European through his wit, and his charming comedy, "Minna
von Barnhelm," has won no place on a foreign stage.   Of
course, we do not pretend to an exhaustive acquaintance with
German literature; we not only admit—we are sure—that it
includes much comic writing of which we know nothing.   We
simply state the fact, that no German production of that kind,
before the present century, ranked as European—a fact which
does not, indeed, determine the amount of the national facetiousness, but which is quite decisive as to its quality.   Whatever may be the stock of fun which Germany yields for home
consumption, she has provided little for the palate of other
lands.   All honor to her for the still greater things she has
done for us!   She has fought the hardest fight for freedom of
thought, has produced the grandest inventions, has made magnificent contributions to science, has given us some of the
divinest poetry, and quite the divinest music, in the world.
We revere and treasure the products of the German mind.
To say that that mind is not fertile in wit, is only like saying
that excellent wheat-land is not rich pasture; to say that we
do not enjoy German facetiousness, is no more than to say,
that though the horse is the finest of quadrupeds, we do not
like him to lay his hoof playfully on our shoulder.   Still, as
we have noticed that the pointless puns and stupid jocularity
of the boy may ultimately be developed into the epigrammatic
brilliancy and polished playfulness of the man; as we believe
that racy wit and chastened delicate humor are inevitably the
results of invigorated and refined mental activity,—we can also

believe that Germany will one day yield a crop of wits and humorists.

Perhaps there is already an earnest of that future crop in the existence of Heinrich Heine, a German born with the present century, who, to Teutonic imagination, sensibility, and humor, adds an amount of *esprit* that would make him brilliant among the most brilliant of Frenchmen. True, this unique German wit is half a Hebrew; but he and his ancestors spent their youth in German air, and were reared on *Wurst* and *Sauerkraut*, so that he is as much a German as a pheasant is an English bird, or a potato an Irish vegetable. But whatever else he may be, Heine is one of the most remarkable men of this age; no echo, but a real voice, and therefore, like all genuine things in this world, worth studying; a surpassing lyric poet, who has uttered our feelings for us in delicious song; a humorist, who touches leaden folly with the magic wand of his fancy, and transmutes it into the fine gold of art —who sheds his sunny smile on human tears, and makes them a beauteous rainbow on the cloudy background of life; a wit, who holds in his mighty hand the most scorching lightnings of satire; an artist in prose literature, who has shown even more completely than Goethe the possibilities of German prose; and—in spite of all charges against him, true as well as false —a lover of freedom, who has spoken wise and brave words on behalf of his fellow-men. He is, moreover, a suffering man, who, with all the highly wrought sensibility of genius, has to endure terrible physical ills; and as such he calls forth more than an intellectual interest. It is true, alas! that there is a heavy weight in the other scale—that Heine's magnificent powers have often served only to give electric force to the expression of debased feeling, so that his works are no Phidian statue of gold, and ivory, and gems, but have not a little brass, and iron, and miry clay mingled with the precious metal. The audacity of his occasional coarseness and personality is unparalleled in contemporary literature, and has hardly been exceeded by the license of former days. Hence, before his volumes are put within the reach of immature minds, there is need of a friendly penknife to exercise a strict censorship. Yet, when all coarseness, all scurrility, all Mephistophelean contempt for the reverent feelings of other men, is removed, there will be a plenteous remainder of exquisite poetry, of wit, humor, and just thought. It is apparently too often a congenial task to write severe words about the transgressions committed by men of genius, especially when the censor has the advantage of being himself a man of no genius, so that those transgressions seem to him quite gratuitous; he, forsooth, never lacerated any one by his wit, or gave irresistible piquancy to a coarse allusion, and his indignation is not mitigated by any knowledge of the temptation that lies in transcendent power. We are also apt to measure what a gifted man has done by our arbitrary conception of what he might have done, rather than by a comparison of his actual doings with our own or those of other ordinary men. We make ourselves over-zealous agents of heaven, and demand that our brother should bring usurious interest for his five Talents, forgetting that it is less easy to manage five Talents than two. Whatever benefit there may be in denouncing the evil, it is after all more edifying, and certainly more cheering, to appreciate the good. Hence, in endeavoring to give our readers some account of Heine and his works, we shall not dwell lengthily on his failings; we shall not hold the candle up to dusty, vermin-haunted corners, but let the light fall as much as possible on the nobler and more attractive details. Our sketch of Heine's life, which has been drawn from various sources, will be free from everything like intrusive gossip, and will derive its coloring chiefly from the autobiographical hints and descriptions scattered through his own writings. Those of our readers who happen to know nothing of Heine, will in this way be making their acquaintance with the writer while they are learning the outline of his career.

We have said that Heine was born with the present century; but this statement is not precise, for we learn that, according to his certificate of baptism, he was born December 12, 1799. However, as he himself says, the important point is, that he was born, and born on the banks of the Rhine, at Düsseldorf, where his father was a merchant. In his "Reisebilder" he gives us some recollections, in his wild poetic way, of the dear old town where he spent his childhood, and of his

schoolboy troubles there. We shall quote from these in butterfly fashion, sipping a little nectar here and there, without
regard to any strict order:—

"I first saw the light on the banks of that lovely stream, where Folly
grows on the green hills, and in autumn is plucked, pressed, poured into
casks, and sent into foreign lands. Believe me, I yesterday heard some
one utter folly which, in anno 1811, lay in a bunch of grapes I then saw
growing on the Johannisberg. . . . Mon Dieu! if I had only such faith
in me that I could remove mountains, the Johannisberg would be the
very mountain I should send for wherever I might be; but as my faith
is not so strong, imagination must help me, and it transports me at once
to the lovely Rhine. . . . I am again a child, and playing with other
children on the Schlossplatz, at Düsseldorf on the Rhine. Yes, madam,
there was I born; and I note this expressly, in case, after my death,
seven cities—Schilda, Krähwinkel, Polkwitz, Bockum, Dülken, Göttingen, and Schöppenstadt—should contend for the honor of being my birthplace. Düsseldorf is a town on the Rhine; sixteen thousand men live
there, and many hundred thousand men besides lie buried there. . . .
Among them, many of whom my mother says, that it would be better if
they were still living; for example, my grandfather and my uncle, the
old Herr Von Geldern and the young Herr Von Geldern, both such celebrated doctors, who saved so many men from death, and yet must die
themselves. And the pious Ursula, who carried me in her arms when I
was a child, also lies buried there, and a rose-bush grows on her grave;
she loved the scent of roses so well in life, and her heart was pure rose-
incense and goodness. The knowing old Canon, too, lies buried there.
Heavens, what an object he looked when I last saw him! *He was made
up of nothing but mind and plasters*, and nevertheless studied day and
night, as if he were alarmed lest the worms should find an idea too little
in his head. And the little William lies there, and for this I am to
blame. We were schoolfellows in the Franciscan monastery, and were
playing on that side of it where the Düssel flows between stone walls,
and I said—' William, fetch out the kitten that has just fallen in'—and
merrily he went down on to the plank which lay across the brook,
snatched the kitten out of the water, but fell in himself, and was dragged
out dripping and dead. *The kitten lived to a good old age.* . . . Princes
in that day were not the tormented race they are now; the crown grew
firmly on their heads, and at night they drew a nightcap over it, and
slept peacefully, and peacefully slept the people at their feet; and when
the people waked in the morning, they said ' Good-morning, father!'—
and the princes answered, ' Good-morning, dear children!' But it was
suddenly quite otherwise; for when we awoke one morning at Düsseldorf, and were ready to say, ' Good-morning, father!'—lo! the father
was gone away; and in the whole town there was nothing but dumb
sorrow, everywhere a sort of funeral disposition; and people glided
along silently to the market, and read the long placard placed on the

door of the Town Hall. It was dismal weather; yet the lean tailor,
Kilian, stood in his nankeen jacket which he usually wore only in the
house, and his blue worsted stockings hung down so that his naked legs
peeped out mournfully, and his thin lips trembled while he muttered the
announcement to himself. And an old soldier read rather louder, and
at many a word a crystal tear trickled down to his brave old mustache.
I stood near him and wept in company, and asked him, '*Why we wept?*'
He answered, 'The Elector has abdicated.' And then he read again,
and at the words, 'for the long-manifested fidelity of my subjects,' and
'hereby set you free from your allegiance,' he wept more than ever. It
is strangely touching to see an old man like that, with faded uniform
and scarred face, weep so bitterly all of a sudden. While we were reading, the Electoral arms were taken down from the Town Hall; everything had such a desolate air, that it was as if an eclipse of the sun were
expected. . . . I went home and wept, and wailed out, 'The Elector
has abdicated!' In vain my mother took a world of trouble to explain
the thing to me. I knew what I knew; I was not to be persuaded, but
went crying to bed, and in the night dreamed that the world was at an
end."

The next morning, however, the sun rises as usual, and
Joachim Murat is proclaimed Grand Duke, whereupon there
is a holiday at the public school, and Heinrich (or Harry, for
that was his baptismal name, which he afterward had the
good taste to change), perched on the bronze horse of the
Electoral statue, sees quite a different scene from yesterday's :—

"The next day the world was again all in order, and we had school as
before, and things were got by heart as before—the Roman emperors,
chronology, the nouns in *im*, the *verba irregularia*, Greek, Hebrew,
geography, mental arithmetic!—heavens! my head is still dizzy with
it,—all must be learned by heart! And a great deal of this came in
very conveniently for me in after life. For if I had not known the
Roman kings by heart, it would subsequently have been quite indifferent to me whether Niebuhr had proved or had not proved that they never
really existed. . . . But oh! the trouble I had at school with the endless dates. And with arithmetic it was still worse. What I understood
best was subtraction, for that has a very practical rule: 'Four can't be
taken from three, therefore I must borrow one.' But I advise every one
in such a case to borrow a few extra pence, for no one can tell what may
happen. . . . As for Latin, you have no idea, madam, what a com-
plicated affair it is. The Romans would never have found time to
conquer the world if they had first had to learn Latin. Luckily for
them, they already knew in their cradles what nouns have their accusa-
tive in *im*. I, on the contrary, had to learn them by heart in the sweat
of my brow; nevertheless, it is fortunate for me that I know them; . . .
and the fact that I have them at my finger-ends if I should ever happen

to want them suddenly, affords me much inward repose and consolation in many troubled hours of life. . . . Of Greek I will not say a word; I should get too much irritated. The monks in the middle ages were not so far wrong when they maintained that Greek was an invention of the devil. God knows the suffering I endured over it. . . . With Hebrew it went somewhat better, for I had always a great liking for the Jews, though to this very hour they crucify my good name; but I could never get on so far in Hebrew as my watch, which had much familiar intercourse with pawnbrokers, and in this way contracted many Jewish habits —for example, it wouldn't go on Saturdays."

Heine's parents were apparently not wealthy, but his education was cared for by his uncle, Solomon Heine, a great banker in Hamburg, so that he had no early pecuniary disadvantages to struggle with. He seems to have been very happy in his mother, who was not of Hebrew, but of Teutonic blood; he often mentions her with reverence and affection, and in the "Buch der Lieder" there are two exquisite sonnets addressed to her, which tell how his proud spirit was always subdued by the charm of her presence, and how her love was the home of his heart after restless weary wandering:—

> "Wie mächtig auch mein stolzer Muth sich blähe,
> In deiner selig süssen, trauten Nähe
> Ergreift mich oft ein demuthvolle Zagen.
>
> .   .   .   .   .   .
>
> Und immer irrte ich nach Liebe, immer
> Nach Liebe, doch die Liebe fand ich nimmer,
> Und kehrte um nach Hause, krank und trübe.
> Doch da bist du entgegen mir gekommen,
> Und ach! was da in deinem Aug' geschwommen,
> Das war die süsse, langgesuchte Liebe."

He was at first destined for a mercantile life, but Nature declared too strongly against this plan. "God knows," he has lately said in conversation with his brother, "I would willingly have become a banker, but I could never bring myself to that pass. I very early discerned that bankers would one day be the rulers of the world." So commerce was at length given up for law, the study of which he began in 1819 at the University of Bonn. He had already published some poems in the corner of a newspaper, and among them was one

5

on Napoleon, the object of his youthful enthusiasm. This poem, he says in a letter to St. René Taillandier, was written when he was only sixteen. It is still to be found in the "Buch der Lieder" under the title "Die Grenadiere," and it proves that even in its earliest efforts his genius showed a strongly specific character.

It will be easily imagined that the germs of poetry sprouted too vigorously in Heine's brain for jurisprudence to find much room there. Lectures on history and literature, we are told, were more diligently attended than lectures on law. He had taken care, too, to furnish his trunk with abundant editions of the poets, and the poet he especially studied at that time was Byron. At a later period we find his taste taking another direction, for he writes: "Of all authors, Byron is precisely the one who excites in me the most intolerable emotion; whereas Scott, in every one of his works, gladdens my heart, soothes and invigorates me." Another indication of his bent in these Bonn days was a newspaper essay, in which he attacked the Romantic school; and here also he went through that chicken-pox of authorship—the production of a tragedy. Heine's tragedy—"Almansor"—is, as might be expected, better than the majority of these youthful mistakes. The tragic collision lies in the conflict between natural affection and the deadly hatred of religion and of race—in the sacrifice of youthful lovers to the strife between Moor and Spaniard, Moslem and Christian. Some of the situations are striking, and there are passages of considerable poetic merit; but the characters are little more than shadowy vehicles for the poetry, and there is a want of clearness and probability in the structure. It was published two years later, in company with another tragedy, in one act, called "William Ratcliffe," in which there is rather a feeble use of the Scotch second-sight after the manner of the Fate in the Greek tragedy. We smile to find Heine saying of his tragedies, in a letter to a friend soon after their publication: "I know they will be terribly cut up, but I will confess to you in confidence that they are very good,—better than my collection of poems, which are not worth a shot." Elsewhere he tells us, that when, after one of Paganini's concerts, he was passionately complimenting the

great master on his violin-playing, Paganini interrupted him
thus: "But how were you pleased with my *bows?*"

In 1820, Heine left Bonn for Göttingen. He there pursued
his omission of law studies; and at the end of three months
he was rusticated for a breach of the laws against duelling.
While there, he had attempted a negotiation with Brockhaus
for the printing of a volume of poems, and had endured that
first ordeal of lovers and poets—a refusal. It was not until a
year after, that he found a Berlin publisher for his first volume of poems, subsequently transformed, with additions, into
the "Buch der Lieder." He remained between two and three
years at Berlin, and the society he found there seems to have
made these years an important epoch in his culture. He was
one of the youngest members of a circle which assembled at
the house of the poetess Elise von Hohenhausen, the translator
of Byron—a circle which included Chamisso, Varnhagen, and
Rahel (Varnhagen's wife). For Rahel, Heine had a profound
admiration and regard. He afterward dedicated to her the
poems included under the title "Heimkehr"; and he frequently refers to her or quotes her in a way that indicates how
he valued her influence. According to his friend, F. von Hohenhausen, the opinions concerning Heine's talent were very
various among his Berlin friends, and it was only a small
minority that had any presentiment of his future fame. In
this minority was Elise von Hohenhausen, who proclaimed
Heine as the Byron of Germany; but her opinion was met
with much head-shaking and opposition. We can imagine
how precious was such a recognition as hers to the young poet,
then only two or three and twenty, and with by no means an
impressive personality for superficial eyes. Perhaps even the
deep-sighted were far from detecting in that small, blond,
pale young man, with quiet, gentle manners, the latent powers of ridicule and sarcasm—the terrible talons that were one
day to be thrust out from the velvet paw of the young leopard.

It was apparently during this residence in Berlin that Heine
united himself with the Lutheran Church. He would willingly, like many of his friends, he tells us, have remained
free from all ecclesiastical ties if the authorities there had not
forbidden residence in Prussia, and especially in Berlin, to

every one who did not belong to one of the positive religions recognized by the State:—

> "As Henry IV. once laughingly said, '*Paris vaut bien une messe,*' so I might with reason say, '*Berlin vaut bien une prêche*'; and I could afterward, as before, accommodate myself to the very enlightened Christianity, filtrated from all superstition, which could then be had in the churches of Berlin, and which was even free from the divinity of Christ, like turtle-soup without turtle."

At the same period, too, Heine became acquainted with Hegel. In his lately published "Geständnisse" (Confessions), he throws on Hegel's influence over him the blue light of demoniacal wit, and confounds us by the most bewildering, double-edged sarcasms; but that influence seems to have been at least more wholesome than the one which produced the mocking retractations of the "Geständnisse." Through all his self-satire, we discern that in those days he had something like real earnestness and enthusiasm, which are certainly not apparent in his present theistic confession of faith:—

> "On the whole, I never felt a strong enthusiasm for this philosophy, and conviction on the subject was out of the question. I never was an abstract thinker, and I accepted the synthesis of the Hegelian doctrine without demanding any proof, since its consequences flattered my vanity. I was young and proud, and it pleased my vainglory when I learned from Hegel that the true God was not, as my grandmother believed, the God who lives in heaven, but myself here upon earth. This foolish pride had not in the least a pernicious influence on my feelings; on the contrary, it heightened these to the pitch of heroism. I was at that time so lavish in generosity and self-sacrifice, that I must assuredly have eclipsed the most brilliant deeds of those good *bourgeois* of virtue who acted merely from a sense of duty, and simply obeyed the laws of morality."

His sketch of Hegel is irresistibly amusing; but we must warn the reader that Heine's anecdotes are often mere devices of style by which he conveys his satire or opinions. The reader will see that he does not neglect an opportunity of giving a sarcastic lash or two, in passing, to Meyerbeer, for whose music he has a great contempt. The sarcasm conveyed in the substitution of *reputation* for *music* and *journalists* for *musicians* might perhaps escape any one unfamiliar with the sly and unexpected turns of Heine's ridicule:—

"To speak frankly, I seldom understood him, and only arrived at the meaning of his words by subsequent reflection. I believe he wished not to be understood; and hence his practice of sprinkling his discourse with modifying parentheses; hence, perhaps, his preference for persons of whom he knew that they did not understand him, and to whom he all the more willingly granted the honor of his familiar acquaintance. Thus every one in Berlin wondered at the intimate companionship of the profound Hegel with the late Heinrich Beer, a brother of Giacomo Meyerbeer, who is universally known by his reputation, and who has been celebrated by the cleverest journalists. This Beer, namely Heinrich, was a thoroughly stupid fellow, and indeed was afterward actually declared imbecile by his family, and placed under guardianship, because instead of making a name for himself in art or in science by means of his great fortune, he squandered his money on childish trifles; and, for example, one day bought six thousand thalers' worth of walking-sticks. This poor man, who had no wish to pass either for a great tragic dramatist, or for a great star-gazer, or for a laurel-crowned musical genius, a rival of Mozart and Rossini, and preferred giving his money for walking-sticks—this degenerate Beer enjoyed Hegel's most confidential society; he was the philosopher's bosom friend, his Pylades, and accompanied him everywhere like his shadow. The equally witty and gifted Felix Mendelssohn once sought to explain this phenomenon by maintaining that Hegel did not understand Heinrich Beer. I now believe, however, that the real ground of that intimacy consisted in this—Hegel was convinced that no word of what he said was understood by Heinrich Beer; and he could therefore, in his presence, give himself up to all the intellectual outpourings of the moment. In general, Hegel's conversation was a sort of monologue, sighed forth by starts in a noiseless voice: the odd roughness of his expressions often struck me, and many of them have remained in my memory. One beautiful starlight evening we stood together at the window, and I, a young man of one-and-twenty, having just had a good dinner and finished my coffee, spoke with enthusiasm of the stars, and called them the habitations of the departed. But the master muttered to himself, 'The stars! hum! hum! The stars are only a brilliant leprosy on the face of the heavens.' 'For God's sake,' I cried, 'is there, then, no happy place above, where virtue is rewarded after death?' But he, staring at me with his pale eyes, said, cuttingly, 'So you want a bonus for having taken care of your sick mother, and refrained from poisoning your worthy brother?' At these words he looked anxiously round, but appeared immediately set at rest when he observed that it was only Heinrich Beer, who had approached to invite him to a game of whist."

In 1823, Heine returned to Göttingen to complete his career as a law-student, and this time he gave evidence of advanced mental maturity, not only by producing many of the charming poems subsequently included in the "Reisebilder," but also by prosecuting his professional studies diligently enough to leave Göttingen in 1825 as *Doctor juris.* Hereupon he settled at Hamburg as an advocate, but his profession seems to have been the least pressing of his occupations. In those days, a small blond young man, with the brim of his hat drawn over his nose, his coat flying open, and his hands stuck in his trouser-pockets, might be seen stumbling along the streets of Hamburg, staring from side to side, and appearing to have small regard to the figure he made in the eyes of the good citizens. Occasionally an inhabitant, more literary than usual, would point out this young man to his companion as *Heinrich Heine ;* but in general, the young poet had not to endure the inconveniences of being a lion. His poems were devoured, but he was not asked to devour flattery in return. Whether because the fair Hamburgers acted in the spirit of Johnson's advice to Hannah More—to "consider what her flattery was worth before she choked him with it"—or for some other reason, Heine, according to the testimony of August Lewald, to whom we owe these particulars of his Hamburg life, was left free from the persecution of tea-parties. Not, however, from another persecution of genius—nervous headaches, which some persons, we are told, regarded as an improbable fiction, intended as a pretext for raising a delicate white hand to his forehead. It is probable that the sceptical persons alluded to were themselves untroubled with nervous headache, and that their hands were not delicate. Slight details these, but worth telling about a man of genius, because they help us to keep in mind that he is, after all, our brother, having to endure the petty every-day ills of life as we have; with this difference, that his heightened sensibility converts what are mere insect-stings for us into scorpion-stings for him.

It was perhaps in these Hamburg days that Heine paid the visit to Goethe, of which he gives us this charming little picture :—

"When I visited him in Weimar, and stood before him, I involuntarily glanced at his side to see whether the eagle was not there with the lightning in his beak. I was nearly speaking Greek to him ; but, as I observed that he understood German, I stated to him, in German, that the plums on the road between Jena and Weimar were very good. I had for so many long winter nights thought over what lofty and profound things I would say to Goethe, if ever I saw him. And when I saw him at last, I said to him, that the Saxon plums were very good! And Goethe smiled."

During the next few years, Heine produced the most popular of all his works—those which have won him his place as the greatest of living German poets and humorists. Between 1826 and 1829 appeared the four volumes of the "Reisebilder" (Pictures of Travel), and the "Buch der Lieder" (Book of Songs)—a volume of lyrics, of which it is hard to say whether their greatest charm is the lightness and finish of their style, their vivid and original imaginativeness, or their simple, pure sensibility. In his "Reisebilder," Heine carries us with him to the Harz, to the isle of Norderney, to his native town Düsseldorf, to Italy, and to England, sketching scenery and character, now with the wildest, most fantastic humor, now with the finest idyllic sensibility,—letting his thoughts wander from poetry to politics, from criticism to dreamy revery, and blending fun, imagination, reflection, and satire in a sort of exquisite, ever-varying shimmer, like the hues of the opal.

Heine's journey to England did not at all heighten his regard for the English. He calls our language the "hiss of egoism" (*Zischlaute des Egoismus*); and his ridicule of English awkwardness is as merciless as—English ridicule of German awkwardness. His antipathy toward us seems to have grown in intensity, like many of his other antipathies; and in his "Vermischte Schriften" he is more bitter than ever. Let us quote one of his philippics; since bitters are understood to be wholesome:—

"It is certainly a frightful injustice to pronounce sentence of condemnation on an entire people. But with regard to the English, momentary disgust might betray me into this injustice; and on looking at the mass, I easily forget the many brave and noble men who distinguished themselves by intellect and love of freedom. But these, especially the British poets, were always all the more glaringly in contrast with the rest of the nation; they were isolated martyrs to their national relations; and besides, great geniuses do not belong to the particular land of their birth: they scarcely belong to this earth, the Golgotha of their sufferings. The mass—the English blockheads, God forgive me! —are hateful to me in my inmost soul; and I often regard them not at all as my fellow-men, but as miserable automata—machines, whose

motive-power is egoism. In these moods, it seems to me as if I heard
the whizzing wheel-work by which they think, feel, reckon, digest, and
pray: their praying, their mechanical Anglican church-going, with the
gilt Prayer-book under their arms, their stupid, tiresome Sunday, their
awkward piety, is most of all odious to me. I am firmly convinced that
a blaspheming Frenchman is a more pleasing sight for the Divinity than
a praying Englishman."

On his return from England, Heine was employed at Munich
in editing the *Allgemeinen Politischen Annalen;* but in 1830
he was again in the north, and the news of the July Revolution surprised him on the island of Heligoland. He has given
us a graphic picture of his democratic enthusiasm in those
days in some letters, apparently written from Heligoland,
which he has inserted in his book on Börne. We quote some
passages, not only for their biographic interest as showing a
phase of Heine's mental history, but because they are a specimen of his power in that kind of dithyrambic writing which,
in less masterly hands, easily becomes ridiculous:—

"The thick packet of newspapers arrived from the Continent with
these warm, glowing-hot tidings. They were sunbeams wrapped up in
packing-paper, and they inflamed my soul till it burst into the wildest
conflagration. . . . It is all like a dream to me; especially the name
Lafayette sounds to me like a legend out of my earliest childhood. Does
he really sit again on horseback, commanding the National Guard? I
almost fear it may not be true, for it is in print. I will myself go to
Paris, to be convinced of it with my bodily eyes. . . . It must be splendid, when he rides through the streets, the citizen of two worlds, the
god-like old man, with his silver locks streaming down his sacred
shoulder. . . . He greets, with his dear old eyes, the grandchildren of
those who once fought with him for freedom and equality. . . . It is
now sixty years since he returned from America with the Declaration
of Human Rights—the decalogue of the world's new creed, which was
revealed to him amid the thunders and lightnings of cannon. . . . And
the tricolored flag waves again on the towers of Paris, and its streets
resound with the Marseillaise! . . . It is all over with my yearning
for repose. I know now again what I will do, what I ought to do, what
I must do. . . . I am the son of the Revolution, and seize again the
hallowed weapons on which my mother pronounced her magic benedic-
tion. . . . Flowers! flowers! I will crown my head for the death-fight.
And the lyre too—reach me the lyre, that I may sing a battle-song. . . .
Words like flaming stars, that shoot down from the heavens, and burn
up the palaces, and illuminate the huts. . . . Words like bright javelins,
that whirr up to the seventh heaven and strike the pious hypocrites who
have skulked into the Holy of Holies. . . . I am all joy and song, all

sword and flame! Perhaps, too, all delirium. . . . One of those sunbeams wrapped in brown paper has flown to my brain, and set my thoughts aglow. In vain I dip my head into the sea. No water extinguishes this Greek fire. . . . Even the poor Heligolanders shout for joy, although they have only a sort of dim instinct of what has occurred. The fisherman who yesterday took me over to the little sand island, which is the bathing-place here, said to me, smilingly, ' The poor people have won!' Yes; instinctively the people comprehend such events—perhaps better than we, with all our means of knowledge. Thus Frau von Varnhagen once told me that when the issue of the battle of Leipzig was not yet known, the maid-servant suddenly rushed into the room, with the sorrowful cry, ' The nobles have won!' . . . This morning another packet of newspapers is come. I devour them like manna. Child that I am, affecting details touch me yet more than the momentous whole. Oh, if I could but see the dog Medor! . . . The dog Medor brought his master his gun and cartridge-box, and when his master fell, and was buried with his fellow-heroes in the Court of the Louvre, there stayed the poor dog, like a monument of faithfulness, sitting motionless on the grave, day and night, eating but little of the food that was offered him —burying the greater part of it in the earth, perhaps as nourishment for his buried master!"

The enthusiasm which was kept thus at boiling-heat by imagination, cooled down rapidly when brought into contact with reality. In the same book he indicates, in his caustic way, the commencement of that change in his political *temperature* —for it cannot be called a change in opinion—which has drawn down on him immense vituperation from some of the patriotic party, but which seems to have resulted simply from the essential antagonism between keen wit and fanaticism :—

"On the very first days of my arrival in Paris, I observed that things wore, in reality, quite different colors from those which had been shed on them, when in perspective, by the light of my enthusiasm. The silver locks which I saw fluttering so majestically on the shoulders of Lafayette, the hero of two worlds, were metamorphosed into a brown perruque, which made a pitiable covering for a narrow skull. And even the dog Medor, which I visited in the Court of the Louvre, and which, encamped under tricolored flags and trophies, very quietly allowed himself to be fed—he was not at all the right dog, but quite an ordinary brute, who assumed to himself merits not his own, as often happens with the French ; and, like many others, he made a profit out of the glory of the Revolution. . . . He was pampered and patronized, perhaps promoted to the highest posts, while the true Medor, some days after the battle, modestly slunk out of sight, like the true people who created the Revolution."

That it was not merely interest in French politics which
sent Heine to Paris in 1831, but also a perception that German
air was not friendly to sympathizers in July revolutions, is
humorously intimated in the " Gestándnisse " :—

"I had done much and suffered much, and when the sun of the July
Revolution arose in France, I had become very weary, and needed some
recreation. Also, my native air was every day more unhealthy for me,
and it was time I should seriously think of a change of climate. I had
visions: the clouds terrified me, and made all sorts of ugly faces at me.
It often seemed to me as if the sun were a Prussian cockade; at night I
dreamed of a hideous black eagle, which gnawed my liver; and I was
very melancholy. Add to this, I had become acquainted with an old
Berlin Justizrath, who had spent many years in the fortress of Spandau,
and he related to me how unpleasant it is when one is obliged to wear
irons in winter. For myself I thought it very unchristian that the
irons were not warmed a trifle. If the irons were warmed a little for us
they would not make so unpleasant an impression, and even chilly natures
might then bear them very well; it would be only proper consideration,
too, if the fetters were perfumed with essence of roses and laurels, as is
the case in this country (France). I asked my Justizrath whether he
often got oysters to eat at Spandau? He said, No; Spandau was too far
from the sea. Moreover, he said meat was very scarce there, and there
was no kind of *volaille* except flies, which fell into one's soup. . . .
Now, as I really needed some recreation, and as Spandau is too far from
the sea for oysters to be got there, and the Spandau fly-soup did not seem
very appetizing to me; as, besides all this, the Prussian chains are very
cold in winter, and could not be conducive to my health, I resolved to
visit Paris."

Since this time Paris has been Heine's home, and his best
prose works have been written either to inform the Germans
on French affairs or to inform the French on German philosophy and literature. He became a correspondent of the " Allgemeine Zeitung," and his correspondence, which extends,
with an interruption of several years, from 1831 to 1844,
forms the volume entitled " Französische Zustände " (French
Affairs), and the second and third volumes of his " Vermischte
Schriften." It is a witty and often wise commentary on public men and public events: Louis Philippe, Casimir Périer,
Thiers, Guizot, Rothschild, the Catholic party, the Socialist
party, have their turn of satire and appreciation, for Heine
deals out both with an impartiality which made his less favorable critics—Börne, for example—charge him with the rather

incompatible sins of reckless caprice and venality. Literature and art alternate with politics: we have now a sketch of George Sand, or a description of one of Horace Vernet's pictures,—now a criticism of Victor Hugo, or of Liszt,—now an irresistible caricature of Spontini, or Kalkbrenner,—and occasionally the predominant satire is relieved by a fine saying or a genial word of admiration. And all is done with that airy lightness, yet precision of touch, which distinguishes Heine beyond any living writer. The charge of venality was loudly made against Heine in Germany: first, it was said that he was paid to write; then, that he was paid to abstain from writing; and the accusations were supposed to have an irrefragable basis in the fact that he accepted a stipend from the French Government. He has never attempted to conceal the reception of that stipend, and we think his statement (in the "Vermischte Schriften") of the circumstances under which it was offered and received is a sufficient vindication of himself and M. Guizot from any dishonor in the matter.

It may be readily imagined that Heine, with so large a share of the Gallic element as he has in his composition, was soon at his ease in Parisian society, and the years here were bright with intellectual activity and social enjoyment. "His wit," wrote August Lewald, "is a perpetual gushing fountain; he throws off the most delicious descriptions with amazing facility, and sketches the most comic characters in conversation." Such a man could not be neglected in Paris, and Heine was sought on all sides—as a guest in distinguished *salons*, as a possible proselyte in the circle of the Saint Simonians. His literary productiveness seems to have been furthered by this congenial life, which, however, was soon to some extent imbittered by the sense of exile; for since 1835 both his works and his person have been the object of denunciation by the German Governments. Between 1833 and 1845 appeared the four volumes of the "Salon," "Die Romantische Schule" (both written, in the first instance, in French); the book on Börne; "Atta Troll," a romantic poem; "Deutschland," an exquisitely humorous poem, describing his last visit to Germany, and containing some grand passages of serious writing; and the "Neue Gedichte," a collection of lyrical poems.

Among the most interesting of his prose works are the second
volume of the "Salon," which contains a survey of religion
and philosophy in Germany, and the "Romantische Schule,"
a delightful introduction to that phase of German literature
known as the Romantic School.   The book on Börne, which
appeared in 1840, two or three years after the death of that
writer, excited great indignation in Germany, as a wreaking
of vengeance on the dead, an insult to the memory of a man
who had worked and suffered in the cause of freedom—a cause
which was Heine's own.   Börne, we may observe parentheti-
cally, for the information of those who are not familiar with
recent German literature, was a remarkable political writer of
the ultra-liberal party in Germany, who resided in Paris at
the same time as Heine,—a man of stern uncompromising partisanship, and bitter humor.   Without justifying Heine's production of this book, we see excuses for him which should
temper the condemnation passed on it.   There was a radical
opposition of nature between him and Börne: to use his own
distinction, Heine is a Hellene—sensuous, realistic, exquisitely
alive to the beautiful; while Börne was a Nazarene—ascetic,
spiritualistic, despising the pure artist as destitute of earnestness.   Heine has too keen a perception of practical absurdities
and damaging exaggerations ever to become a thoroughgoing
partisan; and with a love of freedom, a faith in the ultimate
triumph of democratic principles, of which we see no just
reason to doubt the genuineness and consistency, he has been
unable to satisfy more zealous and one-sided Liberals by giv·
ing his adhesion to their views and measures, or by adopting a denunciatory tone against those in the opposite ranks.
Börne could not forgive what he regarded as Heine's epicurean
indifference and artistic dalliance, and he at length gave vent
to his antipathy in savage attacks on him through the press,
accusing him of utterly lacking character and principle, and
even of writing under the influence of venal motives.   To
these attacks Heine remained absolutely mute—from contempt, according to his own account; but the retort, which he
resolutely refrained from making during Börne's life, comes
in this volume published after his death with the concentrated force of long-gathering thunder.   The utterly inexcusable

part of the book is the caricature of Börne's friend, Madame Wohl, and the scurrilous insinuations concerning Börne's domestic life. It is said, we know not with how much truth, that Heine had to answer for these in a duel with Madame Wohl's husband, and that, after receiving a serious wound, he promised to withdraw the offensive matter from a future edition. That edition, however, has not been called for. Whatever else we may think of the book, it is impossible to deny its transcendent talent—the dramatic vigor with which Börne is made present to us, the critical acumen with which he is characterized, and the wonderful play of wit, pathos, and thought which runs through the whole. But we will let Heine speak for himself, and first we will give part of his graphic description of the way in which Börne's mind and manners grated on his taste:—

"To the disgust which, in intercourse with Börne, I was in danger of feeling toward those who surrounded him, was added the annoyance I felt from his perpetual talk about politics. Nothing but political argument, and again political argument, even at table, where he managed to hunt me out. At dinner, when I so gladly forget all the vexations of the world, he spoiled the best dishes for me by his patriotic gall, which he poured as a bitter sauce over everything. Calf's feet, à la maître d'hôtel, then my innocent bonne bouche, he completely spoiled for me by Job's tidings from Germany, which he scraped together out of the most unreliable newspapers. And then his accursed remarks, which spoiled one's appetite ! . . . This was a sort of table-talk which did not greatly exhilarate me, and I avenged myself by affecting an excessive, almost impassioned indifference for the objects of Börne's enthusiasm. For example, Börne was indignant that immediately on my arrival in Paris, I had nothing better to do than to write for German papers a long account of the Exhibition of Pictures. I omit all discussion as to whether that interest in Art which induced me to undertake this work was so utterly irreconcilable with the revolutionary interests of the day ; but Börne saw in it a proof of my indifference toward the sacred cause of humanity, and I could in my turn spoil the taste of his patriotic Sauerkraut for him by talking all dinner-time of nothing but pictures, of Robert's Reapers, Horace Vernet's Judith, and Scheffer's Faust. . . . That I never thought it worth while to discuss my political principles with him it is needless to say ; and once when he declared that he had found a contradiction in my writings, I satisfied myself with the ironical answer, 'You are mistaken, mon cher; such contradictions never occur in my works, for always before I begin to write I read over the statement of my political principles in my previous writings, that I may not contradict myself, and that no one may be able to reproach me with apostasy from my liberal principles.'"

And here is his own account of the spirit in which the book was written:—

"I was never Börne's friend, nor was I ever his enemy. The displeasure which he could often excite in me was never very important, and he atoned for it sufficiently by the cold silence which I opposed to all his accusations and raillery. While he lived I wrote not a line against him, I never thought about him, I ignored him completely; and that enraged him beyond measure. If I now speak of him, I do so neither out of enthusiasm nor out of uneasiness; I am conscious of the coolest impartiality. I write here neither an apology nor a critique, and as in painting the man I go on my own observation, the image I present of him ought perhaps to be regarded as a real portrait. And such a monument is due to him—to the great wrestler who, in the arena of our political games, wrestled so courageously, and earned, if not the laurel, certainly the crown of oak leaves. I give an image with his true features, without idealization—the more like him the more honorable for his memory. He was neither a genius nor a hero; he was no Olympian god. He was a man, a denizen of this earth; he was a good writer and a great patriot. . . . Beautiful delicious peace, which I feel at this moment in the depths of my soul! thou rewardest me sufficiently for everything I have done and for everything I have despised. . . . I shall defend myself neither from the reproach of indifference nor from the suspicion of venality. I have for years, during the life of the insinuator, held such self-justification unworthy of me; now even decency demands silence. That would be a frightful spectacle!—polemics between Death and Exile! Dost thou stretch out to me a beseeching hand from the grave? Without rancor I reach mine toward thee. . . . See how noble it is and pure! It was never soiled by pressing the hands of the mob, any more than by the impure gold of the people's enemy. In reality thou hast never injured me. . . . In all thy insinuations there is not a *louis-d'or's* worth of truth."

In one of these years Heine was married, and, in deference to the sentiments of his wife, married according to the rites of the Catholic Church. On this fact busy rumor afterward founded the story of his conversion to Catholicism, and could of course name the day and the spot on which he abjured Protestantism. In his "Geständnisse" Heine publishes a denial of this rumor; less, he says, for the sake of depriving the Catholics of the solace they may derive from their belief in a new convert, than in order to cut off from another party the more spiteful satisfaction of bewailing his instability:—

"That statement of time and place was entirely correct. I was actually on the specified day in the specified church, which was, moreover, a Jesuit church—namely, St. Sulpice; and I then went through a religious act. But this act was no odious abjuration, but a very innocent conjugation; that is to say, my marriage, already performed according to the civil law, there received the ecclesiastical consecration, because my wife, whose family are stanch Catholics, would not have thought her marriage sacred enough without such a ceremony. And I would on no account cause this beloved being any uneasiness or disturbance in her religious views."

For sixteen years—from 1831 to 1847—Heine lived that rapid concentrated life which is known only in Paris; but then, alas! stole on the "days of darkness," and they were to be many. In 1847 he felt the approach of the terrible spinal disease which has for seven years chained him to his bed in acute suffering. The last time he went out of doors, he tells us, was in May, 1848:

"With difficulty I dragged myself to the Louvre, and I almost sank down as I entered the magnificent hall where the ever-blessed goddess of beauty, our beloved Lady of Milo, stands on her pedestal. At her feet I lay long, and wept so bitterly that a stone must have pitied me. The goddess looked compassionately on me, but at the same time disconsolately, as if she would say: Dost thou not see, then, that I have no arms, and thus cannot help thee?"

Since 1848, then, this poet, whom the lovely objects of Nature have always "haunted like a passion," has not descended from the second story of a Parisian house; this man of hungry intellect has been shut out from all direct observation of life, all contact with society, except such as is derived from visitors to his sick-room. The terrible nervous disease has affected his eyes; the sight of one is utterly gone, and he can only raise the lid of the other by lifting it with his finger. Opium alone is the beneficent genius that stills his pain. We hardly know whether to call it an alleviation or an intensification of the torture that Heine retains his mental vigor, his poetic imagination, and his incisive wit; for if his intellectual activity fills up a blank, it widens the sphere of suffering. His brother described him in 1851 as still, in moments when the hand of pain was not too heavy on him, the same Heinrich Heine, poet and satirist by turns. In such moments, he would narrate the strangest things in the gravest manner. But when he came to an end, he would roguishly lift up the lid of his right eye with his finger to see the impression he had produced; and if his audience had been listening with a serious face, he would break into Homeric laughter. We have other proof than personal testimony that Heine's disease allows his genius to retain much of its energy, in the "Romanzero," a volume of poems published in 1851, and written chiefly during the first three years of his illness; and in the first volume of the "Vermischte Schriften," also the product of recent years. Very plaintive is the poet's own description of his condition, in the epilogue to the "Romanzero":—

"Do I really exist? My body is so shrunken that I am hardly anything but a voice; and my bed reminds me of the singing grave of the magician Merlin, which lies in the forest of Brozeliand, in Brittany, under tall oaks whose tops soar like green flames toward heaven. Alas! I envy thee those trees and the fresh breeze that moves their branches, brother Merlin, for no green leaf rustles about my mattress-grave in Paris, where early and late I hear nothing but the rolling of vehicles, hammering, quarrelling, and piano-strumming. A grave without repose, death without the privileges of the dead, who have no debts to pay, and need write neither letters nor books—that is a piteous condition. Long ago the measure has been taken for my coffin and for my necrology; but I die so slowly, that the process is tedious for me as well as my friends. But patience; everything has an end. You will one day find the booth closed where the puppet-show of my humor has so often delighted you."

As early as 1850, it was rumored that since Heine's illness a change had taken place in his religious views; and as rumor seldom stops short of extremes, it was soon said that he had become a thorough pietist, Catholics and Protestants by turns claiming him as a convert. Such a change in so uncompromising an iconoclast, in a man who had been so zealous in his negations as Heine, naturally excited considerable sensation in the camp he was supposed to have quitted, as well as in that he was supposed to have joined. In the second volume of the "Salon" and in the "Romantische Schule," written in 1834 and '35, the doctrine of Pantheism is dwelt on with a fervor and unmixed seriousness which show that Pantheism was then an animating faith to Heine, and he attacks what he considers the false spiritualism and asceticism of Christianity

as the enemy of true beauty in Art, and of social well-being.
Now, however, it was said that Heine had recanted all his
heresies; but from the fact that visitors to his sick-room
brought away very various impressions as to his actual religious views, it seemed probable that his love of mystification
had found a tempting opportunity for exercise on this subject,
and that, as one of his friends said, he was not inclined to
pour out unmixed wine to those who asked for a sample out
of mere curiosity. At length, in the epilogue to the "Romanzero," dated 1851, there appeared, amidst much mystifying
banter, a declaration that he had embraced Theism and the
belief in a future life; and what chiefly lent an air of seriousness and reliability to this affirmation, was the fact that he
took care to accompany it with certain negations:—

"As concerns myself, I can boast of no particular progress in politics;
I adhered (after 1848) to the same democratic principles which had the
homage of my youth, and for which I have ever since glowed with increasing fervor. In theology, on the contrary, I must accuse myself of
retrogression, since, as I have already confessed, I returned to the old
superstition—to a personal God. This fact is, once for all, not to be
stifled, as many enlightened and well-meaning friends would fain have
had it. But I must expressly contradict the report that my retrograde
movement has carried me as far as to the threshold of a Church, and
that I have even been received into her lap. No: my religious convictions and views have remained free from any tincture of ecclesiasticism;
no chiming of bells has allured me, no altar-candles have dazzled me.
I have dallied with no dogmas, and have not utterly renounced my
reason."

This sounds like a serious statement. But what shall we
say to a convert who plays with his newly acquired belief in
a future life as Heine does in the very next page? He says
to his reader:—

"Console thyself; we shall meet again in a better world, where I also
mean to write thee better books. I take for granted that my health
will there be improved, and that Swedenborg has not deceived me.
He relates, namely, with great confidence, that we shall peacefully carry
on our old occupations in the other world, just as we have done in this;
that we shall there preserve our individuality unaltered, and that death
will produce no particular change in our organic development. Swedenborg is a thoroughly honorable fellow, and quite worthy of credit in
what he tells us about the other world, where he saw with his own eyes

6

the persons who had played a great part on our earth. Most of them, he says, remained unchanged, and busied themselves with the same things as formerly; they remained stationary, were old-fashioned, *rococo*—which now and then produced a ludicrous effect. For example, our dear Dr. Martin Luther kept fast by his doctrine of Grace, about which he had for three hundred years daily written down the same mouldy arguments—just in the same way as the late Baron Ekstein, who during twenty years printed in the 'Allgemeine Zeitung' one and the same article, perpetually chewing over again the old cud of Jesuitical doctrine. But, as we have said, all persons who once figured here below were not found by Swedenborg in such a state of fossil immutability: many have considerably developed their character, both for good and evil, in the other world; and this gave rise to some singular results. Some who had been heroes and saints on earth had *there* sunk into scamps and good-for-nothings; and there were examples, too, of a contrary transformation. For instance, the fumes of self-conceit mounted to St. Anthony's head when he learned what immense veneration and adoration had been paid to him by all Christendom; and he who here below withstood the most terrible temptations, was now quite an impertinent rascal and dissolute gallows-bird, who vied with his pig in rolling himself in the mud. The chaste Susanna, from having been excessively vain of her virtue, which she thought indomitable, came to a shameful fall, and she who once so gloriously resisted the two old men, was a victim to the seductions of the young Absalom, the son of David. On the contrary, Lot's daughters had in the lapse of time become very virtuous, and passed in the other world for models of propriety: the old man, alas! had stuck to the wine-flask."

In his "Geständnisse," the retractation of former opinions and profession of Theism are renewed, but in a strain of irony that repels our sympathy and baffles our psychology. Yet what strange, deep pathos is mingled with the audacity of the following passage!—

"What avails it me, that enthusiastic youths and maidens crown my marble bust with laurel, when the withered hands of an aged nurse are pressing Spanish flies behind my ears? What avails it me, that all the roses of Shiraz glow and waft incense for me? Alas! Shiraz is two thousand miles from the Rue d'Amsterdam, where, in the wearisome loneliness of my sick-room, I get no scent except it be, perhaps, the perfume of warmed towels. Alas! God's satire weighs heavily on me. The great Author of the universe, the Aristophanes of Heaven, was bent on demonstrating, with crushing force, to me, the little, earthly, German Aristophanes, how my wittiest sarcasms are only pitiful attempts at jesting in comparison with His, and how miserably I am beneath Him in humor, in colossal mockery."

For our own part, we regard the paradoxical irreverence with which Heine professes his theoretical reverence as pathological, as the diseased exhibition of a predominant tendency urged into anomalous action by the pressure of pain and mental privation—as the delirium of wit starved of its proper nourishment. It is not for us to condemn, who have never had the same burden laid on us; it is not for pygmies at their ease to criticise the writhings of the Titan chained to the rock.

On one other point we must touch before quitting Heine's personal history. There is a standing accusation against him in some quarters of wanting political principle, of wishing to denationalize himself, and of indulging in insults against his native country. Whatever ground may exist for these accusations, that ground is not, so far as we see, to be found in his writings. He may not have much faith in German revolutions and revolutionists; experience, in his case as in that of others, may have thrown his millennial anticipations into more distant perspective; but we see no evidence that he has ever swerved from his attachment to the principles of freedom, or written anything which to a philosophic mind is incompatible with true patriotism. He has expressly denied the report that he wished to become naturalized in France; and his yearning toward his native land and the accents of his native language is expressed with a pathos the more reliable from the fact that he is sparing in such effusions. We do not see why Heine's satire of the blunders and foibles of his fellow-countrymen should be denounced as the crime of *lèse-patrie*, any more than the political caricatures of any other satirist. The real offences of Heine are his occasional coarseness and his unscrupulous personalities, which are reprehensible, not because they are directed against his fellow-countrymen, but because they are *personalities*. That these offences have their precedents in men whose memory the world delights to honor, does not remove their turpitude, but it is a fact which should modify our condemnation in a particular case—unless, indeed, we are to deliver our judgments on a principle of compensation, making up for our indulgence in one direction by our severity in another. On this ground of coarseness and personality, a true

bill may be found against Heine — not, we think, on the ground that he has laughed at what is laughable in his compatriots. Here is a specimen of the satire under which we suppose German patriots wince:—

"Rhenish Bavaria was to be the starting-point of the German revolution. Zweibrücken was the Bethlehem in which the infant Saviour—Freedom—lay in the cradle, and gave whimpering promise of redeeming the world. Near his cradle bellowed many an ox, who afterward, when his horns were reckoned on, showed himself a very harmless brute. It was confidently believed that the German revolution would begin in Zweibrücken, and everything was there ripe for an outbreak. But, as has been hinted, the tender-heartedness of some persons frustrated that illegal undertaking. For example, among the Bipontine conspirators there was a tremendous braggart, who was always loudest in his rage, who boiled over with the hatred of tyranny, and this man was fixed on to strike the first blow, by cutting down a sentinel who kept an important post. . . . 'What!' cried the man, when this order was given him—'what!—me! Can you expect so horrible, so bloodthirsty an act of me? I—I, kill an innocent sentinel? I, who am father of a family! And this sentinel is perhaps also father of a family. One father of a family kill another father of a family? Yes! Kill—murder!'"

In political matters, Heine, like all men whose intellect and taste predominate too far over their impulses to allow of their becoming partisans, is offensive alike to the aristocrat and the democrat. By the one he is denounced as a man who holds incendiary principles, by the other as a half-hearted "trimmer." He has no sympathy, as he says, with "that vague, barren pathos, that useless effervescence of enthusiasm, which plunges, with the spirit of a martyr, into an ocean of generalities, and which always reminds me of the American sailor, who had so fervent an enthusiasm for General Jackson that he at last sprang from the top of a mast into the sea, crying, '*I die for General Jackson!*'"

"But thou liest, Brutus, thou liest, Cassius, and thou, too, liest, Asinius, in maintaining that my ridicule attacks those ideas which are the precious acquisition of Humanity, and for which I myself have so striven and suffered. No! for the very reason that those ideas constantly hover before the poet in glorious splendor and majesty, he is the more irresistibly overcome by laughter when he sees how rudely, awkwardly, and clumsily those ideas are seized and mirrored in the contracted minds of contemporaries. . . . There are mirrors which have so rough a surface that even an Apollo reflected in them becomes a caricature, and excites our laughter. *But we laugh then only at the caricature, not at the god.*"

For the rest, why should we demand of Heine that he should be a hero, a patriot, a solemn prophet, any more than we should demand of a gazelle that it should draw well in harness? Nature has not made him of her sterner stuff—not of iron and adamant, but of pollen of flowers, the juice of the grape, and Puck's mischievous brain, plenteously mixing also the dews of kindly affection and the gold-dust of noble thoughts. It is, after all, a *tribute* which his enemies pay him when they utter their bitterest dictum—namely, that he is "*nur Dichter*"—only a poet. Let us accept this point of view for the present, and, leaving all consideration of him as a man, look at him simply as a poet and literary artist.

Heine is essentially a lyric poet. The finest products of his genius are

> "Short swallow-flights of song that dip
> Their wings in tears, and skim away";

and they are so emphatically songs, that, in reading them, we feel as if each must have a twin melody born in the same moment and by the same inspiration. Heine is too impressible and mercurial for any sustained production: even in his short lyrics his tears sometimes pass into laughter, and his laughter into tears; and his longer poems, "Atta Troll" and "Deutschland," are full of Ariosto-like transitions. His song has a wide compass of notes: he can take us to the shores of the Northern Sea and thrill us by the sombre sublimity of his pictures and dreamy fancies; he can draw forth our tears by the voice he gives to our own sorrows, or to the sorrows of "Poor Peter"; he can throw a cold shudder over us by a mysterious legend, a ghost-story, or a still more ghastly rendering of hard reality; he can charm us by a quiet idyl, shake us with laughter at his overflowing fun, or give us a piquant sensation of surprise by the ingenuity of his transitions from the lofty to the ludicrous. This last power is not, indeed, essentially poetical; but only a poet can use it with the same success as Heine, for only a poet can poise our emotion and expectation at such a height as to give effect to the sudden fall.

Heine's greatest power as a poet lies in his simple pathos, in
the ever varied but always natural expression he has given to
the tender emotions. We may perhaps indicate this phase of
his genius by referring to Wordsworth's beautiful little poem,
" She dwelt among the untrodden ways "; the conclusion—

> "She dwelt alone, and few could know
> When Lucy ceased to be ;
> But she is in her grave, and oh !
> The difference to me "—

is entirely in Heine's manner; and so is Tennyson's poem of
a dozen lines, called "Circumstance." Both these poems have
Heine's pregnant simplicity. But lest this comparison should
mislead, we must say that there is no general resemblance
between either Wordsworth, or Tennyson, and Heine. Their
greatest qualities lie quite away from the light, delicate lucid-
ity, the easy, rippling music, of Heine's style. The distinctive charm of his lyrics may best be seen by comparing
them with Goethe's. Both have the same masterly finished
simplicity and rhythmic grace; but there is more thought
mingled with Goethe's feeling—his lyrical genius is a vessel
that draws more water than Heine's, and though it seems to
glide along with equal ease, we have a sense of greater weight
and force accompanying the grace of its movement. But, for
this very reason, Heine touches our hearts more strongly; his
songs are all music and feeling—they are like birds that not
only enchant us with their delicious notes, but nestle against
us with their soft breasts, and make us feel the agitated beating of their hearts. He indicates a whole sad history in a
single quatrain: there is not an image in it, not a thought;
but it is beautiful, simple, and perfect as a " big round tear "
—it is pure feeling breathed in pure music:

> "Anfangs wollt' ich fast verzagen
> Und ich glaubt' ich trug es nie,
> Und ich hab' es doch getragen,—
> Aber fragt mich nur nicht, wie."[1]

He excels equally in the more imaginative expression of

[1] At first I was almost in despair, and I thought I could never bear it
and yet I have borne it—only do not ask me *how ?*

feeling: he represents it by a brief image, like a finely cut
cameo; he expands it into a mysterious dream, or dramatizes
it in a little story, half ballad, half idyl; and in all these
forms his art is so perfect, that we never have a sense of artificiality or of unsuccessful effort; but all seems to have developed itself by the same beautiful necessity that brings forth
vine-leaves and grapes and the natural curls of childhood.   Of
Heine's humorous poetry, "Deutschland" is the most charming specimen—charming especially, because its wit and humor
grow out of a rich loam of thought. "Atta Troll" is more
original, more various, more fantastic; but it is too great a
strain on the imagination to be a general favorite. We have
said that feeling is the element in which Heine's poetic genius
habitually floats; but he can occasionally soar to a higher
region, and impart deep significance to picturesque symbolism; he can flash a sublime thought over the past and into
the future; he can pour forth a lofty strain of hope or indignation. Few could forget, after once hearing them, the
stanzas at the close of "Deutschland," in which he warns the
King of Prussia not to incur the irredeemable hell which
the injured poet can create for him—the *singing flames* of a
Dante's *terza rima!*

> "Kennst du die Hölle des Dante nicht,
> Die schrecklichen Terzetten?
> Wen da der Dichter hineingesperrt
> Den kann kein Gott mehr retten.
>
> "Kein Gott, kein Heiland, erlöst ihn je
> Aus diesen singenden flammen!
> Nimm dich in Acht, dass wir dich nicht
> Zu solcher Hölle verdammen." [1]

As a prosaist, Heine is, in one point of view, even more
distinguished than as a poet. The German language easily

---

[1] It is not fair to the English reader to indulge in German quotations,
but in our opinion poetical translations are usually worse than valueless.
For those who think differently, however, we may mention that Mr.
Stores Smith has published a modest little book, containing "Selections
from the Poetry of Heinrich Heine," and that a meritorious (American)
translation of Heine's complete works, by Charles Leland, is now appearing in shilling numbers.

lends itself to all the purposes of poetry; like the ladies of
the Middle Ages, it is gracious and compliant to the Trouba-
dours. But as these same ladies were often crusty and repulsive to their unmusical mates, so the German language generally appears awkward and unmanageable in the hands of prose
writers. Indeed the number of really fine German prosaists
before Heine would hardly have exceeded the numerating
powers of a New Hollander, who can count three and no more.
Persons the most familiar with German prose testify that
there is an extra fatigue in reading it, just as we feel an extra
fatigue from our walk when it takes us over ploughed clay.
But in Heine's hands German prose, usually so heavy, so
clumsy, so dull, becomes, like clay in the hands of the chem-
ist, compact, metallic, brilliant; it is German in an *allotropic*
condition. No dreary, labyrinthine sentences in which you
find "no end in wandering mazes lost"; no chains of adjective
in linked harshness long drawn out; no digressions thrown in
as parentheses; but crystalline definiteness and clearness, fine
and varied rhythm, and all that delicate precision, all those
felicities of word and cadence, which belong to the highest
order of prose. And Heine has proved—what Madame de
Staël seems to have doubted—that it is possible to be witty in
German; indeed, in reading him, you might imagine that
German was pre-eminently the language of wit, so flexible, so
subtle, so piquant does it become under his management. He
is far more an artist in prose than Goethe. He has not the
breadth and repose, and the calm development which belong
to Goethe's style, for they are foreign to his mental character;
but he excels Goethe in susceptibility to the manifold qualities of prose, and in mastery over its effects. Heine is full
of variety, of light and shadow: he alternates between epigrammatic pith, imaginative grace, sly allusion, and daring
piquancy; and athwart all these there runs a vein of sadness,
tenderness, and grandeur which reveals the poet. He continually throws out those finely chiselled sayings which stamp
themselves on the memory, and become familiar by quotation.
For example: "The People have time enough, they are immortal: kings only are mortal." "Wherever a great soul
utters its thoughts, there is Golgotha." "Nature wanted to

see how she looked, and she created Goethe." "Only the man who has known bodily suffering is truly a *man;* his limbs have their Passion-history, they are spiritualized." He calls Rubens "this Flemish Titan, the wings of whose genius were so strong that he soared as high as the sun, in spite of the hundred-weight of Dutch cheeses that hung on his legs." Speaking of Börne's dislike to the calm creations of the true artist, he says, "He was like a child which, insensible to the glowing significance of a Greek statue, only touches the marble and complains of cold."

The most poetic and specifically humorous of Heine's prose writings are the "Reisebilder." The comparison with Sterne is inevitable here; but Heine does not suffer from it, for if he falls below Sterne in raciness of humor, he is far above him in poetic sensibility, and in reach and variety of thought. Heine's humor is never persistent, it never flows on long in easy gayety and drollery; where it is not swelled by the tide of poetic feeling, it is continually dashing down the precipice of a witticism. It is not broad and unctuous; it is aerial and sprite-like, a momentary resting-place between his poetry and his wit. In the "Reisebilder" he runs through the whole gamut of his powers, and gives us every hue of thought, from the wildly droll and fantastic to the sombre and the terrible. Here is a passage almost Dantesque in its conception:—

"Alas! one ought in truth to write against no one in this world. Each of us is sick enough in this great *lazaretto,* and many a polemical writing reminds me involuntarily of a revolting quarrel, in a little hospital at Cracow, of which I chanced to be a witness, and where it was horrible to hear how the patients mockingly reproached each other with their infirmities : how one who was wasted by consumption jeered at another who was bloated by dropsy; how one laughed at another's cancer in the nose, and this one again at his neighbor's locked-jaw or squint, until at last the delirious fever-patient sprang out of bed and tore away the coverings from the wounded bodies of his companions, and nothing was to be seen but hideous misery and mutilation."

And how fine is the transition in the very next chapter where, after quoting the Homeric description of the feasting gods, he says:—

"Then suddenly approached, panting, a pale Jew, with drops of blood on his brow, with a crown of thorns on his head, and a great cross laid on his shoulders ; and he threw the cross on the high table of the gods, so that the golden cups tottered, and the gods became dumb and pale, and grew even paler, till they at last melted away into vapor."

The richest specimens of Heine's wit are perhaps to be found in the works which have appeared since the "Reise-bilder." The years, if they have intensified his satirical bit-terness, have also given his wit a finer edge and polish. His sarcasms are so subtly prepared and so slyly allusive, that they may often escape readers whose sense of wit is not very acute; but for those who delight in the subtle and delicate flavors of style, there can hardly be any wit more irresistible than Heine's. We may measure its force by the degree in which it has subdued the German language to its purposes, and made that language brilliant in spite of a long hereditary transmission of dulness. As one of the most harmless exam-ples of his satire, take this on a man who has certainly had his share of adulation :—

"Assuredly it is far from my purpose to depreciate M. Victor Cousin. The titles of this celebrated philosopher even lay me under an obligation to praise him. He belongs to that living pantheon of France, which we call the peerage, and his intelligent legs rest on the velvet benches of the Luxembourg. I must indeed sternly repress all private feelings which might seduce me into an excessive enthusiasm. Otherwise I might be suspected of servility ; for M. Cousin is very influential in the State by means of his position and his tongue. This consideration might even move me to speak of his faults as frankly as of his virtues. Will he himself disprove of this? Assuredly not. I know that we cannot do higher honor to great minds than when we throw as strong a light on their demerits as on their merits. When we sing the praises of a Her-cules, we must also mention that he once laid aside the lion's skin and sat down to the distaff : what then? he remains notwithstanding a Her-cules! So when we relate similar circumstances concerning M. Cousin, we must nevertheless add, with discriminating eulogy : *M. Cousin, if he has sometimes sat twaddling at the distaff, has never laid aside the lion's skin.* . . . It is true that, having been suspected of demagogy, he spent some time in a German prison, just as Lafayette and Richard Cœur de Lion. But that M. Cousin there in his leisure hours studied Kant's ' Critique of Pure Reason ' is to be doubted on three grounds. First, this book is written in German. Secondly, in order to read this book, a man must understand German. Thirdly, M. Cousin does not under-stand German. . . . I fear I am passing unawares from the sweet waters of praise into the bitter ocean of blame. Yes, on one account I cannot refrain from bitterly blaming M. Cousin—namely, that he who loves

truth far more than he loves Plato and Tenneman, is unjust to himself
when he wants to persuade us that he has borrowed something from the
philosophy of Schelling and Hegel. Against this self-accusation, I must
take M. Cousin under my protection. On my word and conscience!
this honorable man has not stolen a jot from Schelling and Hegel, and
if he brought home anything of theirs, it was merely their friendship.
That does honor to his heart. But there are many instances of such false
self-accusation in psychology. I knew a man who declared that he had
stolen silver spoons at the king's table; and yet we all knew that the
poor devil had never been presented at Court, and accused himself of
stealing these spoons to make us believe that he had been a guest at the
palace. No! In German philosophy M. Cousin has always kept the
sixth commandment; here he has never pocketed a single idea, not so
much as a salt-spoon of an idea. All witnesses agree in attesting that
in this respect M. Cousin is honor itself. . . . I prophesy to you that
the renown of M. Cousin, like the French Revolution, will go round
the world! I hear some one wickedly add: Undeniably the renown of
M. Cousin is going round the world, and *it has already taken its departure
from France.*"

The following "symbolical myth" about Louis Philippe is
very characteristic of Heine's manner:—

"I remember very well that immediately on my arrival [in Paris] I
hastened to the Palais Royal to see Louis Philippe. The friend who
conducted me told me that the king now appeared on the terrace only at
stated hours, but that formerly he was to be seen at any time for five
francs. 'For five francs!' I cried, with amazement; 'does he then
show himself for money?' 'No; but he is shown for money, and it
happens in this way: there is a society of *claqueurs, marchands de con-
tremarques*, and such riff-raff, who offered every foreigner to show him
the king for five francs: if he would give ten francs, he might see the
king raise his eyes to heaven, and lay his hand protestingly on his heart;
if he would give twenty francs, the king would sing the Marseillaise.
If the foreigner gave five francs, they raised a loud cheering under the
king's windows, and his Majesty appeared on the terrace, bowed, and
retired. If ten francs, they shouted still louder, and gesticulated as if
they had been possessed, when the king appeared, who then, as a sign
of silent emotion, raised his eyes to heaven, and laid his hand on his
heart. English visitors, however, would sometimes spend as much as
twenty francs, and then the enthusiasm mounted to the highest pitch:
no sooner did the king appear on the terrace, than the Marseillaise was
struck up and roared out frightfully, until Louis Philippe, perhaps only
for the sake of putting an end to the singing, bowed, laid his hand on
his heart, and joined in the Marseillaise. Whether, as is asserted, he
beat time with his foot, I cannot say.'"

EVANGELICAL TEACHING: DR. CUMMING.

GIVEN, a man with moderate intellect, a moral standard not higher than the average, some rhetorical affluence and great glibness of speech, what is the career in which, without the aid of birth or money, he may most easily attain power and reputation in English society? Where is that Goshen of mediocrity in which a smattering of science and learning will pass for profound instruction, where platitudes will be accepted as wisdom, bigoted narrowness as holy zeal, unctuous egoism as God-given piety? Let such a man become an evangelical preacher; he will then find it possible to reconcile small ability with great ambition, superficial knowledge with the prestige of erudition, a middling morale with a high reputation for sanctity. Let him shun practical extremes and be ultra only in what is purely theoretic: let him be stringent on predestination, but latitudinarian on fasting; unflinching in insisting on the eternity of punishment, but diffident of curtailing the substantial comforts of time; ardent and imaginative on the premillennial advent of Christ, but cold and cautious toward every other infringement of the *status quo*. Let him fish for souls not with the bait of inconvenient singularity, but with the drag-net of comfortable conformity. Let him be hard and literal in his interpretation only when he wants to hurl texts at the heads of unbelievers and adversaries, but when the letter of the Scriptures presses too closely on the genteel Christianity of the nineteenth century, let him use his spiritualizing alembic and disperse it into impalpable ether. Let him preach less of Christ than of Antichrist; let him be less definite in showing what sin is than in showing who is the Man of Sin, less expansive on the blessedness of faith than on the accursedness of infidelity. Above all, let him set up as an interpreter of prophecy, and rival Moore's Almanack in the prediction of political events, tickling the interests of hearers

who are but moderately spiritual by showing how the Holy
Spirit has dictated problems and charades for their benefit,
and how, if they are ingenious enough to solve these, they may
have their Christian graces nourished by learning precisely to
whom they may point as the "horn that had eyes," "the lying
prophet," and the "unclean spirits." In this way he will
draw men to him by the strong cords of their passions, made
reason-proof by being baptized with the name of piety. In
this way he may gain a metropolitan pulpit; the avenues to
his church will be as crowded as the passages to the opera;
he has but to print his prophetic sermons and bind them in
lilac and gold, and they will adorn the drawing-room table of
all evangelical ladies, who will regard as a sort of pious "light
reading" the demonstration that the prophecy of the locusts
whose sting is in their tail, is fulfilled in the fact of the Turk-
ish commander's having taken a horse's tail for his standard,
and that the French are the very frogs predicted in the Revelation.

Pleasant to the clerical flesh under such circumstances is
the arrival of Sunday! Somewhat at a disadvantage during
the week, in the presence of working-day interests and lay
splendors, on Sunday the preacher becomes the cynosure of
a thousand eyes, and predominates at once over the Amphi-
tryon with whom he dines, and the most captious member of
his church or vestry. He has an immense advantage over all
other public speakers. The platform orator is subject to the
criticism of hisses and groans. Council for the plaintiff expects the retort of council for the defendant. The honorable
gentleman on one side of the House is liable to have his facts
and figures shown up by his honorable friend on the opposite
side. Even the scientific or literary lecturer, if he is dull or
incompetent, may see the best part of his audience slip quietly
out one by one. But the preacher is completely master of the
situation: no one may hiss, no one may depart. Like the
writer of imaginary conversations, he may put what imbecili-
ties he pleases into the mouths of his antagonists, and swell
with triumph when he has refuted them. He may riot in
gratuitous assertions, confident that no man will contradict
him; he may exercise perfect free-will in logic, and invent

illustrative experience; he may give an evangelical edition of
history with the inconvenient facts omitted;—all this he may
do with impunity, certain that those of his hearers who are
not sympathizing are not listening.   For the Press has no
band of critics who go the round of the churches and chapels,
and are on the watch for a slip or defect in the preacher, to
make a "feature" in their article: the clergy are, practically,
the most irresponsible of all talkers.   For this reason, at least,
it is well that they do not always allow their discourses to
be merely fugitive, but are often induced to fix them in that
black and white in which they are open to the criticism of any
man who has the courage and patience to treat them with
thorough freedom of speech and pen.

It is because we think this criticism of clerical teaching desirable for the public good, that we devote some pages to Dr.
Cumming.   He is, as every one knows, a preacher of immense
popularity, and of the numerous publications in which he per-
petuates his pulpit labors, all circulate widely, and some, according to their title-page, have reached the sixteenth thousand.   Now our opinion of these publications is the very
opposite of that given by a newspaper eulogist: we do *not*
"believe that the repeated issues of Dr. Cumming's thoughts
are having a beneficial effect on society," but the reverse; and
hence, little inclined as we are to dwell on his pages, we think
it worth while to do so, for the sake of pointing out in them
what we believe to be profoundly mistaken and pernicious.
Of Dr. Cumming personally we know absolutely nothing: our
acquaintance with him is confined to a perusal of his works;
our judgment of him is founded solely on the manner in which
he has written himself down on his pages.   We know neither
how he looks nor how he lives.   We are ignorant whether,
like St. Paul, he has a bodily presence that is weak and con-
temptible, or whether his person is as florid and as prone to
amplification as his style.   For aught we know, he may not
only have the gift of prophecy, but may bestow the profits of
all his works to feed the poor, and be ready to give his own
body to be burned with as much alacrity as he infers the everlasting burning of Roman Catholics and Puseyites.   Out of
the pulpit he may be a model of justice, truthfulness, and the

love that thinketh no evil; but we are obliged to judge of his charity by the spirit we find in his sermons, and shall only be glad to learn that his practice is, in many respects, an amiable *non sequitur* from his teaching.

Dr. Cumming's mind is evidently not of the pietistic order. There is not the slightest leaning toward mysticism in his Christianity—no indication of religious raptures, of delight in God, of spiritual communion with the Father. He is most at home in the forensic view of Justification, and dwells on salvation as a scheme rather than as an experience. He insists on good works as the sign of justifying faith, as labors to be achieved to the glory of God, but he rarely represents them as the spontaneous, necessary outflow of a soul filled with Divine love. He is at home in the external, the polemical, the historical, the circumstantial, and is only episodically devout and practical. The great majority of his published sermons are occupied with argument or philippic against Romanists and unbelievers, with "vindications" of the Bible, with the political interpretation of prophecy, or the criticism of public events; and the devout aspiration, or the spiritual and practical exhortation, is tacked to them as a sort of fringe in a hurried sentence or two at the end. He revels in the demonstration that the Pope is the Man of Sin; he is copious on the downfall of the Ottoman empire; he appears to glow with satisfaction in turning a story which tends to show how he abashed an "infidel"; it is a favorite exercise with him to form conjectures of the process by which the earth is to be burned up, and to picture Dr. Chalmers and Mr. Wilberforce being caught up to meet Christ in the air, while Romanists, Puseyites, and infidels are given over to gnashing of teeth. But of really spiritual joys and sorrows, of the life and death of Christ as a manifestation of love that constrains the soul, of sympathy with that yearning over the lost and erring which made Jesus weep over Jerusalem, and prompted the sublime prayer, "Father, forgive them," of the gentler fruits of the Spirit, and the peace of God which passeth understanding—of all this, we find little trace in Dr. Cumming's discourses.

His style is in perfect correspondence with this habit of

mind. Though diffuse, as that of all preachers must be, it
has rapidity of movement, perfect clearness, and some aptness
of illustration. He has much of that literary talent which
makes a good journalist—the power of beating out an idea
over a large space, and of introducing far-fetched *à propos*.
His writings have, indeed, no high merit: they have no originality or force of thought, no striking felicity of presentation, no depth of emotion. Throughout nine volumes we have
alighted on no passage which impressed us as worth extract-
ing and placing among the "beauties" of evangelical writers,
such as Robert Hall, Foster the Essayist, or Isaac Taylor.
Everywhere there is commonplace cleverness, nowhere a spark
of rare thought, of lofty sentiment, or pathetic tenderness.
We feel ourselves in company with a voluble retail talker,
whose language is exuberant but not exact, and to whom we
should never think of referring for precise information, or for
well-digested thought and experience. His argument continually slides into wholesale assertion and vague declamation,
and in his love of ornament he frequently becomes tawdry.
For example, he tells us (Apoc. Sketches, p. 265) that
" Botany weaves around the cross her amaranthine garlands;
and Newton comes from his starry home—Linnæus from his
flowery resting-place—and Werner and Hutton from their sub-
terranean graves at the voice of Chalmers, to acknowledge
that all they learned and elicited in their respective provinces
has only served to show more clearly that Jesus of Nazareth
is enthroned on the riches of the universe." And so prosaic
an injunction to his hearers as that they should choose a
residence within an easy distance of church, is magnificently
draped by him as an exhortation to prefer a house "that basks
in the sunshine of the countenance of God." Like all preachers of his class, he is more fertile in imaginative paraphrase
than in close exposition, and in this way he gives us some
remarkable fragments of what we may call the romance of
Scripture, filling up the outline of the record with an elaborate
coloring quite undreamed of by more literal minds. The serpent, he informs us, said to Eve, "Can it be so? Surely you
are mistaken, that God hath said you shall die, a creature so
fair, so lovely, so beautiful. It is impossible. *The laws of*

nature and physical science tell you that my interpretation is correct; you shall not die. I can tell you by my own experience as an angel that you shall be as gods, knowing good and evil."—(Apoc. Sketches, p. 294.) Again, according to Dr. Cumming, Abel had so clear an idea of the Incarnation and Atonement, that when he offered his sacrifice "he must have said, 'I feel myself a guilty sinner, and that in myself I cannot meet Thee alive; I lay on Thine altar this victim, and I shed its blood as my testimony that mine should be shed; and I look for forgiveness and undeserved mercy through Him who is to bruise the serpent's head, and whose atonement this typifies.'"—(Occas. Disc., vol. i. p. 23.) Indeed his productions are essentially ephemeral; he is essentially a journalist, who writes sermons instead of leading articles, who, instead of venting diatribes against her Majesty's Ministers, directs his power of invective against Cardinal Wiseman and the Puseyites,—instead of declaiming on public spirit, perorates on the "glory of God." We fancy he is called, in the more refined evangelical circles, an "intellectual preacher"; by the plainer sort of Christians, a "flowery preacher"; and we are inclined to think that the more spiritually minded class of believers, who look with greater anxiety for the kingdom of God within them than for the visible advent of Christ in 1864, will be likely to find Dr. Cumming's declamatory flights and historico-prophetical exercitations as little better than "clouts o' cauld parritch."

Such is our general impression from his writings after an attentive perusal. There are some particular characteristics which we shall consider more closely, but in doing so we must be understood as altogether declining any doctrinal discussion. We have no intention to consider the grounds of Dr. Cumming's dogmatic system, to examine the principles of his prophetic exegesis, or to question his opinion concerning the little horn, the river Euphrates, or the seven vials. We identify ourselves with no one of the bodies whom he regards it as his special mission to attack: not giving adhesion either to Romanism, to Puseyism, or to that anomalous combination of opinions which he introduces to us under the name of infidelity. It is simply as spectators that we criticise Dr. Cumming's

7

mode of warfare: as spectators concerned less with what he
holds to be Christian truth than with his manner of enforcing
that truth, less with the doctrines he teaches than with the
moral spirit and tendencies of his teaching.

One of the most striking characteristics of Dr. Cumming's
writings is *unscrupulosity of statement*.   His motto apparently
is, *Christianitatem, quocunque modo, Christianitatem ;* and the
only system he includes under the term Christianity is Calvin-
istic Protestantism.   Experience has so long shown that the
human brain is a congenial nidus for inconsistent beliefs, that
we do not pause to inquire how Dr. Cumming, who attributes
the conversion of the unbelieving to the. Divine Spirit, can
think it necessary to co-operate with that Spirit by argumentative white lies.   Nor do we for a moment impugn the genuineness of his zeal for Christianity, or the sincerity of his
conviction that the doctrines he preaches are necessary to salvation; on the contrary, we regard the flagrant unveracity
found on his pages as an indirect result of that conviction—as
a result, namely, of the intellectual and moral distortion of
view which is inevitably produced by assigning to dogmas,
based on a very complex structure of evidence, the place and
authority of first truths.   A distinct appreciation of the value
of evidence—in other words, the intellectual perception of
truth—is more closely allied to truthfulness of statement,
or the moral quality of veracity, than is generally admitted.
That highest moral habit, the constant preference of truth,
both theoretically and practically, pre-eminently demands the
co-operation of the intellect with the impulses—as is indicated
by the fact that it is only found in anything like completeness
in the highest class of minds.   And it is commonly seen that,
in proportion as religious sects believe themselves to be guided
by direct inspiration rather than by a spontaneous exertion
of their faculties, their sense of truthfulness is misty and
confused.   No one can have talked to the more enthusiastic
Methodists and listened to their stories of miracles without
perceiving that they require no other passport to a statement
than that it accords with their wishes and their general conception of God's dealings; nay, they regard as a symptom
of sinful scepticism an inquiry into the evidence for a story

which they think unquestionably tends to the glory of God, and in retailing such stories, new particulars, further tending to His glory, are "borne in" upon their minds. Now, Dr. Cumming, as we have said, is no enthusiastic pietist: within a certain circle—within the mill of evangelical orthodoxy—his intellect is perpetually at work; but that principle of sophistication which our friends the Methodists derive from the predominance of their pietistic feelings, is involved for him in the doctrine of verbal inspiration; what is for them a state of emotion submerging the intellect, is with him a formula imprisoning the intellect, depriving it of its proper function—the free search for truth—and making it the mere servant-of-all-work to a foregone conclusion. Minds fettered by this doctrine no longer inquire concerning a proposition whether it is attested by sufficient evidence, but whether it accords with Scripture; they do not search for facts, as such, but for facts that will bear out their doctrine. They become accustomed to reject the more direct evidence in favor of the less direct, and where adverse evidence reaches demonstration they must resort to devices and expedients in order to explain away contradiction. It is easy to see that this mental habit blunts not only the perception of truth, but the sense of truthfulness, and that the man whose faith drives him into fallacies, treads close upon the precipice of falsehood.

We have entered into this digression for the sake of mitigating the inference that is likely to be drawn from that characteristic of Dr. Cumming's works to which we have pointed. He is much in the same intellectual condition as that professor of Padua, who, in order to disprove Galileo's discovery of Jupiter's satellites, urged that as there were only seven metals there could not be more than seven planets—a mental condition scarcely compatible with candor. And we may well suppose that if the professor had held the belief in seven planets, and no more, to be a necessary condition of salvation, his mental vision would have been so dazed that even if he had consented to look through Galileo's telescope, his eyes would have reported in accordance with his inward alarms rather than with the external fact. So long as a belief in propositions is regarded as indispensable to salvation, the pursuit of

truth *as such* is not possible, any more than it is possible for
a man who is swimming for his life to make meteorological
observations on the storm which threatens to overwhelm him.
The sense of alarm and haste, the anxiety for personal safety,
which Dr. Cumming insists upon as the proper religious attitude, unmans the nature, and allows no thorough, calm thinking, no truly noble, disinterested feeling.   Hence, we by no
means suspect that the unscrupulosity of statement with which
we charge Dr. Cumming, extends beyond the sphere of his
theological prejudices : religion apart, he probably appreciates
and practises veracity.

A grave general accusation must be supported by details,
and in adducing these, we purposely select the most obvious
cases of misrepresentation—such as require no argument to
expose them, but can be perceived at a glance.   Among Dr.
Cumming's numerous books, one of the most notable for unscrupulosity of statement is the " Manual of Christian Evidences," written, as he tells us in his Preface, not to give the
deepest solutions of the difficulties in question, but to furnish
Scripture-readers, city missionaries, and Sunday-school teachers with a " ready reply " to sceptical arguments.   This announcement that *readiness* was the chief quality sought for
in the solutions here given, modifies our inference from the
other qualities which those solutions present; and it is but
fair to presume, that when the Christian disputant is not in
a hurry, Dr. Cumming would recommend replies less ready
and more veracious.   Here is an example of what in another
place[1] he tells his readers is "change in their pocket, . . .
a little ready argument which they can employ, and therewith
answer a fool according to his folly."   From the nature of
this argumentative small-coin, we are inclined to think Dr.
Cumming understands answering a fool according to his folly
to mean, giving him a foolish answer.   We quote from the
" Manual of Christian Evidences," p. 62 :—

"Some of the gods which the heathen worshipped were among the
greatest monsters that ever walked the earth. Mercury was a thief; and
because he was an expert thief he was enrolled among the gods. Bacchus
was a mere sensualist and drunkard; and therefore he was enrolled

[1] Lect. on Daniel, p. 6.

among the gods. Venus was a dissipated and abandoned courtesan; and therefore she was enrolled among the goddesses. Mars was a savage, that gloried in battle and in blood; and therefore he was deified and enrolled among the gods."

Does Dr. Cumming believe the purport of these sentences? If so, this passage is worth handing down as his theory of the Greek myth—as a specimen of the astounding ignorance which was possible in a metropolitan preacher A.D. 1854. And if he does not believe them . . . The inference must then be, that he thinks delicate veracity about the ancient Greeks is not a Christian virtue, but only a "splendid sin" of the unregenerate. This inference is rendered the more probable by our finding, a little further on, that he is not more scrupulous about the moderns, if they come under his definition of "Infidels." But the passage we are about to quote in proof of this has a worse quality than its discrepancy with fact. Who that has a spark of generous feeling, that rejoices in the presence of good in a fellow-being, has not dwelt with pleasure on the thought that Lord Byron's unhappy career was ennobled and purified toward its close by a high and sympathetic purpose, by honest and energetic efforts for his fellow-men? Who has not read with deep emotion those last pathetic lines, beautiful as the after-glow of sunset, in which love and resignation are mingled with something of a melancholy heroism? Who has not lingered with compassion over the dying scene at Missolonghi—the sufferer's inability to make his farewell messages of love intelligible, and the last long hours of silent pain? Yet for the sake of furnishing his disciples with a "ready reply," Dr. Cumming can prevail on himself to inoculate them with a bad-spirited falsity like the following:—

"We have one striking exhibition of *an infidel's brightest thoughts*, in some lines *written in his dying moments* by a man, gifted with great genius, capable of prodigious intellectual prowess, but of worthless principle, and yet more worthless practices—I mean the celebrated Lord Byron. He says,—

> "'Though gay companions o'er the bowl
> Dispel awhile the sense of ill,
> Though pleasure fills the maddening soul,
> The heart—*the heart* is lonely still.

>"'Ay, but to die, and go, alas!
>   Where all have gone and all must go;
> To be the *Nothing* that I was,
>   Ere born to life and living woe!

>"'Count o'er the joys thine hours have seen,
>   Count o'er thy days from anguish free,
> And know, whatever thou hast been,
>   'Tis *something better* not to be.

>"'Nay, for myself, so dark my fate
>   Through every turn of life hath been,
> *Man* and the *world* so much *I hate*,
>   I care not when I quit the scene.'"

It is difficult to suppose that Dr. Cumming can have been so grossly imposed upon—that he can be so ill informed as really to believe that these lines were "written" by Lord Byron in his dying moments; but, allowing him the full benefit of that possibility, how shall we explain his introduction of this feebly rabid doggerel as "an infidel's brightest thoughts"?

In marshalling the evidences of Christianity, Dr. Cumming directs most of his arguments against opinions that are either totally imaginary, or that belong to the past rather than to the present; while he entirely fails to meet the difficulties actually felt and urged by those who are unable to accept Revelation. There can hardly be a stronger proof of misconception as to the character of free-thinking in the present day than the recommendation of Leland's "Short and Easy Method with the Deists,"—a method which is unquestionably short and easy for preachers disinclined to consider their stereotyped modes of thinking and arguing, but which has quite ceased to realize those epithets in the conversion of Deists. Yet Dr. Cumming not only recommends this book, but takes the trouble himself to write a feebler version of its arguments. For example, on the question of the genuineness and authenticity of the New Testament writings, he says:—

"If therefore, at a period long subsequent to the death of Christ, a number of men had appeared in the world, drawn up a book which they christened by the name of Holy Scripture, and recorded these things which appear in it as facts when they were only the fancies of their own imagination, surely the *Jews* would have instantly reclaimed that no such events transpired, that no such person as Jesus Christ appeared in their capital, and that *their* crucifixion of Him, and their alleged evil treatment of His apostles, were mere fictions." [1]

It is scarcely necessary to say that, in such argument as this, Dr. Cumming is beating the air. He is meeting a hypothesis which no one holds, and totally missing the real question. The only type of "infidel" whose existence Dr. Cumming recognizes is that fossil personage who "calls the Bible a lie and a forgery." He seems to be ignorant—or he chooses to ignore the fact—that there is a large body of eminently instructed and earnest men who regard the Hebrew and Christian Scriptures as a series of historical documents, to be dealt with according to the rules of historical criticism; and that an equally large number of men, who are not historical critics, find the dogmatic scheme built on the letter of the Scriptures opposed to their profoundest moral convictions. Dr. Cumming's infidel is a man who, because his life is vicious, tries to convince himself that there is no God, and that Christianity is an imposture, but who is all the while secretly conscious that he is opposing the truth, and cannot help "letting out" admissions "that the Bible is the Book of God." We are favored with the following "Creed of the Infidel":—

"I believe that there is no God, but that matter is God, and God is matter; and that it is no matter whether there is any God or not. I believe also that the world was not made, but that the world made itself or that it had no beginning, and that it will last forever. I believe that man is a beast; that the soul is the body, and that the body is the soul; and that after death there is neither body nor soul. I believe that there is no religion, that *natural religion is the only religion, and all religion unnatural.* I believe not in Moses; I believe in the first philosophers. I believe not in the evangelists; I believe in Chubb, Collins, Toland, Tindal, and Hobbes. I believe in Lord Bolingbroke, and I believe not in St. Paul. I believe not in revelation; *I believe in tradition; I believe in the Talmud: I believe in the Koran*; I believe not in the Bible. I believe in Socrates; I believe in Confucius; I believe in Mahomet; I believe not in Christ. And lastly, *I believe in all unbelief.*"

The intellectual and moral monster whose creed is this complex web of contradictions is, moreover, according to Dr. Cum-

[1] Man. of Ev., p. 81.

ming, a being who unites much simplicity and imbecility with
his Satanic hardihood,—much tenderness of conscience with
his obdurate vice.   Hear the "proof":—

"I once met with an acute and enlightened infidel, with whom I
reasoned day after day, and for hours together; I submitted to him the
internal, the external, and the experimental evidences, but made no impression on his scorn and unbelief.   At length I entertained a suspicion
that there was something morally, rather than intellectually wrong, and
that the bias was not in the intellect, but in the heart; one day therefore I said to him—' I must now state my conviction, and you may call
me uncharitable, but duty compels me: you are living in some known
and gross sin.'   *The man's countenance became pale; he bowed and left
me.*"—Man. of Evidences, p. 254.

Here we have the remarkable psychological phenomenon of
an "acute and enlightened" man who, deliberately purposing
to indulge in a favorite sin, and regarding the Gospel with
scorn and unbelief, is nevertheless so much more scrupulous
than the majority of Christians, that he cannot "embrace sin
and the Gospel simultaneously"; who is so alarmed at the
Gospel in which he does not believe, that he cannot be easy
without trying to crush it; whose acuteness and enlightenment
suggest to him, as a means of crushing the Gospel, to argue
from day to day with Dr. Cumming; and who is withal so
naïve that he is taken by surprise when Dr. Cumming, failing
in argument, resorts to accusation, and so tender in conscience
that, at the mention of his sin, he turns pale and leaves the
spot.   If there be any human mind in existence capable of
holding Dr. Cumming's "Creed of the Infidel," of at the same
time believing in tradition and "believing in all unbelief," it
must be the mind of the infidel just described, for whose existence we have Dr. Cumming's *ex officio* word as a theologian;
and to theologians we may apply what Sancho Panza says of
the bachelors of Salamanca, that they never tell lies—except
when it suits their purpose.

The total absence from Dr. Cumming's theological mind of
any demarcation between fact and rhetoric is exhibited in another passage, where he adopts the dramatic form:—

"Ask the peasant on the hills—*and I have asked amid the mountains
of Braemar and Deeside*—' How do you know that this book is divine,

and that the religion you profess is true? You never read Paley?'
'No, I never heard of him.' 'You have never read Butler?' 'No, I
have never heard of him.' 'Nor Chalmers?' 'No, I do not know him.'
'You have never read any books on evidence?' 'No, I have read no such
books.' 'Then, how do you know this book is true?' 'Know it! Tell
me that the Dee, the Clunie, and the Garrawalt, the streams at my feet,
do not run; that the winds do not sigh amid the gorges of these blue
hills; that the sun does not kindle the peaks of Loch-na-Gar,—tell me
my heart does not beat, and I will believe you; but do not tell me the
Bible is not divine. I have found its truth illuminating my footsteps;
its consolations sustaining my heart. May my tongue cleave to my
mouth's roof, and my right hand forget its cunning, if I ever deny what
is my deepest inner experience, that this blessed book is the Book of
God.'"—Church before the Flood, p. 35.

Dr. Cumming is so slippery and lax in his mode of presentation, that we find it impossible to gather whether he means
to assert, that this is what a peasant on the mountains of
Braemar *did* say, or that it is what such a peasant *would* say:
in the one case, the passage may be taken as a measure of his
truthfulness; in the other, of his judgment.

His own faith, apparently, has not been altogether intuitive,
like that of his rhetorical peasant, for he tells us (Apoc.
Sketches, p. 405) that he has himself experienced what it is
to have religious doubts. "I was tainted while at the University by this spirit of scepticism. I thought Christianity
might not be true. The very possibility of its being true was
the thought I felt I must meet and settle. Conscience could
give me no peace till I had settled it. I read, and I have
read from that day, for fourteen or fifteen years, till this, and
now I am as convinced, upon the clearest evidence, that this
book is the Book of God, as that I now address you." This
experience, however, instead of impressing on him the fact
that doubt may be the stamp of a truth-loving mind—that
sunt quibus non credidisse honor est, et fidei futuræ pignus—
seems to have produced precisely the contrary effect. It has
not enabled him even to conceive the condition of a mind
"perplext in faith but pure in deed," craving light, yearning
for a faith that will harmonize and cherish its highest powers
and aspirations, but unable to find that faith in dogmatic
Christianity. His own doubts apparently were of a different
kind. Nowhere in his pages have we found a humble, can-

did, sympathetic attempt to meet the difficulties that may be
felt by an ingenuous mind.   Everywhere he supposes that the
doubter is hardened, conceited, consciously shutting his eyes
to the light—a fool who is to be answered according to his
folly—that is, with ready replies made up of reckless assertions, of apocryphal anecdotes, and, where other resources
fail, of vituperative imputations.   As to the reading which he
has prosecuted for fifteen years—*either* it has left him totally
ignorant of the relation which his own religious creed bears to
the criticism and philosophy of the nineteenth century, *or* he
systematically blinks that criticism and that philosophy; and
instead of honestly and seriously endeavoring to meet and
solve what he knows to be the real difficulties, contents himself with setting up popinjays to shoot at, for the sake of
confirming the ignorance and winning the cheap admiration
of his evangelical hearers and readers.   Like the Catholic
preacher who, after throwing down his cap and apostrophizing
it as Luther, turned to his audience and said, " You see this
heretical fellow has not a word to say for himself," Dr. Cumming, having drawn his ugly portrait of the infidel, and put
arguments of a convenient quality into his mouth, finds a
" short and easy method " of confounding this " croaking frog."

   In his treatment of infidels, we imagine he is guided by a
mental process which may be expressed in the following syllo-
gism: Whatever tends to the glory of God is true; it is for
the glory of God that infidels should be as bad as possible;
therefore, whatever tends to show that infidels are as bad as
possible is true.   All infidels, he tells us, have been men of
" gross and licentious lives."   Is there not some well-known
unbeliever—David Hume, for example—of whom even Dr.
Cumming's readers may have heard as an exception?   No matter.   Some one suspected that he was *not* an exception; and
as that suspicion tends to the glory of God, it is one for a
Christian to entertain.—(See Man. of Ev., p. 73.)   If we
were unable to imagine this kind of self-sophistication, we
should be obliged to suppose that, relying on the ignorance
of his evangelical disciples, he fed them with direct and conscious falsehoods.   " Voltaire," he informs them, " declares
there is no God "; he was " an antitheist—that is, one who

deliberately and avowedly opposed and hated God; who swore in his blasphemy that he would dethrone Him"; and "advocated the very depths of the lowest sensuality." With regard to many statements of a similar kind, equally at variance with truth, in Dr. Cumming's volumes, we presume that he has been misled by hearsay or by the second-hand character of his acquaintance with free-thinking literature. An evangelical preacher is not obliged to be well read. Here, however, is a case which the extremest supposition of educated ignorance will not reach. Even books of "evidences" quote from Voltaire the line—

"Si Dieu n'existait pas, il faudrait l'inventer";

even persons fed on the mere whey and buttermilk of literature must know that in philosophy Voltaire was nothing if not a theist—must know that he wrote not against God, but against Jehovah, the God of the Jews, whom he believed to be a false God—must know that to say Voltaire was an atheist on this ground is as absurd as to say that a Jacobite opposed hereditary monarchy because he declared the Brunswick family had no title to the throne. That Dr. Cumming should repeat the vulgar fables about Voltaire's death is merely what we might expect from the specimens we have seen of his illustrative stories. A man whose accounts of his own experience are apocryphal is not likely to put borrowed narratives to any severe test.

The alliance between intellectual and moral perversion is strikingly typified by the way in which he alternates from the unveracious to the absurd, from misrepresentation to contradiction. Side by side with the adduction of "facts" such as those we have quoted, we find him arguing on one page that the doctrine of the Trinity was too grand to have been conceived by man, and was *therefore* Divine; and on another page, that the Incarnation *had* been preconceived by man, and is *therefore* to be accepted as Divine. But we are less concerned with the fallacy of his "ready replies" than with their falsity; and even of this we can only afford space for a very few specimens. Here is one: "There is a *thousand times* more proof that the Gospel of John was written by him than there is that the 'Ανάβασις was written by Xenophon, or the 'Ars Poetica' by Horace." If Dr. Cumming had chosen Plato's Epistles or Anacreon's Poems, instead of the "Anabasis" or the "Ars Poetica," he would have reduced the extent of the falsehood, and would have furnished a ready reply, which would have been equally effective with his Sunday-school teachers and their disputants. Hence we conclude this prodigality of misstatement, this exuberance of mendacity, is an effervescence of zeal *in majorem gloriam Dei.* Elsewhere he tells us that " the idea of the author of the 'Vestiges' is, that man is the development of a monkey, that the monkey is the embryo man; so that *if you keep a baboon long enough, it will develop itself into a man.*" How well Dr. Cumming has qualified himself to judge of the ideas in " that very unphilosophical book," as he pronounces it, may be inferred from the fact that he implies the author of the " Vestiges " to have *originated* the nebular hypothesis.

In the volume from which the last extract is taken, even the hardihood of assertion is surpassed by the suicidal character of the argument. It is called "The Church before the Flood," and is devoted chiefly to the adjustment of the question between the Bible and Geology. Keeping within the limits we have prescribed to ourselves, we do not enter into the matter of this discussion; we merely pause a little over the volume in order to point out Dr. Cumming's mode of treating the question. He first tells us that " the Bible has not a single scientific error in it "; that " *its slightest intimations of scientific principles or natural phenomena have in every instance been demonstrated to be exactly and strictly true* " ; and he asks:—

" How is it that Moses, with no greater education than the Hindoo or the ancient philosopher, has written his book, touching science at a thousand points, so accurately, that scientific research has discovered no flaws in it; and yet in those investigations which have taken place in more recent centuries, it has not been shown that he has committed one single error, or made one solitary assertion which can be proved by the maturest science, or by the most eagle-eyed philosopher, to be incorrect, scientifically or historically?"

According to this, the relation of the Bible to science should be one of the strong points of apologists for revelation: the

scientific accuracy of Moses should stand at the head of their
evidences; and they might urge with some cogency, that since
Aristotle, who devoted himself to science, and lived many
ages after Moses, does little else than err ingeniously, this
fact, that the Jewish lawgiver, though touching science at a
thousand points, has written nothing that has not been "demonstrated to be exactly and strictly true," is an irrefragable
proof of his having derived his knowledge from a supernatural
source. How does it happen, then, that Dr. Cumming for-
sakes this strong position? How is it that we find him, some
pages further on, engaged in reconciling Genesis with the discoveries of science, by means of imaginative hypotheses and
feats of "interpretation"? Surely that which has been demonstrated to be exactly and strictly true does not require hypothesis and critical argument, in order to show that it may
possibly agree with those very discoveries by means of which
its exact and strict truth has been demonstrated. And why
should Dr. Cumming suppose, as we shall presently find him
supposing, that men of science hesitate to accept the Bible
because it appears to contradict their discoveries? By his
own statement, that appearance of contradiction does not
exist; on the contrary, it has been demonstrated that the
Bible precisely agrees with their discoveries. Perhaps, however, in saying of the Bible that its "slightest intimations of
scientific principles or natural phenomena have in every instance been demonstrated to be exactly and strictly true," Dr.
Cumming merely means to imply that theologians have found
out a way of explaining the Biblical text so that it no longer,
in their opinion, appears to be in contradiction with the discoveries of science. One of two things, therefore: either, he
uses language without the slightest appreciation of its real
meaning; or, the assertions he makes on one page are directly
contradicted by the arguments he urges on another.

Dr. Cumming's principles—or, we should rather say, confused notions—of Biblical interpretation, as exhibited in this
volume, are particularly significant of his mental calibre.
He says ("Church before the Flood," p. 93):—

"Men of science, who are full of scientific investigation, and en-
amoured of scientific discovery, will hesitate before they accept a book

which, they think, contradicts the plainest and the most unequivocal disclosures they have made in the bowels of the earth, or among the stars of the sky. To all these we answer, as we have already indicated, there is not the least dissonance between God's written book and the most mature discoveries of geological science. One thing, however, there may be : *there may be a contradiction between the discoveries of geology and our preconceived interpretations of the Bible.* But this is not because the Bible is wrong, but because our interpretation is wrong." (The italics in all cases are our own.)

Elsewhere he says :—

"It seems to me plainly evident that the record of Genesis, when read fairly, and not in the light of our prejudices,—*and mind you, the essence of Popery is to read the Bible in the light of our opinions, instead of viewing our opinions in the light of the Bible, in its plain and obvious sense,*—falls in perfectly with the assertion of geologists."

On comparing these two passages, we gather that when Dr. Cumming, under stress of geological discovery, assigns to the Biblical text a meaning entirely different from that which, on his own showing, was universally ascribed to it for more than three thousand years, he regards himself as "viewing his opinions in the light of the Bible in its plain and obvious sense" ! Now he is reduced to one of two alternatives : either, he must hold that the "plain and obvious meaning" lies in the sum of knowledge possessed by each successive age—the Bible being an elastic garment for the growing thought of mankind; or, he must hold that some portions are amenable to this criterion, and others not so. In the former case, he accepts the principle of interpretation adopted by the early German rationalists; in the latter case, he has to show a further criterion by which we can judge what parts of the Bible are elastic and what rigid. If he says that the interpretation of the text is rigid wherever it treats of doctrines necessary to salvation, we answer, that for doctrines to be necessary to salvation they must first be true; and in order to be true, according to his own principle, they must be founded on a correct interpretation of the Biblical text. Thus he makes the necessity of doctrines to salvation the criterion of infallible interpretation, and infallible interpretation the criterion of doctrines being necessary to salvation. He is whirled round in a circle, having,

by admitting the principle of novelty in interpretation, completely deprived himself of a basis. That he should seize the
very moment in which he is most palpably betraying that he
has no test of Biblical truth beyond his own opinion, as an
appropriate occasion for flinging the rather novel reproach
against Popery that its essence is to "read the Bible in the
light of our opinions," would be an almost pathetic self-
exposure, if it were not disgusting. Imbecility that is not
even meek, ceases to be pitiable, and becomes simply odious.

Parenthetic lashes of this kind against Popery are very
frequent with Dr. Cumming, and occur even in his more devout
passages, where their introduction must surely disturb the
spiritual exercises of his hearers. Indeed, Roman Catholics
fare worse with him even than infidels. Infidels are the small
vermin—the mice to be bagged *en passant*. The main object
of his chase—the rats which are to be nailed up as trophies
—are the Roman Catholics. Romanism is the masterpiece
of Satan. But reassure yourselves! Dr. Cumming has been
created. Antichrist is enthroned in the Vatican; but he is
stoutly withstood by the Boanerges of Crown Court. The
personality of Satan, as might be expected, is a very prominent tenet in Dr. Cumming's discourses; those who doubt it
are, he thinks, "generally specimens of the victims of Satan
as a triumphant seducer"; and it is through the medium of
this doctrine that he habitually contemplates Roman Catholics.
They are the puppets of which the devil holds the strings. It
is only exceptionally that he speaks of them as fellow-men,
acted on by the same desires, fears, and hopes as himself; his
rule is to hold them up to his hearers as foredoomed instruments of Satan, and vessels of wrath. If he is obliged to
admit that they are "no shams," that they are "thoroughly in
earnest"—that is because they are inspired by hell, because
they are under an "infra-natural" influence. If their missionaries are found wherever Protestant missionaries go, this
zeal in propagating their faith is not in them a consistent virtue, as it is in Protestants, but a "melancholy fact," affording
additional evidence that they are instigated and assisted by
the devil. And Dr. Cumming is inclined to think that they
work miracles, because that is no more than might be ex

pected from the known ability of Satan who inspires them.[1]
He admits, indeed, that "there is a fragment of the Church
of Christ in the very bosom of that awful apostasy," [2] and that
there are members of the Church of Rome in glory; but this
admission is rare and episodical—is a declaration, *pro formâ*,
about as influential on the general disposition and habits as an
aristocrat's profession of democracy.

This leads us to mention another conspicuous characteristic
of Dr. Cumming's teaching—the *absence of genuine charity*.
It is true that he makes large profession of tolerance and liberality within a certain circle; he exhorts Christians to unity;
he would have Churchmen fraternize with Dissenters, and
exhorts these two branches of God's family to defer the settle-
ment of their differences till the millennium. But the love
thus taught is the love of the *clan*, which is the correlative of
antagonism to the rest of mankind. It is not sympathy and
helpfulness toward men as men, but toward men as Christians,
and as Christians in the sense of a small minority. Dr. Cumming's religion may demand a tribute of love, but it gives a
charter to hatred; it may enjoin charity, but it fosters all
uncharitableness. If I believe that God tells me to love my
enemies, but at the same time hates His own enemies and
requires me to have one will with Him, which has the larger
scope, love or hatred? And we refer to those pages of Dr.
Cumming's in which he opposes Roman Catholics, Puseyites,
and infidels—pages which form the larger proportion of what
he has published—for proof that the idea of God which both
the logic and spirit of his discourses keep present to his hearers
is that of a God who hates His enemies, a God who teaches
love by fierce denunciations of wrath—a God who encourages
obedience to His precepts by elaborately revealing to us that
His own government is in precise opposition to those precepts.
We know the usual evasions on this subject. We know Dr.
Cumming would say that even Roman Catholics are to be
loved and succored as men; that he would help even that
"unclean spirit," Cardinal Wiseman, out of a ditch. But
who that is in the slightest degree acquainted with the action
of the human mind, will believe that any genuine and large

[1] Signs of the Times, p. 38.   [2] Apoc. Sketches, p. 243.

charity can grow out of an exercise of love which is always to have an *arrière-pensée* of hatred? Of what quality would be the conjugal love of a husband who loved his spouse as a wife, but hated her as a woman? It is reserved for the regenerate mind, according to Dr. Cumming's conception of it, to be "wise, amazed, temperate and furious, loyal and neutral, in a moment." Precepts of charity uttered with faint breath at the end of a sermon are perfectly futile, when all the force of the lungs has been spent in keeping the hearer's mind fixed on the conception of his fellow-men, not as fellow-sinners and fellow-sufferers, but as agents of hell, as automata through whom Satan plays his game upon earth,—not on objects which call forth their reverence, their love, their hope of good even in the most strayed and perverted, but on a minute identification of human things with such symbols as the scarlet whore, the beast out of the abyss, scorpions whose sting is in their tails, men who have the mark of the beast, and unclean spirits like frogs. You might as well attempt to educate a child's sense of beauty by hanging its nursery with the horrible and grotesque pictures in which the early painters represented the Last Judgment, as expect Christian graces to flourish on that prophetic interpretation which Dr. Cumming offers as the principal nutriment of his flock. Quite apart from the critical basis of that interpretation, quite apart from the degree of truth there may be in Dr. Cumming's prognostications—questions into which we do not choose to enter—his use of prophecy must be *à priori* condemned in the judgment of right-minded persons, by its results as testified in the net moral effect of his sermons. The best minds that accept Christianity as a divinely inspired system, believe that the great end of the Gospel is not merely the saving but the educating of men's souls, the creating within them of holy dispositions, the subduing of egoistical pretensions, and the perpetual enhancing of the desire that the will of God—a will synonymous with goodness and truth—may be done on earth. But what relation to all this has a system of interpretation which keeps the mind of the Christian in the position of a spectator at a gladiatorial show, of which Satan is the wild beast in the shape of the great red dragon, and two-thirds of mankind the victims—

8

the whole provided and got up by God for the edification of the saints? The demonstration that the Second Advent is at hand, if true, can have no really holy, spiritual effect; the highest state of mind inculcated by the Gospel is resignation to the disposal of God's providence—"Whether we live, we live unto the Lord; whether we die, we die unto the Lord" —not an eagerness to see a temporal manifestation which shall confound the enemies of God and give exaltation to the saints; it is to dwell in Christ by spiritual communion with His nature, not to fix the date when He shall appear in the sky. Dr. Cumming's delight in shadowing forth the downfall of the Man of Sin, in prognosticating the battle of Gog and Magog, and in advertising the premillennial Advent, is simply the transportation of political passions on to a so-called religious platform; it is the anticipation of the triumph of "our party," accomplished by our principal men being "sent for" into the clouds. Let us be understood to speak in all seriousness. If we were in search of amusement, we should not seek for it by examining Dr. Cumming's works in order to ridicule them. We are simply discharging a disagreeable duty in delivering our opinion that, judged by the highest standard even of orthodox Christianity, they are little calculated to produce

"A closer walk with God,
    A calm and heavenly frame";

but are more likely to nourish egoistic complacency and pretension, a hard and condemnatory spirit toward one's fellowmen, and a busy occupation with the minutiæ of events, instead of a reverent contemplation of great facts and a wise application of great principles. It would be idle to consider Dr. Cumming's theory of prophecy in any other light,—as a philosophy of history or a specimen of Biblical interpretation; it bears about the same relation to the extension of genuine knowledge as the astrological "house" in the heavens bears to the true structure and relations of the universe.

The slight degree in which Dr. Cumming's faith is imbued with truly human sympathies is exhibited in the way he treats the doctrine of Eternal Punishment. *Here* a little of that readiness to strain the letter of the Scriptures which he so often manifests when his object is to prove a point against Romanism, would have been an amiable frailty if it had been applied on the side of mercy. When he is bent on proving that the prophecy concerning the Man of Sin, in the Second Epistle to the Thessalonians, refers to the Pope, he can extort from the innocent word *καθίσαι* the meaning *cathedrise;* though why we are to translate " He as God cathedrises in the temple of God," any more than we are to translate " cathedrise here, while I go and pray yonder," it is for Dr. Cumming to show more clearly than he has yet done. But when rigorous literality will favor the conclusion that the greater proportion of the human race will be eternally miserable, *then* he is rigorously literal. He says—

"The Greek words, *εἰς τοὺς αἰῶνας τῶν αἰώνων,* here translated ' everlasting,' signify literally ' unto the ages of ages '; *αἰεὶ ὤν,* ' always being,' that is, everlasting, ceaseless existence. Plato uses the word in this sense when he says, ' The gods that live for ever.' *But I must also admit,* that this word is used several times in a limited extent,—as for instance, ' The everlasting hills.' Of course, this does not mean that there never will be a time when the hills will cease to stand; the expression here is evidently figurative, but it implies eternity. The hills shall remain as long as the earth lasts, and no hand has power to remove them but that Eternal One which first called them into being; *so the state of the soul* remains the same after death as long as the soul exists, and no one has power to alter it. The same word is often applied to denote the existence of God—' the Eternal God.' Can we limit the word when applied to Him? Because occasionally used in a limited sense, we must not infer it is always so. ' Everlasting ' plainly means in Scripture ' without end '; it is only to be explained figuratively when it is evident it cannot be interpreted in any other way."

We do not discuss whether Dr. Cumming's interpretation accords with the meaning of the New Testament writers: we simply point to the fact that the text becomes elastic for him when he wants freer play for his prejudices; while he makes it an adamantine barrier against the admission that mercy will ultimately triumph, that God—*i.e.,* Love—will be all in all. He assures us that he does not " delight to dwell on the misery of the lost"; and we believe him. That misery does not seem to be a question of feeling with him, either one way or the other. He does not merely resign himself to the awful mystery of eternal punishment; he contends for it. Do we object,

he asks,[1] to everlasting happiness? then why object to everlasting misery?—reasoning which is perhaps felt to be cogent
by theologians who anticipate the everlasting happiness for
themselves, and the everlasting misery for their neighbors.

The compassion of some Christians has been glad to take
refuge in the opinion, that the Bible allows the supposition of
annihilation for the impenitent; but the rigid sequence of Dr.
Cumming's reasoning will not admit of this idea. He sees
that flax is made into linen, and linen into paper; that paper,
when burnt, partly ascends as smoke, and then again descends
in rain, or in dust and carbon. "Not one particle of the original flax is lost, although there may be not one particle that
has not undergone an entire change: annihilation is not, but
change of form is. *It will be thus with our bodies at the resurrection.* The death of the body means not annihilation. *Not
one feature of the face* will be annihilated." Having established the perpetuity of the body by this close and clear analogy—namely, that *as* there is a total change in the particles
of flax in consequence of which they no longer appear as flax,
so there will *not* be a total change in the particles of the human
body, but they will reappear as the human body—he does not
seem to consider that the perpetuity of the body involves the
perpetuity of the soul, but requires separate evidence for this,
and finds such evidence by begging the very question at issue
—namely, by asserting that the text of the Scriptures implies
"the perpetuity of the punishment of the lost, and the consciousness of the punishment which they endure." Yet it is
drivelling like this which is listened to and lauded as eloquence by hundreds, and which a Doctor of Divinity can believe that he has his "reward as a saint" for preaching and
publishing!

One more characteristic of Dr. Cumming's writings, and we
have done. This is the *perverted moral judgment* that everywhere reigns in them. Not that this perversion is peculiar
to Dr. Cumming; it belongs to the dogmatic system which he
shares with all evangelical believers. But the abstract tendencies of systems are represented in very different degrees,
according to the different characters of those who embrace

[1] Man. of Christ. Ev., p. 184.

them; just as the same food tells differently on different constitutions: and there are certain qualities in Dr. Cumming that cause the perversion of which we speak to exhibit itself with peculiar prominence in his teaching. A single extract will enable us to explain what we mean:—

"The ' thoughts ' are evil. If it were possible for human eye to discern and to detect the thoughts that flutter round the heart of an unregenerate man—to mark their hue and their multitude—it would be found that they are indeed ' evil.' We speak not of the thief, and the murderer, and the adulterer, and suchlike, whose crimes draw down the cognizance of earthly tribunals, and whose unenviable character it is to take the lead in the paths of sin ; but we refer to the men who are marked out by their practice of many of the seemliest moralities of life—by the exercise of the kindliest affections, and the interchange of the sweetest reciprocities—and of these men, if unrenewed and unchanged, we pronounce that their thoughts are evil. To ascertain this, we must refer to the object around which our thoughts ought continually to circulate. The Scriptures assert that this object is *the glory of God;* that for this we ought to think, to act, and to speak ; and that in thus thinking, acting, and speaking, there is involved the purest and most endearing bliss. Now it will be found true of the most amiable men, that with all their good society and kindliness of heart, and all their strict and unbending integrity, they never or rarely think of the glory of God. The question never occurs to them—Will this redound to the glory of God? Will this make His name more known, His being more loved, His praise more sung? And just inasmuch as their every thought comes short of this lofty aim, in so much does it come short of good, and entitle itself to the character of evil. If the glory of God is not the absorbing and the influential aim of their thoughts, then they are evil ; but God's glory never enters into their minds. They are amiable, because it chances to be one of the constitutional tendencies of their individual character, left uneffaced by the Fall ; and *they are just and upright, because they have perhaps no occasion to be otherwise, or find it subservient to their interests to maintain such a character."*—Occ. Disc., vol. i. p. 8.

Again we read (Ibid., p. 236) :—

"There are traits in the Christian character which the mere worldly man cannot understand. He can understand the outward morality, but he cannot understand the inner spring of it ; he can understand Dorcas's liberality to the poor, but he cannot penetrate the ground of Dorcas's liberality. *Some men give to the poor because they are ostentatious, or because they think the poor will ultimately avenge their neglect ; but the Christian gives to the poor, not only because he has sensibilities like other men,* but because inasmuch as ye did it to the least of these my brethren, ye did it unto me."

Before entering on the more general question involved in
these quotations, we must point to the clauses we have marked
with italics, where Dr. Cumming appears to express sentiments which, we are happy to think, are not shared by the
majority of his brethren in the faith. Dr. Cumming, it seems,
is unable to conceive that the natural man can have any other
motive for being just and upright than that it is useless to be
otherwise, or that a character for honesty is profitable; according to his experience, between the feelings of ostentation
and selfish alarm and the feeling of love to Christ, there lie
no sensibilities which can lead a man to relieve want. Granting, as we should prefer to think, that it is Dr. Cumming's
exposition of his sentiments which is deficient rather than his
sentiments themselves, still, the fact that the deficiency lies
precisely here, and that he can overlook it not only in the
haste of oral delivery but in the examination of proof-sheets,
is strongly significant of his mental bias—of the faint degree
in which he sympathizes with the disinterested elements of
human feeling, and of the fact, which we are about to dwell
upon, that those feelings are totally absent from his religious
theory. Now, Dr. Cumming invariably assumes that, in ful-
minating against those who differ from him, he is standing on
a moral elevation to which they are compelled reluctantly to
look up; that his theory of motives and conduct is in its loftiness and purity a perpetual rebuke to their low and vicious
desires and practice. It is time he should be told that the
reverse is the fact; that there are men who do not merely
cast a superficial glance at his doctrine, and fail to see its
beauty or justice, but who, after a close consideration of that
doctrine, pronounce it to be subversive of true moral development, and therefore positively noxious. Dr. Cumming is fond
of showing up the teaching of Romanism, and accusing it of
undermining true morality: it is time he should be told that
there is a large body, both of thinkers and practical men, who
hold precisely the same opinion of his own teaching—with
this difference, that they do not regard it as the inspiration
of Satan, but as the natural crop of a human mind where
the soil is chiefly made up of egoistic passions and dogmatic
beliefs.

Dr. Cumming's theory, as we have seen, is that actions are good or evil according as they are prompted or not prompted by an exclusive reference to the "glory of God." God, then, in Dr. Cumming's conception, is a Being who has no pleasure in the exercise of love and truthfulness and justice, considered as affecting the well-being of His creatures; He has satisfaction in us only in so far as we exhaust our motives and dispositions of all relation to our fellow-beings, and replace sympathy with men by anxiety for the "glory of God." The deed of Grace Darling, when she took a boat in the storm to rescue drowning men and women, was not good if it was only compassion that nerved her arm and impelled her to brave death for the chance of saving others; it was only good if she asked herself—Will this redound to the glory of God? The man who endures tortures rather than betray a trust, the man who spends years in toil in order to discharge an obligation from which the law declares him free, must be animated not by the spirit of fidelity to his fellow-man, but by a desire to make "the name of God more known." The sweet charities of domestic life—the ready hand and the soothing word in sickness, the forbearance toward frailties, the prompt helpfulness in all efforts and sympathy in all joys—are simply evil if they result from a "constitutional tendency" or from dispositions disciplined by the experience of suffering and the perception of moral loveliness. A wife is not to devote herself to her husband out of love to him and a sense of the duties implied by a close relation—she is to be a faithful wife for the glory of God; if she feels her natural affections welling up too strongly, she is to repress them; it will not do to act from natural affection—she must think of the glory of God. A man is to guide his affairs with energy and discretion, not from an honest desire to fulfil his responsibilities as a member of society and a father, but—that "God's praise may be sung." Dr. Cumming's Christian pays his debts for the glory of God: were it not for the coercion of that supreme motive, it would be evil to pay them. A man is not to be just from a feeling of justice; he is not to help his fellow-men out of good-will to his fellow-men; he is not to be a tender husband and father out of affection: all these natural muscles and

fibres are to be torn away and replaced by a patent steel spring
—anxiety for the "glory of God."

Happily, the constitution of human nature forbids the complete prevalence of such a theory. Fatally powerful as religious systems have been, human nature is stronger and wider
than religious systems, and though dogmas may hamper, they
cannot absolutely repress its growth: build walls round the
living tree as you will, the bricks and mortar have by and by
to give way before the slow and sure operation of the sap.
But next to that hatred of the enemies of God which is the
principle of persecution, there perhaps has been no perversion
more obstructive of true moral development than this substitution of a reference to the glory of God for the direct prompt-
ings of the sympathetic feelings. Benevolence and justice are
strong only in proportion as they are directly and inevitably
called into activity by their proper objects: pity is strong only
because we are strongly impressed by suffering; and only in
proportion as it is compassion that speaks through the eyes
when we soothe, and moves the arm when we succor, is a deed
strictly benevolent. If the soothing or the succor be given
because another being wishes or approves it, the deed ceases to
be one of benevolence, and becomes one of deference, of obedience, of self-interest, or vanity. Accessory motives may aid
in producing an *action*, but they presuppose the weakness of
the direct motive; and conversely, when the direct motive is
strong, the action of accessory motives will be excluded. If
then, as Dr. Cumming inculcates, the glory of God is to be
"the absorbing and the influential aim" in our thoughts and
actions, this must tend to neutralize the human sympathies;
the stream of feeling will be diverted from its natural current
in order to feed an artificial canal. The idea of God is really
moral in its influence—it really cherishes all that is best and
loveliest in man—only when God is contemplated as sympathizing with the pure elements of human feeling, as possessing
infinitely all those attributes which we recognize to be moral
in humanity. In this light, the idea of God and the sense of
His presence intensify all noble feeling, and encourage all
noble effort, on the same principle that human sympathy is
found a source of strength: the brave man feels braver when

he knows that another stout heart is beating time with his; the devoted woman who is wearing out her years in patient effort to alleviate suffering or save vice from the last stages of degradation, finds aid in the pressure of a friendly hand which tells her that there is one who understands her deeds, and in her place would do the like. The idea of a God who not only sympathizes with all we feel and endure for our fellow-men, but who will pour new life into our too languid love, and give firmness to our vacillating purpose, is an extension and multiplication of the effects produced by human sympathy; and it has been intensified for the better spirits who have been under the influence of orthodox Christianity, by the contemplation of Jesus as "God manifest in the flesh." But Dr. Cumming's God is the very opposite of all this: He is a God who, instead of sharing and aiding our human sympathies, is directly in collision with them; who, instead of strengthening the bond between man and man, by encouraging the sense that they are both alike the objects of His love and care, thrusts Himself between them and forbids them to feel for each other except as they have relation to Him. He is a God who, instead of adding His solar force to swell the tide of those impulses that tend to give humanity a common life in which the good of one is the good of all, commands us to check those impulses, lest they should prevent us from thinking of His glory. It is in vain for Dr. Cumming to say that we are to love man for God's sake: with the conception of God which his teaching presents, the love of man for God's sake involves, as his writings abundantly show, a strong principle of hatred. We can only love one being for the sake of another when there is an habitual delight in associating the idea of those two beings—that is, when the object of our indirect love is a source of joy and honor to the object of our direct love. But, according to Dr. Cumming's theory, the majority of mankind—the majority of his neighbors—are in precisely the opposite relation to God. His soul has no pleasure in them: they belong more to Satan than to Him; and if they contribute to His glory, it is against their will. Dr. Cumming, then, can only love *some* men for God's sake; the rest he must in consistency *hate* for God's sake.

There must be many, even in the circle of Dr. Cumming's admirers, who would be revolted by the doctrine we have just exposed, if their natural good sense and healthy feeling were not early stifled by dogmatic beliefs, and their reverence misled by pious phrases.   But as it is, many a rational question, many a generous instinct, is repelled as the suggestion of a supernatural enemy, or as the ebullition of human pride and corruption.   This state of inward contradiction can be put an end to only by the conviction that the free and diligent exertion of the intellect, instead of being a sin, is a part of their responsibility—that Right and Reason are synonymous.   The fundamental faith for man is faith in the result of a brave, honest, and steady use of all his faculties:—

> "Let knowledge grow from more to more,
> But more of reverence in us dwell;
> That mind and soul, according well,
> May make one music as before,
> But vaster."

Before taking leave of Dr. Cumming, let us express a hope that we have in no case exaggerated the unfavorable character of the inferences to be drawn from his pages.   His creed often obliges him to hope the worst of men, and to exert himself in proving that the worst is true; but thus far we are happier than he.   We have no theory which requires us to attribute unworthy motives to Dr. Cumming, no opinions, religious or irreligious, which can make it a gratification to us to detect him in delinquencies.   On the contrary, the better we are able to think of him as a man, while we are obliged to disapprove him as a theologian, the stronger will be the evidence for our conviction, that the tendency toward good in human nature has a force which no creed can utterly counteract, and which insures the ultimate triumph of that tendency over all dogmatic perversions.

THE INFLUENCE OF RATIONALISM:
LECKY'S HISTORY.

THERE is a valuable class of books on great subjects which have something of the character and functions of good popular lecturing. They are not original, not subtle, not of close logical texture, not exquisite either in thought or style; but by virtue of these negatives they are all the more fit to act on the average intelligence. They have enough of organizing purpose in them to make their facts illustrative, and to leave a distinct result in the mind, even when most of the facts are forgotten; and they have enough of vagueness and vacillation in their theory to win them ready acceptance from a mixed audience. The vagueness and vacillation are not devices of timidity; they are the honest result of the writer's own mental character, which adapts him to be the instructor and the favorite of "the general reader." For the most part, the general reader of the present day does not exactly know what distance he goes; he only knows that he does not go "too far." Of any remarkable thinker whose writings have excited controversy, he likes to have it said that "his errors are to be deplored," leaving it not too certain what those errors are: he is fond of what may be called disembodied opinions, that float in vapory phrases above all systems of thought or action; he likes an undefined Christianity which opposes itself to nothing in particular, an undefined education of the people, an undefined amelioration of all things: in fact, he likes sound views,— nothing extreme, but something between the excesses of the past and the excesses of the present. This modern type of the general reader may be known in conversation by the cordiality with which he assents to indistinct, blurred statements: say that black is black, he will shake his head and hardly think it; say that black is not so very black, he will reply, "Exactly." He has no hesitation, if you wish it, even to get up at a public meeting and express his conviction that at times, and within certain limits, the radii of a circle have a tendency to be equal; but, on the other hand, he would urge that the spirit of geometry may be carried a little too far. His only bigotry is a bigotry against any clearly defined opinion; not in the least based on a scientific scepticism, but belonging to a lack of coherent thought,—a spongy texture of mind, that gravitates strongly to nothing. The one thing he is stanch for is the utmost liberty of private haziness.

But precisely these characteristics of the general reader, rendering him incapable of assimilating ideas unless they are administered in a highly diluted form, make it a matter of rejoicing that there are clever, fair-minded men, who will write books for him,—men very much above him in knowledge and ability, but not too remote from him in their habits of thinking, and who can thus prepare for him infusions of history and science that will leave some solidifying deposit, and save him from a fatal softening of the intellectual skeleton. Among such serviceable writers, Mr. Lecky's "History of the Rise and Influence of the Spirit of Rationalism in Europe" entitles him to a high place. He has prepared himself for its production by an unusual amount of well-directed reading; he has chosen his facts and quotations with much judgment; and he gives proof of those important moral qualifications—impartiality, seriousness, and modesty. This praise is chiefly applicable to the long chapter on the history of magic and witchcraft which opens the work, and to the two chapters on the antecedents and history of persecution, which occur, the one at the end of the first volume, the other at the beginning of the second. In these chapters Mr. Lecky has a narrower and better-traced path before him than in other portions of his work; he is more occupied with presenting a particular class of facts in their historical sequence, and in their relation to certain grand tide-marks of opinion, than with disquisition; and his writing is freer than elsewhere from an apparent confusedness of thought and an exuberance of approximative phrases, which can be serviceable in no other way than as diluents needful for the sort of reader we have just described.

The history of magic and witchcraft has been judiciously

chosen by Mr. Lecky as the subject of his first section on the Declining Sense of the Miraculous, because it is strikingly illustrative of a position with the truth of which he is strongly impressed, though he may not always treat of it with desirable clearness and precision—namely, that certain beliefs become obsolete, not in consequence of direct arguments against them, but because of their incongruity with prevalent habits of thought. Here is his statement of the two "classes of influences," by which the mass of men, in what is called civilized society, get their beliefs gradually modified:—

"If we ask why it is that the world has rejected what was once so universally and so intensely believed, why a narrative of an old woman who had been seen riding on a broomstick, or who was proved to have transformed herself into a wolf, and to have devoured the flocks of her neighbors, is deemed so entirely incredible, most persons would probably be unable to give a very definite answer to the question. It is not because we have examined the evidence and found it insufficient, for the disbelief always precedes, when it does not prevent, examination. · It is rather because the idea of absurdity is so strongly attached to such narratives, that it is difficult even to consider them with gravity. Yet at one time no such improbability was felt, and hundreds of persons have been burnt simply on the two grounds I have mentioned.

"When so complete a change takes place in public opinion, it may be ascribed to one or other of two causes. It may be the result of a controversy which has conclusively settled the question, establishing to the satisfaction of all parties a clear preponderance of argument or fact in favor of one opinion, and making that opinion a truism which is accepted by all enlightened men, even though they have not themselves examined the evidence on which it rests. Thus, if any one in a company of ordinarily educated persons were to deny the motion of the earth, or the circulation of the blood, his statement would be received with derision, though it is probable that some of his audience would be unable to demonstrate the first truth, and that very few of them could give sufficient reasons for the second. They may not themselves be able to defend their position; but they are aware that, at certain known periods of history, controversies on those subjects took place, and that known writers then brought forward some definite arguments or experiments, which were ultimately accepted by the whole learned world as rigid and conclusive demonstrations. It is possible, also, for as complete a change to be effected by what is called the spirit of the age. The general intellectual tendencies pervading the literature of a century profoundly modify the character of the public mind. They form a new tone and habit of thought. They alter the measure of probability. They create new attractions and new antipathies, and they eventually cause as absolute a rejection of certain old opinions as could be produced by the most cogent and definite arguments."

Mr. Lecky proceeds to some questionable views concerning the evidences of witchcraft, which seem to be irreconcilable even with his own remarks later on; but they lead him to the statement, thoroughly made out by his historical survey, that "the movement was mainly silent, unargumentative, and insensible; that men came gradually to disbelieve in witchcraft, because they came gradually to look upon it as absurd; and that this new tone of thought appeared, first of all, in those who were least subject to theological influences, and soon spread through the educated laity, and, last of all, took possession of the clergy."

We have rather painful proof that this "second class of influences" with a vast number go hardly deeper than fashion, and that withcraft to many of us is absurd only on the same ground that our grandfathers' gigs are absurd. It is felt preposterous to think of spiritual agencies in connection with ragged beldames soaring on broomsticks, in an age when it is known that mediums of communication with the invisible world are usually unctuous personages dressed in excellent broadcloth, who soar above the curtain-poles without any broomstick, and who are not given to unprofitable intrigues. The enlightened imagination rejects the figure of a witch with her profile in dark relief against the moon and her broomstick cutting a constellation. No undiscovered natural laws, no names of "respectable" witnesses, are invoked to make us feel our presumption in questioning the diabolic intimacies of that obsolete old woman, for it is known now that the undiscovered laws, and the witnesses qualified by the payment of income-tax, are all in favor of a different conception—the image of a heavy gentleman in boots and black coat-tails foreshortened against the cornice. Yet no less a person than Sir Thomas Browne once wrote that those who denied there were witches, inasmuch as they thereby denied spirits also, were "obliquely and upon consequence a sort, not of infidels, but of atheists." At present, doubtless, in certain circles, unbelievers in heavy gentlemen who float in the air by means of undiscovered laws are also taxed with atheism; illiberal as it is not to admit that

mere weakness of understanding may prevent one from seeing
how that phenomenon is necessarily involved in the Divine
origin of things. With still more remarkable parallelism, Sir
Thomas Browne goes on: "Those that, to refute their incredulity, desire to see apparitions, shall questionless never behold any, nor have the power to be so much as witches. The
devil hath made them already in a heresy as capital as witchcraft, *and to appear to them were but to convert them.*" It
would be difficult to see what has been changed here but the
mere drapery of circumstance, if it were not for this prominent difference between our own days and the days of witchcraft, that instead of torturing, drowning, or burning the
innocent, we give hospitality and large pay to—the highly
distinguished medium. At least we are safely rid of certain
horrors; but if the multitude—that "farraginous concurrence
of all conditions, tempers, sexes, and ages"—do not roll back
even to a superstition that carries cruelty in its train, it is not
because they possess a cultivated Reason, but because they are
pressed upon and held up by what we may call an external
Reason—the sum of conditions resulting from the laws of material growth, from changes produced by great historical colli-
sions shattering the structures of ages and making new high-
ways for events and ideas, and from the activities of higher
minds no longer existing merely as opinions and teaching, but
as institutions and organizations with which the interests, the
affections, and the habits of the multitude are inextricably
interwoven. No undiscovered laws accounting for small phenomena going forward under drawing-room tables are likely
to affect the tremendous facts of the increase of population,
the rejection of convicts by our colonies, the exhaustion of the
soil by cotton plantations, which urge even upon the foolish
certain questions, certain claims, certain views concerning the
scheme of the world, that can never again be silenced. If
right reason is a right representation of the coexistences and
sequences of things, here are coexistences and sequences that
do not wait to be discovered, but press themselves upon us
like bars of iron. No *séances* at a guinea a head for the sake
of being pinched by "Mary Jane" can annihilate railways,
steamships, and electric telegraphs, which are demonstrating

the interdependence of all human interests, and making self-
interest a duct for sympathy. These things are part of the
external Reason to which internal silliness has inevitably to
accommodate itself.

Three points in the history of magic and witchcraft are well
brought out by Mr. Lecky. First, that the cruelties connected
with it did not begin until men's minds had ceased to repose
implicitly in a sacramental system which made them feel well
armed against evil spirits—that is, until the eleventh century,
when there came a sort of morning dream of doubt and heresy,
bringing on the one side the terror of timid consciences, and
on the other the terrorism of authority or zeal bent on check-
ing the rising struggle. In that time of comparative mental
repose, says Mr. Lecky—

"All those conceptions of diabolical presence; all that predisposition
toward the miraculous, which acted so fearfully upon the imaginations
of the fifteenth and sixteenth centuries, existed; but the implicit faith,
the boundless and triumphant credulity with which the virtue of ecclesiastical rites was accepted, rendered them comparatively innocuous.
If men had been a little less superstitious, the effects of their superstition would have been much more terrible. It was firmly believed that
any one who deviated from the strict line of orthodoxy must soon suc-
cumb beneath the power of Satan; but as there was no spirit of rebellion
or doubt, this persuasion did not produce any extraordinary terrorism."

The Church was disposed to confound heretical opinion with
sorcery; false doctrine was especially the devil's work, and it
was a ready conclusion that a denier or innovator had held
consultation with the father of lies. It is a saying of a zealous Catholic in the sixteenth century, quoted by Maury in his
excellent work, 'De la Magie'—" *Crescit cum magia hæresis,
cum hæresi magia.*" Even those who doubted were terrified
at their doubts, for trust is more easily undermined than terror.
Fear is earlier born than hope, lays a stronger grasp on man's
system than any other passion, and remains master of a larger
group of involuntary actions. A chief aspect of man's moral
development is the slow subduing of fear by the gradual growth
of intelligence, and its suppression as a motive by the presence
of impulses less animally selfish; so that in relation to invisible Power, fear at last ceases to exist, save in that interfusion
with higher faculties which we call awe.

Secondly, Mr. Lecky shows clearly that dogmatic Protestantism, holding the vivid belief in Satanic agency to be an essential of piety, would have felt it shame to be a whit behind
Catholicism in severity against the devil's servants.   Luther's
sentiment was that he would not suffer a witch to live (he was
not much more merciful to Jews); and, in spite of his fond-
ness for children, believing a certain child to have been begotten by the devil, he recommended the parents to throw it into
the river.   The torch must be turned on the worst errors of
heroic minds—not in irreverent ingratitude, but for the sake
of measuring our vast and various debt to all the influences
which have concurred, in the intervening ages, to make us
recognize as detestable errors the honest convictions of men
who, in mére individual capacity and moral force, were very
much above us.   Again, the Scotch Puritans, during the
comparatively short period of their ascendency, surpassed all
Christians before them in the elaborate ingenuity of the tortures they applied for the discovery of witchcraft and sorcery,
and did their utmost to prove that if Scotch Calvinism was
the true religion, the chief "note" of the true religion was
cruelty.   It is hardly an endurable task to read the story of
their doings; thoroughly to imagine them as a past reality is
already a sort of torture.   One detail is enough, and it is a
comparatively mild one.   It was the regular profession of men
called "prickers" to thrust long pins into the body of a suspected witch in order to detect the insensible spot which was
the infallible sign of her guilt.   On a superficial view one
would be in danger of saying that the main difference between
the teachers who sanctioned these things and the much-
despised ancestors who offered human victims inside a huge
wicker idol, was that they arrived at a more elaborate barbar-
ity by a longer series of dependent propositions.   I do not
share Mr. Buckle's opinion that a Scotch minister's groans
were a part of his deliberate plan for keeping the people in a
state of terrified subjection; the ministers themselves held the
belief they taught, and might well groan over it.   What a
blessing has a little false logic been to the world!   Seeing that
men are so slow to question their premises, they must have
made each other much more miserable, if pity had not some-

9

times drawn tender conclusion not warranted by Major and
Minor; if there had not been people with an amiable imbecility of reasoning which enabled them at once to cling to hideous beliefs, and to be conscientiously inconsistent with them
in their conduct.   There is nothing like acute deductive reasoning for keeping a man in the dark: it might be called the
technique of the intellect, and the concentration of the mind
upon it corresponds to that predominance of technical skill in
art which ends in degradation of the artist's function, unless
new inspiration and invention come to guide it.

And of this there is some good illustration furnished by that
third node in the history of witchcraft, the beginning of its
end, which is treated in an interesting manner by Mr. Lecky.
It is worth noticing, that the most important defences of the
belief in witchcraft, against the growing scepticism in the latter part of the sixteenth century and in the seventeenth, were
the productions of men who in some departments were among
the foremost thinkers of their time.   One of them was Jean
Bodin, the famous writer on government and jurisprudence,
whose " Republic," Hallam thinks, had an important influence
in England, and furnished " a store of arguments and examples
that were not lost on the thoughtful minds of our countrymen."   In some of his views he was original and bold; for
example, he anticipated Montesquieu in attempting to appreciate the relations of government and climate.   Hallam in-
clines to the opinion that he was a Jew, and attached Divine
authority only to the Old Testament.   But this was enough to
furnish him with his chief data for the existence of witches
and for their capital punishment; and in the account of his
" Republic " given by Hallam, there is enough evidence that
the sagacity which often enabled him to make fine use of his
learning was also often entangled in it, to temper our surprise
at finding a writer on political science of whom it could be
said that, along with Montesquieu, he was " the most philosophical of those who had read so deeply, the most learned of
those who had thought so much," in the van of the forlorn
hope to maintain the reality of witchcraft.   It should be said
that he was equally confident of the unreality of the Coperni-
can hypothesis, on the ground that it was contrary to the tenets

of the theologians and philosophers and to common sense, and therefore subversive of the foundations of every science. Of his work on witchcraft, Mr. Lecky says:—

"The 'Démonomanie des Sorciers' is chiefly an appeal to authority, which the author deemed on this subject so unanimous and so conclusive, that it was scarcely possible for any sane man to resist it. He appealed to the popular belief in all countries, in all ages, and in all religions. He cited the opinions of an immense multitude of the greatest writers of pagan antiquity, and of the most illustrious of the Fathers. He showed how the laws of all nations recognized the existence of witchcraft; and he collected hundreds of cases which had been investigated before the tribunals of his own or of other countries. He relates with the most minute and circumstantial detail, and with the most unfaltering confidence, all the proceedings at the witches' Sabbath, the methods which the witches employed in transporting themselves through the air, their transformations, their carnal intercourse with the Devil, their various means of injuring their enemies, the signs that lead to their detection, their confessions when condemned, and their demeanor at the stake."

Something must be allowed for a lawyer's affection toward a belief which had furnished so many "cases." Bodin's work had been immediately prompted by the treatise "De Prestigiis Dæmonum," written by John Wier, a German physician—a treatise which is worth notice as an example of a transitional form of opinion for which many analogies may be found in the history both of religion and science. Wier believed in demons, and in possession by demons, but his practice as a physician had convinced him that the so-called witches were patients and victims, that the Devil took advantage of their diseased condition to delude them, and that there was no consent of an evil will on the part of the women. He argued that the word in Leviticus translated "witch" meant "poisoner," and besought the princes of Europe to hinder the further spilling of innocent blood. These heresies of Wier threw Bodin into such a state of amazed indignation, that if he had been an ancient Jew instead of a modern economical one, he would have rent his garment. "No one had ever heard of pardon being accorded to sorcerers"; and probably the reason why Charles IX. died young was because he had pardoned the sorcerer, Trois Echelles! We must remember that this was in 1581, when the great scientific movement of the Renaissance had hardly begun—when Galileo was a youth of seventeen, and Kepler a boy of ten.

But directly afterward, on the other side, came Montaigne, whose sceptical acuteness could arrive at negatives without any apparatus of method. A certain keen narrowness of nature will secure a man from many absurd beliefs which the larger soul, vibrating to more manifold influences, would have a long struggle to part with. And so we find the charming, chatty Montaigne—in one of the brightest of his essays, "Des Boiteux," where he declares that, from his own observation of witches and sorcerers, he should have recommended them to be treated with curative hellebore—stating in his own way a pregnant doctrine, since taught more gravely. It seems to him much less of a prodigy that men should lie, or that their imaginations should deceive them, than that a human body should be carried through the air on a broomstick, or up a chimney, by some unknown spirit. He thinks it a sad business to persuade one's self that the test of truth lies in the multitude of believers—"en une presse où les fols surpassent de tant les sages en nombre." Ordinarily, he has observed, when men have something stated to them as a fact, they are more ready to explain it than to inquire whether it is real: "Ils passent par-dessus les propositions, mais ils examinent les conséquences; *ils laissent les choses, et courent aux causes.*" There is a sort of strong and generous ignorance which is as honorable and courageous as science—"ignorance pour laquelle concevoir il n'y a pas moins de science qu'à concevoir la science." And *à propos* of the immense traditional evidence which weighed with such men as Bodin, he says: "As for the proofs and arguments founded on experience and facts, I do not pretend to unravel these. What end of a thread is there to lay hold of? I often cut them as Alexander did his knot. *Après tout, c'est mettre ses conjectures à bien haut prix, que d'en faire cuire un homme tout vif.*"

Writing like this, when it finds eager readers, is a sign that the weather is changing; yet much later, namely, after 1665, when the Royal Society had been founded, our own Glanvil, the author of the "Scepsis Scientifica," a work that was a remarkable advance toward a true definition of the limits of inquiry, and that won him his election as fellow of the Society, published an energetic vindication of the belief in witchcraft, of which Mr. Lecky gives the following sketch:—

"The 'Sadducismus Triumphatus,' which is probably the ablest book ever published in defence of the superstition, opens with a striking picture of the rapid progress of the scepticism in England. Everywhere a disbelief in witchcraft was becoming fashionable in the upper classes; but it was a disbelief that arose entirely from a strong sense of its antecedent improbability. All who were opposed to the orthodox faith united in discrediting witchcraft. They laughed at it, as palpably absurd, as involving the most grotesque and ludicrous conceptions, as so essentially incredible that it would be a waste of time to examine it. This spirit had arisen since the Restoration, although the laws were still in force, and although little or no direct reasoning had been brought to bear upon the subject. In order to combat it, Glanvil proceeded to examine the general question of the credibility of the miraculous. He saw that the reason why witchcraft was ridiculed was, because it was a phase of the miraculous and the work of the Devil; that the scepticism was chiefly due to those who disbelieved in miracles and the Devil; and that the instances of witchcraft or possession in the Bible were invariably placed on a level with those that were tried in the law courts of England. That the evidence of the belief was overwhelming, he firmly believed—and this, indeed, was scarcely disputed; but, until the sense of à priori improbability was removed, no possible accumulation of facts would cause men to believe it. To that task he accordingly addressed himself. Anticipating the idea and almost the words of modern controversialists, he urged that there was such a thing as a credulity of unbelief; and that those who believe so strange a concurrence of delusions, as was necessary on the supposition of the unreality of witchcraft, were far more credulous than those who accepted the belief. He made his very scepticism his principal weapon; and, analyzing with much acuteness the à priori objections, he showed that they rested upon an unwarrantable confidence in our knowledge of the laws of the spirit world; that they implied the existence of some strict analogy between the faculties of men and of spirits; and that, as such analogy most probably did not exist, no reasoning based on the supposition could dispense men from examining the evidence. He concluded with a large collection of cases, the evidence of which was, as he thought, incontestable."

We have quoted this sketch because Glanvil's argument against the à priori objection of absurdity is fatiguingly urged in relation to other alleged marvels which, to busy people seriously occupied with the difficulties of affairs, of science, or of art, seem as little worthy of examination as aëronautic broomsticks. And also because we here see Glanvil, in com-

bating an incredulity that does not happen to be his own, wielding that very argument of traditional evidence which he had made the subject of vigorous attack in his "Scepsis Scientifica." But perhaps large minds have been peculiarly liable to this fluctuation concerning the sphere of tradition, because, while they have attacked its misapplications, they have been the more solicited by the vague sense that tradition is really the basis of our best life. Our sentiments may be called organized traditions; and a large part of our actions gather all their justification, all their attraction and aroma, from the memory of the life lived, of the actions done, before we were born. In the absence of any profound research into psychological functions or into the mysteries of inheritance, in the absence of any comprehensive view of man's historical development and the dependence of one age on another, a mind at all rich in sensibilities must always have had an indefinite uneasiness in an undistinguishing attack on the coercive influence of tradition. And this may be the apology for the apparent inconsistency of Glanvil's acute criticism on the one side, and his indignation at the "looser gentry," who laughed at the evidences for witchcraft, on the other. We have already taken up too much space with this subject of witchcraft, else we should be tempted to dwell on Sir Thomas Browne, who far surpassed Glanvil in magnificent incongruity of opinion, and whose works are the most remarkable combination existing, of witty sarcasm against ancient nonsense and modern obsequiousness, with indications of a capacious credulity. After all, we may be sharing what seems to us the hardness of these men who sat in their studies and argued at their ease about a belief that would be reckoned to have caused more misery and bloodshed than any other superstition, if there had been no such thing as persecution on the ground of religious opinion.   .

On this subject of persecution, Mr. Lecky writes his best: with clearness of conception, with calm justice, bent on appreciating the necessary tendency of ideas, and with an appropriateness of illustration that could be supplied only by extensive and intelligent reading. Persecution, he shows, is not in any sense peculiar to the Catholic Church; it is a direct sequence of the doctrines that salvation is to be had only within the Church, and that erroneous belief is damnatory— doctrines held as fully by Protestant sects as by the Catholics; and in proportion to its power, Protestantism has been as persecuting as Catholicism. He maintains, in opposition to the favorite modern notion of persecution defeating its own object, that the Church, holding the dogma of exclusive salvation, was perfectly consequent, and really achieved its end of spreading one belief and quenching another by calling in the aid of the civil arm. Who will say that Governments, by their power over institutions and patronage, as well as over punishment, have not power also over the interests and inclinations of men, and over most of those external conditions into which subjects are born, and which make them adopt the prevalent belief as a second nature? Hence, to a sincere believer in the doctrine of exclusive salvation, Governments had it in their power to save men from perdition; and wherever the clergy were at the elbow of the civil arm, no matter whether they were Catholic or Protestant, persecution was the result. "Compel them to come in" was a rule that seemed sanctioned by mercy, and the horrible sufferings it led men to inflict seemed small to minds accustomed to contemplate, as a perpetual source of motive, the eternal unmitigated miseries of a hell that was the inevitable destination of a majority amongst mankind.

It is a significant fact, noted by Mr. Lecky, that the only two leaders of the Reformation who advocated tolerance were Zuinglius and Socinus, both of them disbelievers in exclusive salvation. And in corroboration of other evidence that the chief triumphs of the Reformation were due to coercion, he commends to the special attention of his readers the following quotation from a work attributed without question to the famous Protestant theologian, Jurieu, who had himself been hindered, as a Protestant, from exercising his professional functions in France, and was settled as pastor at Rotterdam. It should be remembered that Jurieu's labors fell in the latter part of the seventeenth century and in the beginning of the eighteenth, and that he was the contemporary of Bayle, with whom he was in bitter controversial hostility. He wrote,

then, at a time when there was warm debate on the question
of Toleration; and it was his great object to vindicate himself and his French fellow-Protestants from all laxity on this
point:—

"Peut-on nier que le paganisme est tombé dans le monde par l'autorité
des empereurs Romains? On peut assurer sans témérité que le paganisme seroit encore debout, et que les trois quarts de l'Europe seroient
encore payens si Constantin et ses successeurs n'avaient employé leur
autorité pour l'abolir. Mais, je vous prie, de quelles voies Dieu s'est-il
servi dans ces derniers siècles pour rétablir la véritable religion dans
l'Occident? *Les rois de Suède, ceux de Danemarck, ceux d'Angleterre,
les magistrats souverains de Suisse, des Païs Bas, des villes libres d'Al-
lemagne, les princes électeurs, et autres princes souverains de l'empire,
n'ont-ils pas employé leur autorité pour abbattre le Papisme ?*"

Indeed, wherever the tremendous alternative of everlasting
torments is believed in—believed in so that it becomes a
motive determining the life—not only persecution, but every
other form of severity and gloom, are the legitimate consequences. There is much ready declamation in these days
against the spirit of asceticism and against zeal for doctrinal
conversion; but surely the macerated form of a Saint Francis,
the fierce denunciations of a Saint Dominic, the groans and
prayerful wrestlings of the Puritan who seasoned his bread
with tears and made all pleasurable sensation sin, are more in
keeping with the contemplation of unending anguish as the
destiny of a vast multitude whose nature we share, than the
rubicund cheerfulness of some modern divines, who profess to
unite a smiling liberalism with a well-bred and tacit but un-
shaken confidence in the reality of the bottomless pit. But
in fact, as Mr. Lecky maintains, that awful image, with its
group of associated dogmas concerning the inherited curse,
and the damnation of unbaptized infants, of heathens, and of
heretics, has passed away from what he is fond of calling
"the realizations" of Christendom. These things are no
longer the objects of practical belief. They may be mourned
for in encyclical letters; bishops may regret them; doctors
of divinity may sign testimonials to the excellent character
of these decayed beliefs; but for the mass of Christians they
are no more influential than unrepealed but forgotten statutes.
And with these dogmas has melted away the strong basis for

the defence of persecution. No man now writes eager vindications of himself and his colleagues from the suspicion of adhering to the principle of toleration. And this momentous change, it is Mr. Lecky's object to show, is due to that concurrence of conditions which he has chosen to call "the advance of the Spirit of Rationalism."

In other parts of his work, where he attempts to trace the action of the same conditions on the acceptance of miracles and on other chief phases of our historical development, Mr. Lecky has laid himself open to considerable criticism. The chapters on the Miracles of the Church, the æsthetic, scientific, and moral Development of Rationalism, the Secularization of Politics, and the Industrial history of Rationalism, embrace a wide range of diligently gathered facts; but they are nowhere illuminated by a sufficiently clear conception and statement of the agencies at work, or the mode of their action in the gradual modification of opinion and of life. The writer frequently impresses us as being in a state of hesitation concerning his own standing-point, which may form a desirable stage in private meditation but not in published exposition. Certain epochs in theoretic conception, certain considerations, which should be fundamental to his survey, are introduced quite incidentally in a sentence or two, or in a note which seems to be an afterthought. Great writers and their ideas are touched upon too slightly and with too little discrimination, and important theories are sometimes characterized with a rashness which conscientious revision will correct. There is a fatiguing use of vague or shifting phrases, such as "modern civilization," "spirit of the age," "tone of thought," "intellectual type of the age," "bias of the imagination," "habits of religious thought," unbalanced by any precise definition; and the spirit of rationalism is sometimes treated of as if it lay outside the specific mental activities of which it is a generalized expression. Mr. Curdle's famous definition of the dramatic unities as "a sort of a general oneness," is not totally false; but such luminousness as it has could only be perceived by those who already knew what the unities were. Mr. Lecky has the advantage of being strongly impressed with the great part played by the emotions in the formation of opinion, and with the high complexity of the causes at work in social evolution; but he frequently writes as if he had never yet distinguished between the complexity of the conditions that produce prevalent states of mind, and the inability of particular minds to give distinct reasons for the preferences or persuasions produced by those states.   In brief, he does not discriminate, or does not help his reader to discriminate, between objective complexity and subjective confusion.   But the most muddleheaded gentleman who represents the spirit of the age by observing, as he settles his collar, that the development-theory is quite "the thing," is a result of definite processes, if we could only trace them.   "Mental attitudes" and "predispositions," however vague in consciousness, have not vague causes, any more than the "blind motions of the spring" in plants and animals.

The word "Rationalism" has the misfortune, shared by most words in this gray world, of being somewhat equivocal. This evil may be nearly overcome by careful preliminary definition; but Mr. Lecky does not supply this, and the original specific application of the word to a particular phase of Biblical interpretation seems to have clung about his use of it with a misleading effect.   Through some parts of his book he appears to regard the grand characteristic of modern thought and civilization, compared with ancient, as a radiation in the first instance from a change in religious conceptions.   The supremely important fact, that the gradual reduction of all phenomena within the sphere of established law, which carries as a consequence the rejection of the miraculous, has its determining current in the development of physical science, seems to have engaged comparatively little of his attention; at least, he gives it no prominence.   The great conception of universal regular sequence, without partiality and without caprice—the conception which is the most potent force at work in the modification of our faith, and of the practical form given to our sentiments—could only grow out of that patient watching of external fact, and that silencing of preconceived notions, which are urged upon the mind by the problems of physical science.

THE NATURAL HISTORY OF GERMAN LIFE: RIEHL.

IT is an interesting branch of psychological observation to note the images that are habitually associated with abstract or collective terms—what may be called the picture-writing of the mind, which it carries on concurrently with the more subtle symbolism of language. Perhaps the fixity or variety of these associated images would furnish a tolerably fair test of the amount of concrete knowledge and experience which a given word represents, in the minds of two persons who use it with equal familiarity. The word *railways*, for example, will probably call up, in the mind of a man who is not highly locomotive, the image either of a "Bradshaw," or of the station with which he is most familiar, or of an indefinite length of tram-road; he will alternate between these three images, which represent his stock of concrete acquaintance with railways. But suppose a man to have had successively the experience of a "navvy," an engineer, a traveller, a railway director and shareholder, and a landed proprietor in treaty with a railway company, and it is probable that the range of images which would by turns present themselves to his mind at the mention of the *word* "railways," would include all the essential facts in the existence and relations of the *thing*. Now it is possible for the first-mentioned personage to entertain very expanded views as to the multiplication of railways in the abstract, and their ultimate function in civilization. He may talk of a vast network of railways stretching over the globe, of future "lines" in Madagascar, and elegant refreshment-rooms in the Sandwich Islands, with none the less glibness because his distinct conceptions on the subject do not extend beyond his one station and his indefinite length of tram-road. But it is evident that if we want a railway to be made, or its affairs to be managed, this man of wide views and narrow observation will not serve our purpose.

Probably, if we could ascertain the images called up by the terms "the people," "the masses," "the proletariat," "the peasantry," by many who theorize on those bodies with eloquence, or who legislate for them without eloquence, we should find that they indicate almost as small an amount of concrete knowledge—that they are as far from completely representing the complex facts summed up in the collective term, as the railway images of our non-locomotive gentleman. How little the real characteristics of the working classes are known to those who are outside them, how little their natural history has been studied, is sufficiently disclosed by our Art as well as by our political and social theories. Where, in our picture exhibitions, shall we find a group of true peasantry? What English artist even attempts to rival in truthfulness such studies of popular life as the pictures of Teniers or the ragged boys·of Murillo? Even one of the greatest painters of the pre-eminently realistic school, while, in his picture of "The Hireling Shepherd," he gave us a landscape of marvellous truthfulness, placed a pair of peasants in the foreground who were not much more real than the idyllic swains and damsels of our chimney ornaments. Only a total absence of acquaintance and sympathy with our peasantry could give a moment's popularity to such a picture as "Cross Purposes," where we have a peasant girl who looks as if she knew L. E. L.'s poems by heart, and English rustics, whose costume seems to indicate that they are meant for ploughmen, with exotic features that remind us of a handsome *primo tenore*. Rather than such Cockney sentimentality as this, as an education for the taste and sympathies, we prefer the most crapulous group of boors that Teniers ever painted. But even those among our painters who aim at giving the rustic type of features, who are far above the effeminate feebleness of the "Keepsake" style, treat their subjects under the influence of traditions and prepossessions rather than of direct observation. The notion that peasants are joyous, that the typical moment to represent a man in a smock-frock is when he is cracking a joke and showing a row of sound teeth, that cot-

tage matrons are usually buxom, and village children necessarily rosy and merry, are prejudices difficult to dislodge from
the artistic mind, which looks for its subjects into literature
instead of life. The painter is still under the influence of
idyllic literature, which has always expressed the imagination
of the cultivated and town-bred, rather than the truth of rustic life. Idyllic ploughmen are jocund when they drive their
team afield; idyllic shepherds make bashful love under haw-
thorn-bushes; idyllic villagers dance in the checkered shade
and refresh themselves, not immoderately, with spicy nut-
brown ale. But no one who has seen much of actual ploughmen thinks them jocund; no one who is well acquainted with
the English peasantry can pronounce them merry. The slow
gaze, in which no sense of beauty beams, no humor twinkles,
—the slow utterance, and the heavy slouching walk, remind
one rather of that melancholy animal the camel, than of the
sturdy countryman, with striped stockings, red waistcoat, and
hat aside, who represents the traditional English peasant.
Observe a company of haymakers. When you see them at a
distance, tossing up the forkfuls of hay in the golden light,
while the wagon creeps slowly with its increasing burden over
the meadow, and the bright green space which tells of work
done gets larger and larger, you pronounce the scene "smiling," and you think these companions in labor must be as
bright and cheerful as the picture to which they give anima-
tion. Approach nearer, and you will certainly find that hay-
making-time is a time for joking, especially if there are
women among the laborers; but the coarse laugh that bursts
out every now and then, and expresses the triumphant taunt,
is as far as possible from your conception of idyllic merriment.
That delicious effervescence of the mind which we call fun has
no equivalent for the northern peasant, except tipsy revelry;
the only realm of fancy and imagination for the English clown
exists at the bottom of the third quart-pot.

The conventional countryman of the stage, who picks up
pocket-books and never looks into them, and who is too simple even to know that honesty has its opposite, represents the
still lingering mistake, that an unintelligible dialect is a guaranty for ingenuousness, and that slouching shoulders indicate

an upright disposition. It is quite true that a thresher is likely to be innocent of any adroit arithmetical cheating, but he is not the less likely to carry home his master's corn in his shoes and pocket; a reaper is not given to writing begging-letters, but he is quite capable of cajoling the dairymaid into filling his small-beer bottle with ale. The selfish instincts are not subdued by the sight of buttercups, nor is integrity in the least established by that classic rural occupation, sheep-washing. To make men moral, something more is requisite than to turn them out to grass.

Opera peasants, whose unreality excites Mr. Ruskin's indignation, are surely too frank an idealization to be misleading; and since popular chorus is one of the most effective elements of the opera, we can hardly object to lyric rustics in elegant laced bodices and picturesque motley, unless we are prepared to advocate a chorus of colliers in their pit costume, or a ballet of charwomen and stocking-weavers. But our social novels profess to represent the people as they are, and the unreality of their representations is a grave evil. The greatest benefit we owe to the artist, whether painter, poet, or novelist, is the extension of our sympathies. Appeals founded on generalizations and statistics require a sympathy ready-made, a moral sentiment already in activity; but a picture of human life such as a great artist can give, surprises even the trivial and the selfish into that attention to what is apart from themselves, which may be called the raw material of moral sentiment. When Scott takes us into Luckie Mucklebackit's cottage, or tells the story of "The Two Drovers,"—when Wordsworth sings to us the reverie of "Poor Susan,"—when Kingsley shows us Alton Locke gazing yearningly over the gate which leads from the highway into the first wood he ever saw,—when Hornung paints a group of chimney-sweepers,—more is done toward linking the higher classes with the lower, toward obliterating the vulgarity of exclusiveness, than by hundreds of sermons and philosophical dissertations. Art is the nearest thing to life; it is a mode of amplifying experience and extending our contact with our fellow-men beyond the bounds of our personal lot. All the more sacred is the task of the artist when he undertakes to paint the life of the

People. Falsification here is far more pernicious than in the more artificial aspects of life. It is not so very serious that we should have false ideas about evanescent fashions—about the manners and conversation of beaux and duchesses; but it *is* serious that our sympathy with the perennial joys and struggles, the toil, the tragedy, and the humor in the life of our more heavily laden fellow-men, should be perverted, and turned toward a false object instead of the true one.

This perversion is not the less fatal because the misrepresentation which gives rise to it has what the artist considers a moral end. The thing for mankind to know is, not what are the motives and influences which the moralist thinks *ought* to act on the laborer or the artisan, but what are the motives and influences which *do* act on him. We want to be taught to feel, not for the heroic artisan or the sentimental peasant, but for the peasant in all his coarse apathy, and the artisan in all his suspicious selfishness.

We have one great novelist who is gifted with the utmost power of rendering the external traits of our town population; and if he could give us their psychological character—their conceptions of life, and their emotions—with the same truth as their idiom and manners, his books would be the greatest contribution Art has ever made to the awakening of social sympathies. But while he can copy Mrs. Plornish's colloquial style with the delicate accuracy of a sun-picture, while there is the same startling inspiration in his description of the gestures and phrases of "Boots," as in the speeches of Shakespeare's mobs or numskulls, he scarcely ever passes from the humorous and external to the emotional and tragic, without becoming as transcendent in his unreality as he was a moment before in his artistic truthfulness. But for the precious salt of his humor, which compels him to reproduce external traits that serve, in some degree, as a corrective to his frequently false psychology, his preternaturally virtuous poor children and artisans, his melodramatic boatmen and courtesans, would be as noxious as Eugène Sue's idealized proletaires in encouraging the miserable fallacy that high morality and refined sentiment can grow out of harsh social relations, ignorance, and want; or that the working classes are in a condition to enter at once into a millennial state of *alt·uism*, wherein every one is caring for every one else, and no one for himself.

If we need a true conception of the popular character to guide our sympathies rightly, we need it equally to check our theories, and direct us in their application. The tendency created by the splendid conquests of modern generalization, to believe that all social questions are merged in economical science, and that the relations of men to their neighbors may be settled by algebraic equations,—the dream that the uncultured classes are prepared for a condition which appeals principally to their moral sensibilities,—the aristocratic dilettanteism which attempts to restore the "good old times" by a sort of idyllic masquerading, and to grow feudal fidelity and veneration as we grow prize turnips, by an artificial system of culture,—none of these diverging mistakes can coexist with a real knowledge of the People, with a thorough study of their habits, their ideas, their motives. The land-holder, the clergyman, the mill-owner, the mining-agent, have each an opportunity for making precious observations on different sections of the working classes; but unfortunately their experience is too often not registered at all, or its results are too scattered to be available as a source of information and stimulus to the public mind generally. If any man of sufficient moral and intellectual breadth, whose observations would not be vitiated by a foregone conclusion, or by a professional point of view, would devote himself to studying the natural history of our social classes, especially of the small shopkeepers, artisans, and peasantry,—the degree in which they are influenced by local conditions, their maxims and habits, the points of view from which they regard their religious teachers, and the degree in which they are influenced by religious doctrines, the interaction of the various classes on each other, and what are the tendencies in their position toward disintegration or toward development,—and if, after all this study, he would give us the result of his observations in a book well nourished with specific facts, his work would be a valuable aid to the social and political reformer.

What we are desiring for ourselves has been in some degree done for the Germans by Riehl, the author of the very re-

markable books the titles of which are placed at the bottom of
this page;[1] and we wish to make these books known to our
readers, not only for the sake of the interesting matter they
contain and the important reflections they suggest, but also as
a model for some future or actual student of our own people.
By way of introducing Riehl to those who are unacquainted
with his writings, we will give a rapid sketch from his picture of the German Peasantry, and perhaps this indication of
the mode in which he treats a particular branch of his subject
may prepare them to follow us with more interest when we
enter on the general purpose and contents of his works.

In England, at present, when we speak of the peasantry,
we mean scarcely more than the class of farm-servants and
farm-laborers; and it is only in the most primitive districts—
as in Wales, for example—that farmers are included under
the term. In order to appreciate what Riehl says of the German peasantry, we must remember what the tenant-farmers
and small proprietors were in England half a century ago,
when the master helped to milk his own cows, and the daughters got up at one o'clock in the morning to brew,—when the
family dined in the kitchen with the servants, and sat with
them round the kitchen fire in the evening. In those days
the quarried parlor was innocent of a carpet, and its only
specimens of art were a framed sampler and the best tea-
board; the daughters even of substantial farmers had often
no greater accomplishment in writing and spelling than they
could procure at a dame-school; and, instead of carrying on
sentimental correspondence, they were spinning their future
table-linen, and looking after every saving in butter and eggs
that might enable them to add to the little stock of plate and
china which they were laying in against their marriage. In
our own day, setting aside the superior order of farmers,
whose style of living and mental culture are often equal to
that of the professional class in provincial towns, we can
hardly enter the least imposing farmhouse without finding a
bad piano in the "drawing-room," and some old annuals, disposed with a symmetrical imitation of negligence, on the table;

---

[1] *Die Bürgerliche Gesellschaft.* Von W. H. Riehl. Dritte Auflage,
1855. *Land und Leute.* Von W. H. Riehl. Dritte Auflage, 1856.

10

though the daughters may still drop their *h*'s, their vowels are studiously narrow; and it is only in very primitive regions that they will consent to sit in a covered vehicle without springs, which was once thought an advance in luxury on the pillion.

The condition of the tenant-farmers and small proprietors in Germany is, we imagine, about on a par, not, certainly, in material prosperity, but in mental culture and habits, with that of the English farmers who were beginning to be thought old-fashioned nearly fifty years ago; and if we add to these the farm-servants and laborers, we shall have a class approximating in its characteristics to the *Bauernthum*, or peasantry, described by Riehl.

In Germany, perhaps more than in any other country, it is among the peasantry that we must look for the historical type of the national *physique*. In the towns this type has become so modified to express the personality of the individual, that even "family likeness" is often but faintly marked. But the peasants may still be distinguished into groups by their physical peculiarities. In one part of the country we find a longer-legged, in another a broader-shouldered race, which has inherited these peculiarities for centuries. For example, in certain districts of Hesse are seen long faces, with high foreheads, long straight noses, and small eyes with arched eyebrows and large eyelids. On comparing these physiognomies with the sculptures in the church of St. Elizabeth, at Marburg, executed in the thirteenth century, it will be found that the same old Hessian type of face has subsisted unchanged, with this distinction only, that the sculptures represent princes and nobles, whose features then bore the stamp of their race, while that stamp is now to be found only among the peasants. A painter who wants to draw mediæval characters with historic truth, must seek his models among the peasantry. This explains why the old German painters gave the heads of their subjects a greater uniformity of type than the painters of our day; the race had not attained to a high degree of individualization in features and expression. It indicates, too, that the cultured man acts more as an individual; the peasant, more as one of a group. Hans drives the plough, lives, and thinks just as Kunz does; and it is this fact, that many thousands of men are as like each other in thoughts and habits as so many sheep or oysters, which constitutes the weight of the peasantry in the social and political scale.

In the cultivated world each individual has his style of speaking and writing. But among the peasantry it is the race, the district, the province, that has its style—namely, its dialect, its phraseology, its proverbs, and its songs, which belong alike to the entire body of the people. This provincial style of the peasant is again, like his *physique*, a remnant of history to which he clings with the utmost tenacity. In certain parts of Hungary, there are still descendants of German colonists of the twelfth and thirteenth centuries, who go about the country as reapers, retaining their old Saxon songs and manners, while the more cultivated German emigrants in a very short time forget their own language, and speak Hungarian. Another remarkable case of the same kind is that of the Wends, a Sclavonic race settled in Lusatia, whose numbers amount to 200,000, living either scattered among the German population or in separate parishes. They have their own schools and churches, and are taught in the Sclavonic tongue. The Catholics among them are rigid adherents of the Pope; the Protestants not less rigid adherents of Luther, or *Doctor* Luther, as they are particular in calling him—a custom which, a hundred years ago, was universal in Protestant Germany. The Wend clings tenaciously to the usages of his Church, and perhaps this may contribute not a little to the purity in which he maintains the specific characteristics of his race. German education, German law and government, service in the standing army, and many other agencies, are in antagonism to his national exclusiveness; but the *wives* and *mothers* here, as elsewhere, are a conservative influence, and the habits temporarily laid aside in the outer world are recovered by the fireside. The Wends form several stout regiments in the Saxon army; they are sought far and wide, as diligent and honest servants; and many a weakly Dresden or Leipzig child becomes thriving under the care of a Wendish nurse. In their villages they have the air and habits of genuine, sturdy peasants, and all their customs indicate that they have been, from the first, an agricultural people. For example, they have traditional modes of treating their domestic animals. Each cow has its own name, generally chosen carefully, so as to express the special qualities of the animal; and all important family events are narrated to the *bees*—a custom which is found also in Westphalia. Whether by the help of the bees or not, the Wend farming is especially prosperous; and when a poor Bohemian peasant has a son born to him, he binds him to the end of a long pole and turns his face toward Lusatia, that he may be as lucky as the Wends who live there.

The peculiarity of the peasant's language consists chiefly in his retention of historical peculiarities, which gradually disappear under the friction of cultivated circles. He prefers any proper name that may be given to a day in the calendar, rather than the abstract date, by which he very rarely reckons. In the baptismal names of his children he is guided by the old custom of the country, not at all by whim and fancy. Many old baptismal names, formerly common in Germany, would have become extinct but for their preservation among the peasantry, especially in North Germany; and so firmly have they adhered to local tradition in this matter, that it would be possible to give a sort of topographical statistics of proper names, and distinguish a district by its rustic names as we do by its Flora and Fauna. The continuous inheritance of certain favorite proper names in a family, in some districts, forces the peasant to adopt the princely custom of attaching a numeral to the name, and saying, when three generations are living at once, Hans I., II., and III.; or, in the more antique fashion, Hans the elder, the middle, and the younger. In some of our English counties there is a similar adherence to a narrow range of proper names; and as a mode of distinguishing collateral branches in the same family, you will hear of Jonathan's Bess, Thomas's Bess, and Samuel's Bess—the three Bessies being cousins.

The peasant's adherence to the traditional has much greater inconvenience than that entailed by a paucity of proper names. In the Black Forest and in Hüttenberg you will see him in the dog-days wearing a thick fur cap, because it is a historical fur cap—a cap worn by his grandfather. In the Wetterau, that peasant girl is considered the handsomest who wears the most petticoats. To go to field-labor in seven petticoats can be anything but convenient or agreeable, but it is the traditionally correct thing; and a German peasant girl would think herself as unfavorably conspicuous in an untraditional costume as an English servant-girl would now think herself in a "linsey-woolsey" apron or a thick muslin cap. In many districts no medical advice would induce the rustic to renounce the tight leather belt with which he injures his digestive functions; you could more easily persuade him to smile on a new communal system than on the unhistorical invention of braces. In the eighteenth century, in spite of the philanthropic preachers of potatoes, the peasant for years threw his potatoes to the pigs and the dogs, before he could be persuaded to put them on his own table. However, the unwillingness of the peasant to adopt innovations has a not unreasonable foundation in the fact, that for him experiments are practical, not theoretical, and must be made with expense of money instead of brains—a fact that is not, perhaps, sufficiently taken into account by agricultural theorists, who complain of the farmer's obstinacy. The peasant has the smallest possible faith in theoretic knowledge; he thinks it rather dangerous than otherwise, as is well indicated by a Lower Rhenish proverb: "One is never too old to learn, said an old woman; so she learned to be a witch."

Between many villages an historical feud—once perhaps the occasion of much bloodshed—is still kept up under the milder form of an occasional round of cudgelling, and the launching of traditional nicknames. An historical feud of this kind still exists, for example, among many villages on the Rhine and more inland places in the neighborhood. *Rheinschnacke* (of which the equivalent is perhaps "water-snake") is the standing term of ignominy for the inhabitant of the Rhine village, who repays it in kind by the epithet "karst" (mattock) or "kukuk" (cuckoo), according as the object of his hereditary hatred belongs to the field or the forest. If any Romeo among the "mattocks" were to marry a Juliet among the "water-snakes," there would be no lack of Tybalts and

Mercutios to carry the conflict from words to blows, though neither side knows a reason for the enmity.

A droll instance of peasant conservatism is told of a village on the Taunus, whose inhabitants from time immemorial had been famous for impromptu cudgelling. For this historical offence the magistrates of the district had always inflicted the equally historical punishment of shutting up the most incorrigible offenders, not in prison, but in their own pig-sty. In recent times, however, the Government, wishing to correct the rudeness of these peasants, appointed an "enlightened" man as magistrate, who at once abolished the original penalty above-mentioned. But this relaxation of punishment was so far from being welcome to the villagers, that they presented a petition praying that a more energetic man might be given them as a magistrate, who would have the courage to punish according to law and justice, "as had been beforetime." And the magistrate who abolished incarceration in the pig-sty could never obtain the respect of the neighborhood. This happened no longer ago than the beginning of the present century.

But it must not be supposed that the historical piety of the German peasant extends to anything not immediately connected with himself. He has the warmest piety toward the old tumble-down house which his grandfather built, and which nothing will induce him to improve; but toward the venerable ruins of the old castle that overlooks his village he has no piety at all, and carries off its stones to make a fence for his garden, or tears down the Gothic carving of the old monastic church, which is "nothing to him," to mark off a footpath through his field. It is the same with historical traditions. The peasant has them fresh in his memory, so far as they relate to himself. In districts where the peasantry are unadulterated, you discern the remnants of the feudal relations in innumerable customs and phrases, but you will ask in vain for historical traditions concerning the empire, or even concerning the particular princely house to which the peasant is subject. He can tell you what "half people and whole people" mean; in Hesse you will still hear of "four horses making a whole peasant," or of "four-day and three-day peasants ": but you will ask in vain about Charlemagne and Frederic Barbarossa.

Riehl well observes that the feudal system, which made the peasant the bondman of his lord, was an immense benefit in a country the greater part of which had still to be colonized,—rescued the peasant from vagabondage, and laid the foundation of persistency and endurance in future generations. If a free German peasantry belongs only to modern times, it is to his ancestor who was a serf, and even, in the earliest times, a slave, that the peasant owes the foundation of his independence—namely, his capability of a settled existence,—nay, his unreasoning persistency, which has its important function in the development of the race.

Perhaps the very worst result of that unreasoning persistency is the peasant's inveterate habit of litigation. Every one remembers the immortal description of Dandie Dinmont's importunate application to Lawyer Pleydell to manage his "bit lawsuit," till at length Pleydell consents to help him ruin himself, on the ground that Dandie may fall into worse hands. It seems, this is a scene which has many parallels in Germany. The farmer's lawsuit is his point of honor; and he will carry it through, though he knows from the very first day that he shall get nothing by it. The litigious peasant piques himself, like Mr. Saddletree, on his knowledge of the law, and this vanity is the chief impulse to many a lawsuit. To the mind of the peasant, law presents itself as the "custom of the country," and it is his pride to be versed in all customs. *Custom with him holds the place of sentiment, of theory, and in many cases of affection.* Riehl justly urges the importance of simplifying law proceedings, so as to cut off this vanity at its source, and also of encouraging, by every possible means, the practice of arbitration.

The peasant never begins his lawsuit in summer, for the same reason that he does not make love and marry in summer, —because he has no time for that sort of thing. Anything is easier to him than to move out of his habitual course, and he is attached even to his privations. Some years ago, a peasant youth, out of the poorest and remotest region of the Westerwald, was enlisted as a recruit, at Weilburg in Nassau. The lad having never in his life slept in a bed, when he had to get into one for the first time began to cry like a child; and he deserted twice because he could not reconcile himself to sleeping in a bed, and to the "fine" life of the barracks: he was homesick at the thought of his accustomed poverty and his thatched hut. A strong contrast this with the feeling of the poor in towns, who would be far enough from deserting because their condition was too much improved! The genuine peasant is never ashamed of his rank and calling; he is rather inclined to look down on every one who does not wear a smock-frock, and thinks a man who has the manners of the gentry is likely to be rather windy and unsubstantial. In some places, even in French districts, this feeling is strongly symbolized by the practice of the peasantry, on certain festival days, to dress the images of the saints in peasant's clothing. History tells us of all kinds of peasant insurrections, the object of which was to obtain relief for the peasants from some of their many oppressions; but of an effort on their part to step out of their hereditary rank and calling, to become gentry, to leave the plough and carry on the easier business of capitalists or Government functionaries, there is no example.

The German novelists who undertake to give pictures of peasant life, fall into the same mistake as our English novelists; they transfer their own feelings to ploughmen and woodcutters, and give them both joys and sorrows of which they know nothing. The peasant never questions the obligation of family ties—he questions *no custom*,—but tender affection, as it exists amongst the refined part of mankind, is almost as foreign to him as white hands and filbert-shaped nails. That the aged father who has given up his property to his children on condition of their maintaining him for the remainder of his life, is very far from meeting with delicate attentions, is indicated by the proverb current among the peasantry—"Don't take your clothes off before you go to bed." [1] Among rustic moral tales and parables, not one is more universal than the story of the ungrateful children, who made their gray-headed father, dependent on them for a maintenance, eat at a wooden trough because he shook the food out of his trembling hands.

[1] This proverb is common among the English farmers also.

Then these same ungrateful children observed one day that
their own little boy was making a tiny wooden trough; and
when they asked him what it was for, he answered—that his
father and mother might eat out of it, when he was a man
and had to keep them.

Marriage is a very prudential affair, especially among the
peasants who have the largest share of property.   Politic mar-
riages are as common among them as among princes; and
when a peasant-heiress in Westphalia marries, her husband
adopts her name, and places his own after it with the prefix
geborner (né).   The girls marry young, and the rapidity with
which they get old and ugly is one among the many proofs
that the early years of marriage are fuller of hardships
than of conjugal tenderness.   " When our writers of village
stories," says Riehl, "transferred their own emotional life to
the peasant, they obliterated what is precisely his most predominant characteristic—namely, that with him general custom holds the place of individual feeling."

We pay for greater emotional susceptibility too often by
nervous diseases of which the peasant knows nothing.   To
him headache is the least of physical evils, because he thinks
head-work the easiest and least indispensable of all labor.
Happily, many of the younger sons in peasant families, by
going to seek their living in the towns, carry their hardy nervous system to amalgamate with the over-wrought nerves of
our town population, and refresh them with a little rude vigor.
And a return to the habits of peasant life is the best remedy
for many moral as well as physical diseases induced by perverted civilization.   Riehl points to colonization as presenting
the true field for this regenerative process.   On the other side
of the ocean a man will have the courage to begin life again
as a peasant, while at home, perhaps, opportunity as well as
courage will fail him.   *Apropos* of this subject of emigration,
he remarks the striking fact that the native shrewdness and
mother-wit of the German peasant seem to forsake him entirely when he has to apply them under new circumstances,
and on relations foreign to his experience.   Hence it is that
the German peasant who emigrates, so constantly falls a victim to unprincipled adventurers in the preliminaries to emi-

gration; but if once he gets his foot on the American soil, he exhibits all the first-rate qualities of an agricultural colonist; and among all German emigrants, the peasant class are the most successful.

But many disintegrating forces have been at work on the peasant character, and degeneration is unhappily going on at a greater pace than development. In the wine districts especially, the inability of the small proprietors to bear up under the vicissitudes of the market, or to ensure a high quality of wine by running the risks of a late vintage, and the competition of beer and cider with the inferior wines, have tended to produce that uncertainty of gain which, with the peasant, is the inevitable cause of demoralization. The small peasant proprietors are not a new class in Germany, but many of the evils of their position are new. They are more dependent on ready money than formerly: thus, where a peasant used to get his wood for building and firing from the common forest, he has now to pay for it with hard cash; he used to thatch his own house, with the help perhaps of a neighbor, but now he pays a man to do it for him; he used to pay taxes in kind, he now pays them in money. The chances of the market have to be discounted, and the peasant falls into the hands of money-lenders. Here is one of the cases in which social policy clashes with a purely economical policy.

Political vicissitudes have added their influence to that of economical changes in disturbing that dim instinct, that reverence for traditional custom, which is the peasant's principle of action. He is in the midst of novelties for which he knows no reason—changes in political geography, changes of the Government to which he owes fealty, changes in bureaucratic management and police regulations. He finds himself in a new element before an apparatus for breathing in it is developed in him. His only knowledge of modern history is in some of its results—for instance, that he has to pay heavier taxes from year to year. His chief idea of a Government is of a power that raises his taxes, opposes his harmless customs, and torments him with new formalities. The source of all this is the false system of "enlightening" the peasant which has been adopted by the bureaucratic Governments. A sys-

tem which disregards the traditions and hereditary attach-
ments of the peasant, and appeals only to a logical understanding which is not yet developed in him, is simply disintegrating
and ruinous to the peasant character.   The interference with
the communal regulations has been of this fatal character.
Instead of endeavoring to promote to the utmost the healthy
life of the Commune, as an organism the conditions of which
are bound up with the historical characteristics of the peasant, the bureaucratic plan of government is bent on improvement by its patent machinery of State-appointed functionaries,
and off-hand regulations in accordance with modern enlightenment.   The spirit of communal exclusiveness—the resistance
to the indiscriminate establishment of strangers—is an intense traditional feeling in the peasant.   "This gallows is for
us and our children," is the typical motto of this spirit.   But
such exclusiveness is highly irrational and repugnant to modern liberalism; therefore a bureaucratic Government at once
opposes it, and encourages to the utmost the introduction of new
inhabitants in the provincial communes.   Instead of allowing
the peasants to manage their own affairs, and, if they happen
to believe that five and four make eleven, to unlearn the prejudice by their own experience in calculation, so that they
may gradually understand processes, and not merely see results, bureaucracy comes with its "Ready Reckoner" and
works all the peasant's sums for him—the surest way of
maintaining him in his stupidity, however it may shake his
prejudice.

Another questionable plan for elevating the peasant is the
supposed elevation of the clerical character, by preventing the
clergyman from cultivating more than a trifling part of the
land attached to his benefice,—that he may be as much as
possible of a scientific theologian, and as little as possible of
a peasant.   In this, Riehl observes, lies one great source of
weakness to the Protestant Church as compared with the Catholic, which finds the great majority of its priests among the
owner orders; and we have had the opportunity of making an
analogous comparison in England, where many of us can remember country districts in which the great mass of the people were christianized by illiterate Methodist and Independent

ministers; while the influence of the parish clergyman among the poor did not extend much beyond a few old women in scarlet cloaks, and a few exceptional church-going laborers.

Bearing in mind the general characteristics of the German peasant, it is easy to understand his relation to the revolutionary ideas and revolutionary movements of modern times. The peasant in Germany, as elsewhere, is a born grumbler. He has always plenty of grievances in his pocket, but he does not generalize those grievances; he does not complain of " government " or " society," probably because he has good reason to complain of the burgomaster. When a few sparks from the first French Revolution fell among the German peasantry, and in certain villages of Saxony the country people assembled together to write down their demands, there was no glimpse in their petition of the " universal rights of man," but simply of their own particular affairs as Saxon peasants. Again, after the July revolution of 1830, there were many insignificant peasant insurrections; but the object of almost all was the removal of local grievances. Toll-houses were pulled down; stamped paper was destroyed; in some places there was a persecution of wild boars, in others of that plentiful tame animal, the German *Rath*, or councillor who is never called into council. But in 1848 it seemed as if the movements of the peasants had taken a new character; in the small western states of Germany it seemed as if the whole class of peasantry was in insurrection. But, in fact, the peasant did not know the meaning of the part he was playing. He had heard that everything was being set right in the towns, and that wonderful things were happening there, so he tied up his bundle and set off. Without any distinct object or resolution, the country people presented themselves on the scene of commotion, and were warmly received by the party leaders. But, seen from the windows of ducal palaces and ministerial hotels, these swarms of peasants had quite another aspect, and it was imagined that they had a common plan of co-operation. This, however, the peasants have never had. Systematic co-operation implies general conceptions, and a provisional subordination of egoism, to which even the artisans of towns have rarely shown themselves equal, and

which are as foreign to the mind of the peasant as logarithms
or the doctrine of chemical proportions. And the revolutionary fervor of the peasant was soon cooled. The old mis-
trust of the towns was reawakened on the spot. The Tyrolese peasants saw no great good in the freedom of the press
and the constitution, because these changes "seemed to please
the gentry so much." Peasants who had given their voices
stormily for a German parliament asked afterward, with a
doubtful look, whether it were to consist of infantry or cav-
alry. When royal domains were declared the property of the
State, the peasants in some small principalities rejoiced over
this, because they interpreted it to mean that every one would
have his share in them, after the manner of the old common
and forests rights.

The very practical views of the peasants, with regard to
the demands of the people, were in amusing contrast with the
abstract theorizing of the educated townsmen. The peasant
continually withheld all State payments until he saw how
matters would turn out, and was disposed to reckon up the
solid benefit, in the form of land or money, that might come
to him from the changes obtained. While the townsman was
heating his brains about representation on the broadest basis,
the peasant asked if the relation between tenant and landlord
would continue as before, and whether the removal of the
"feudal obligations" meant that the farmer should become
owner of the land?

It is in the same naïve way that Communism is interpreted
by the German peasantry. The wide spread among them of
communistic doctrines, the eagerness with which they listened
to a plan for the partition of property, seemed to countenance
the notion that it was a delusion to suppose the peasant would
be secured from this intoxication by his love of secure possession and peaceful earnings. But, in fact, the peasant contemplated "partition" by the light of a historical reminiscence
rather than of novel theory. The golden age, in the imagination of the peasant, was the time when every member of the
commune had a right to as much wood from the forest as
would enable him to sell some, after using what he wanted in
firing,--in which the communal possessions were so profit-

able that, instead of his having to pay rates at the end of the
year, each member of the commune was something in pocket.
Hence the peasants in general understood by "partition" that
the State lands, especially the forests, would be divided among
the communes, and that, by some political legerdemain or
other, everybody would have free firewood, free grazing for
his cattle, and, over and above that, a piece of gold without
working for it.   That he should give up a single clod of his
own to further the general "partition" had never entered the
mind of the peasant communist; and the perception that this
was an essential preliminary to "partition" was often a sufficient cure for his Communism.

In villages lying in the neighborhood of large towns, however, where the circumstances of the peasantry are very different, quite another interpretation of Communism is prevalent.
Here the peasant is generally sunk to the position of the pro-
letaire, living from hand to mouth; he has nothing to lose,
but everything to gain by "partition."   The coarse nature of
the peasant has here been corrupted into bestiality by the
disturbance of his instincts, while he is as yet incapable of
principles; and in this type of the degenerate peasant is seen
the worst example of ignorance intoxicated by theory.

A significant hint as to the interpretation the peasants put
on revolutionary theories, may be drawn from the way they
employed the few weeks in which their movements were un-
checked.   They felled the forest trees and shot the game;
they withheld taxes; they shook off the imaginary or real
burdens imposed on them by their mediatized princes, by presenting their "demands" in a very rough way before the ducal or princely "Schloss"; they set their faces against the
bureaucratic management of the communes, deposed the Government functionaries who had been placed over them as bur-
gomasters and magistrates, and abolished the whole bureaucratic system of procedure, simply by taking no notice of its
regulations, and recurring to some tradition—some old order
or disorder of things.   In all this it is clear that they were
animated not in the least by the spirit of modern revolution,
but by a purely narrow and personal impulse toward reaction.

The idea of constitutional government lies quite beyond the

range of the German peasant's conceptions. His only notion of representation is that of a representation of ranks — of classes; his only notion of a deputy is of one who takes care, not of the national welfare, but of the interests of his own order. Herein lay the great mistake of the democratic party, in common with the bureaucratic Governments, that they entirely omitted the peculiar character of the peasant from their political calculations. They talked of the "people," and forgot that the peasants were included in the term. Only a baseless misconception of the peasant's character could induce the supposition that he would feel the slightest enthusiasm about the principles involved in the reconstitution of the Empire, or even about that reconstitution itself. He has no zeal for a written law, as such, but only so far as it takes the form of a living law—a tradition. It was the external authority which the revolutionary party had won in Baden that attracted the peasants into a participation in the struggle.

Such, Riehl tells us, are the general characteristics of the German peasantry—characteristics which subsist amidst a wide variety of circumstances. In Mecklenburg, Pomerania, and Brandenburg, the peasant lives on extensive estates; in Westphalia he lives in large isolated homesteads; in the Westerwald and in Sauerland, in little groups of villages and hamlets; on the Rhine, land is for the most part parcelled out among small proprietors, who live together in large villages. Then, of course, the diversified physical geography of Germany gives rise to equally diversified methods of land-culture; and out of these various circumstances grow numerous specific differences in manner and character. But the generic character of the German peasant is everywhere the same: in the clean mountain-hamlet and in the dirty fishing-village on the coast; in the plains of North Germany and in the backwoods of America. "Everywhere he has the same historical character—everywhere custom is his supreme law. Where religion and patriotism are still a naïve instinct—are still a sacred *custom*—there begins the class of the German Peasantry."

Our readers will perhaps already have gathered from the foregoing portrait of the German peasant, that Riehl is not a

man who looks at objects through the spectacles either of the
doctrinaire or the dreamer; and they will be ready to believe
what he tells us in his Preface—namely, that years ago he
began his wanderings over the hills and plains of Germany
for the sake of obtaining, in immediate intercourse with the
people, that completion of his historical, political, and economical studies which he was unable to find in books.   He
began his investigations with no party prepossessions, and his
present views were evolved entirely from his own gradually
amassed observations.   He was, first of all, a pedestrian, and
only in the second place a political author.   The views at
which he has arrived by this inductive process, he sums up in
the term—*social-political-conservatism;* but his conservatism
is, we conceive, of a thoroughly philosophical kind.   He sees
in European society *incarnate history,* and any attempt to
disengage it from its historical elements must, he believes,
be simply destructive of social vitality.[1]   What has grown up
historically can only die out historically, by the gradual operation of necessary laws.   The external conditions which society has inherited from the past are but the manifestation of
inherited internal conditions in the human beings who com-
pose it; the internal conditions and the external are related
to each other as the organism and its medium, and development can take place only by the gradual consentaneous development of both.   Take the familiar example of attempts to
abolish titles, which have been about as effective as the process of cutting off poppy-heads in a corn-field.   "*Jedem Men-
schen,*" says Riehl, "*ist sein Zopf angeboren, warum soll denn
der sociale Sprachgebrauch nicht auch seinen Zopf haben?*"—
which we may render—"As long as snobbism runs in the
blood, why should it not run in our speech?"   As a necessary
preliminary to a purely rational society, you must obtain
purely rational men, free from the sweet and bitter prejudices
of hereditary affection and antipathy; which is as easy as to
get running streams without springs, or the leafy shade of the
forest without the secular growth of trunk and branch.

[1] Throughout this article, in our statement of Riehl's opinions, we
must be understood not as quoting Riehl, but as interpreting and illus-
trating him.

The historical conditions of society may be compared with those of language. It must be admitted that the language of cultivated nations is in anything but a rational state; the great sections of the civilized world are only approximatively intelligible to each other, and even that, only at the cost of long study; one word stands for many things, and many words for one thing; the subtle shades of meaning, and still subtler echoes of association, make language an instrument which scarcely anything short of genius can wield with definiteness and certainty. Suppose, then, that the effort which has been again and again made to construct a universal language on a rational basis has at length succeeded, and that you have a language which has no uncertainty, no whims of idiom, no cumbrous forms, no fitful shimmer of many-hued significance, no hoary archaisms "familiar with forgotten years"—a patent deodorized and non-resonant language, which effects the purpose of communication as perfectly and rapidly as algebraic signs. Your language may be a perfect medium of expression to science, but will never express *life*, which is a great deal more than science. With the anomalies and inconveniences of historical language, you will have parted with its music and its passion, with its vital qualities as an expression of individual character, with its subtle capabilities of wit, with everything that gives it power over the imagination; and the next step in simplification will be the invention of a talking watch, which will achieve the utmost facility and despatch in the communication of ideas by a graduated adjustment of ticks, to be represented in writing by a corresponding arrangement of dots. A melancholy "language of the future"! The sensory and motor nerves that run in the same sheath, are scarcely bound together by a more necessary and delicate union than that which binds men's affections, imagination, wit, and humor, with the subtle ramifications of historical language. Language must be left to grow in precision, completeness, and unity, as minds grow in clearness, comprehensiveness, and sympathy. And there is an analogous relation between the moral tendencies of men and the social conditions they have inherited. The nature of European men has its roots intertwined with the past, and can only be developed by allowing those roots to remain undisturbed while the process of development is going on, until that perfect ripeness of the seed which carries with it a life independent of the root. This vital connection with the past is much more vividly felt on the Continent than in England, where we have to recall it by an effort of memory and reflection; for though our English life is in its core intensely traditional, Protestantism and commerce have modernized the face of the land and the aspects of society in a far greater degree than in any Continental country:—

"Abroad," says Ruskin, "a building of the eighth or tenth century stands ruinous in the open street; the children play around it, the peasants heap their corn in it, the buildings of yesterday nestle about it, and fit their new stones in its rents, and tremble in sympathy as it trembles. No one wonders at it, or thinks of it as separate, and of another time; we feel the ancient world to be a real thing, and one with the new; antiquity is no dream; it is rather the children playing about the old stones that are the dream. But all is continuous, and the words, 'from generation to generation,' understandable here."

This conception of European society as incarnate history, is the fundamental idea of Riehl's books.

After the notable failure of revolutionary attempts conducted from the point of view of abstract democratic and socialistic theories, after the practical demonstration of the evils resulting from a bureaucratic system which governs by an undiscriminating, dead mechanism, Riehl wishes to urge on the consideration of his countrymen a social policy founded on the special study of the people as they are—on the natural history of the various social ranks. He thinks it wise to pause a little from theorizing, and see what is the material actually present for theory to work upon. It is the glory of the Socialists—in contrast with the democratic doctrinaires who have been too much occupied with the general idea of "the people" to inquire particularly into the actual life of the people—that they have thrown themselves with enthusiastic zeal into the study at least of one social group—namely, the factory operatives; and here lies the secret of their partial success. But, unfortunately, they have made this special study of a single fragment of society the basis of a theory which quietly substitutes for the small group of Parisian proletaires or English factory-workers, the society of all Europe—nay, of the whole world. And in this way they have lost the best fruit of their investigations. For, says Riehl, the more deeply we penetrate into the knowledge of society in its details, the more thoroughly we shall be convinced that *a universal social policy has no validity except on paper*, and can never be carried into successful practice. The conditions of German society are altogether different from those of French, of English, or of Italian society; and to apply the same social theory to these nations indiscriminately, is about as wise a procedure as Triptolemus Yellowley's application of the agricultural directions in Virgil's "Georgics" to his farm in the Shetland Isles.

It is the clear and strong light in which Riehl places this important position, that in our opinion constitutes the suggestive value of his books for foreign as well as German readers. It has not been sufficiently insisted on, that in the various branches of Social Science there is an advance from the general to the special, from the simple to the complex, analogous with that which is found in the series of the sciences, from Mathematics to Biology. To the laws of quantity comprised in Mathematics and Physics are superadded, in Chemistry, laws of quality; to these again are added, in Biology, laws of life; and lastly, the conditions of life in general branch out into its special conditions, or Natural History, on the one hand, and into its abnormal conditions, or Pathology, on the other. And in this series or ramification of the sciences, the more general science will not suffice to solve the problems of the more special. Chemistry embraces phenomena which are not explicable by Physics; Biology embraces phenomena which are not explicable by Chemistry; and no biological generalization will enable us to predict the infinite specialities produced by the complexity of vital conditions. So Social Science, while it has departments which in their fundamental generality correspond to mathematics and physics—namely, those grand and simple generalizations which trace out the inevitable march of the human race as a whole, and, as a ramification of these, the laws of economical science—has also, in the departments of government and jurisprudence, which embrace the conditions of social life in all their complexity, what may be called its Biology, carrying us on to innumerable special phenomena which outlie the sphere of science, and belong to Natural History. And just as the most thorough acquaintance with physics, or chemistry, or general physiology will not enable you at once to establish the balance of life in your private vivarium, so that your particular society of zoöphytes, molluscs, and echinoderms may feel themselves, as the Germans say, at ease in their skin; so the most complete equipment of theory will not enable a statesman or a political and social reformer to adjust his measures wisely, in the absence of a special acquaintance with the section of society for which he legislates, with the peculiar characteristics of the nation, the province, the class whose well-being he has to consult. In other words, a wise social policy must be based not simply on abstract social science, but on the Natural History of social bodies.

Riehl's books are not dedicated merely to the argumentative maintenance of this or of any other position; they are intended chiefly as a contribution to that knowledge of the German people on the importance of which he insists. He is less occupied with urging his own conclusions than with impressing on his readers the facts which have led him to those conclusions. In the volume entitled "Land und Leute," which, though published last, is properly an introduction to the volume entitled "Die Bürgerliche Gesellschaft," he considers the German people in their physical-geographical relations; he compares the natural divisions of the race, as determined by land and climate, and social traditions, with the artificial divisions which are based on diplomacy; and he traces the genesis and influences of what we may call the ecclesiastical geography of Germany—its partition between Catholicism and Protestantism. He shows that the ordinary antithesis of North and South Germany represents no real ethnographical distinction, and that the natural divisions of Germany, founded on its physical geography, are threefold—namely, the low plains, the middle mountain region, and the high mountain region, or Lower, Middle, and Upper Germany; and on this primary natural division all the other broad ethnographical distinctions of Germany will be found to rest. The plains of North or Lower Germany include all the seaboard the nation possesses; and this, together with the fact that they are traversed to the depth of 600 miles by navigable rivers, makes them the natural seat of a trading race. Quite different is the geographical character of Middle Germany. While the northern plains are marked off into great divisions, by such rivers as the Lower Rhine, the Weser, and the Oder, running almost in parallel lines, this central region is cut up like a mosaic, by the capricious lines of valleys and rivers. Here is the region in which you find those famous roofs from which the rain-water runs toward two different seas, and the mountain-tops from which you may look into eight or ten German States. The abundance of water-power and the presence of extensive coal-mines allow of a very diversified industrial development in Middle Germany. In Upper Germany, or the high mountain region, we find the same symmetry in the lines of the rivers as in the north; almost all the great Alpine streams flow parallel with the Danube. But the majority of these rivers are neither navigable nor available for industrial objects, and instead of serving for communication, they shut off one great tract from another. The slow development, the simple peasant-life of many districts, is here determined by the mountain and the river. In the southeast, however, industrial activity spreads through Bohemia toward Austria, and forms a sort of balance to the industrial districts of the Lower Rhine. Of course, the boundaries of these three regions cannot be very strictly defined; but an approximation to the limits of Middle Germany may be obtained by regarding it as a triangle, of which one angle lies in Silesia, another in Aix-la-Chapelle, and a third at Lake Constance.

This triple division corresponds with the broad distinctions of climate. In the northern plains the atmosphere is damp and heavy; in the southern mountain region it is dry and rare, and there are abrupt changes of temperature, sharp contrasts between the seasons, and devastating storms; but in both these zones men are hardened by conflict with the roughnesses of the climate. In Middle Germany, on the contrary, there is little of this struggle; the seasons are more equable, and the mild, soft air of the valleys tends to make the inhabitants luxurious and sensitive to hardships. It is only in exceptional mountain districts that one is here reminded of the rough, bracing air on the heights of Southern Germany. It is a curious fact that, as the air becomes gradually lighter and rarer from the North German coast toward Upper Germany, the average of suicides regularly decreases. Mecklenburg has the highest number, then Prussia, while the fewest suicides occur in Bavaria and Austria.

Both the northern and southern regions have still a large extent of waste lands, downs, morasses, and heaths; and to these are added, in the south, abundance of snow-fields and naked rock; while in Middle Germany culture has almost overspread the face of the land, and there are no large tracts of waste. There is the same proportion in the distribution of forests. Again, in the north we see a monotonous continuity of wheat-fields, potato-grounds, meadow-lands, and vast heaths; and there is the same uniformity of culture over large surfaces in the southern table-lands and the Alpine pastures. In Middle Germany, on the contrary, there is a perpetual variety of crops within a short space: the diversity of land surface, and the corresponding variety in the species of plants, are an invitation to the splitting up of estates, and this again encourages to the utmost the motley character of the cultivation.

According to this threefold division, it appears that there are certain features common to North and South Germany in which they differ from Central Germany, and the nature of this difference Riehl indicates by distinguishing the former as *Centralized Land* and the latter as *Individualized Land*—a distinction which is well symbolized by the fact that North and South Germany possess the great lines of railway which are the medium for the traffic of the world, while Middle Germany is far richer in lines for local communication, and possesses the greatest length of railway within the smallest space. Disregarding superficialities, the East Frieslanders, the Schleswig-Holsteiners, the Mecklenburgers, and the Pomeranians are much more nearly allied to the old Bavarians, the Tyrolese, and the Styrians, than any of these are allied to the Saxons, the Thuringians, or the Rhinelanders. Both in North and South Germany original races are still found in large masses, and popular dialects are spoken; you still find there thoroughly peasant districts, thorough villages, and also, at great intervals, thorough cities; you still find there a sense of rank. In Middle Germany, on the contrary, the original races are fused together or sprinkled hither and thither; the peculiarities of the popular dialects are worn down or confused; there is no very strict line of demarcation between the country and the town population, hundreds of small towns and large villages being hardly distinguishable in their characteristics; and the sense of rank, as part of the organic structure of society, is almost extinguished. Again, both in the north and south there is still a strong ecclesiastical spirit in the people, and the Pomeranian sees Antichrist in the Pope as clearly as the Tyrolese sees him in Doctor Luther; while in Middle Germany the confessions are mingled—they exist peaceably side by side in very narrow space, and tolerance or indifference has spread itself widely even in the popular mind. And the analogy, or rather the causal relation, between the physical geography of the three regions and the development of the population goes still further:—

"For," observes Riehl, "the striking connection which has been pointed out between the local geological formations in Germany and the revolutionary disposition of the people, has more than a metaphorical significance. Where the primeval physical revolutions of the globe have been the wildest in their effects, and the most multiform strata have been tossed together or thrown one upon the other, it is a very intelligible consequence that on a land surface thus broken up, the population should sooner develop itself into small communities, and that the more intense life generated in these smaller communities should become the most favorable nidus for the reception of modern culture, and with this a susceptibility for its revolutionary ideas; while a people settled in a region where its groups are spread over a large space will persist much more obstinately in the retention of its original character. The people of Middle Germany have none of that exclusive one-sidedness which determines the peculiar genius of great national groups, just as this one-sidedness or uniformity is wanting to the geological and geographical character of their land."

This ethnographical outline Riehl fills up with special and typical descriptions, and then makes it the starting-point for a criticism of the actual political condition of Germany. The volume is full of vivid pictures, as well as penetrating glances into the maladies and tendencies of modern society. It would be fascinating as literature, if it were not important for its facts and philosophy. But we can only commend it to our readers, and pass on to the volume entitled "Die Bürgerliche Gesellschaft," from which we have drawn our sketch of the German peasantry. Here Riehl gives us a series of studies in that natural history of the people, which he regards as the proper basis of social policy. He holds that, in European society, there are *three natural ranks or estates:* the hereditary landed aristocracy, the citizens or commercial class, and the peasantry or agricultural class. By *natural ranks* he means ranks which have their roots deep in the historical structure of society, and are still, in the present, showing vitality above ground; he means those great social groups which are not only distinguished externally by their vocation, but essentially by their mental character, their habits, their mode of life,—by the principle they represent in the historical development of society. In his conception of the " Fourth Estate " he differs from the usual interpretation, according to which it is simply equivalent to the Proletariat, or those who are dependent on daily wages, whose only capital is their skill or bodily strength—factory operatives, artisans, agricultural laborers, to whom might be added, especially in Germany, the day-laborers with the quill, the literary proletariat. This, Riehl observes, is a valid basis of economical classification, but not of social classification. In his view, the Fourth Estate is a stratum produced by the perpetual abrasion of the other great social groups; it is the sign and result of the decomposition which is commencing in the organic constitution of society. Its elements are derived alike from the aristocracy, the bourgeoisie, and the peasantry. It assembles under its banner the deserters of historical society, and forms them into a terrible army, which is only just awaking to the consciousness of its corporate power. The tendency of this Fourth Estate, by the very process of its formation, is to do away with the distinctive historical character of the other estates, and to resolve their peculiar rank and vocation into a uniform social relation founded on an abstract conception of society. According to

Riehl's classification, the day-laborers, whom the political economist designates as the Fourth Estate, belong partly to the peasantry or agricultural class, and partly to the citizens or commercial class.

Riehl considers, in the first place, the peasantry and aristocracy as the " Forces of social persistence," and, in the second, the bourgeoisie and the "fourth estate" as the "Forces of social movement."

The aristocracy, he observes, is the only one among these four groups which is denied by others besides Socialists to have any natural basis as a separate rank. It is admitted that there was once an aristocracy which had an intrinsic ground of existence; but now, it is alleged, this is an historical fossil, an antiquarian relic, venerable because gray with age. In what, it is asked, can consist the peculiar vocation of the aristocracy, since it has no longer the monopoly of the land, of the higher military functions, and of Government offices, and since the service of the Court has no longer any political importance? To this Riehl replies that in great revolutionary crises, the "men of progress" have more than once "abolished" the aristocracy. But remarkably enough, the aristocracy has always reappeared. This measure of abolition showed that the nobility were no longer regarded as a real class, for to abolish a real class would be an absurdity. It is quite possible to contemplate a voluntary breaking up of the peasant or citizen class in the socialistic sense, but no man in his senses would think of straightway "abolishing" citizens and peasants. The aristocracy, then, was regarded as a sort of cancer, or excrescence of society. Nevertheless, not only has it been found impossible to annihilate a hereditary nobility by decree; but also, the aristocracy of the eighteenth century outlived even the self-destructive acts of its own perversity. A life which was entirely without object, entirely destitute of functions, would not, says Riehl, be so persistent. He has an acute criticism of those who conduct a polemic against the idea of a hereditary aristocracy while they are proposing an "aristocracy of talent," which after all is based on the principle of inheritance. The Socialists are, therefore, only consistent in declaring against an aristocracy of talent. "But when they have turned the world into a great Foundling Hospital, they will still be unable to eradicate the ' privileges of birth.' "   We must not follow him in his criticism, however; nor can we afford to do more than mention hastily his interesting sketch of the mediæval aristocracy, and his admonition to the German aristocracy of the present day, that the vitality of their class is not to be sustained by romantic attempts to revive mediæval forms and sentiments, but only by the exercise of functions as real and salutary for actual society as those of the mediæval aristocracy were for the feudal age. "In modern society the divisions of rank indicate *division of labor*, according to that distribution of functions in the social organism which the historical constitution of society has determined.   In this way the principle of differentiation and the principle of unity are identical."

The elaborate study of the German bourgeoisie which forms the next division of the volume must be passed over; but we may pause a moment to note Riehl's definition of the social *Philister* (Philistine), an epithet for which we have no equivalent—not at all, however, for want of the object it represents.   Most people who read a little German, know that the epithet *Philister* originated in the *Burschen-Leben*, or student-life in Germany, and that the antithesis of *Bursch* and *Philister* was equivalent to the antithesis of "gown" and "town"; but since the word has passed into ordinary language, it has assumed several shades of significance which have not yet been merged in a single absolute meaning; and one of the questions which an English visitor in Germany will probably take an opportunity of asking is, "What is the strict meaning of the word *Philister?*"   Riehl's answer is, that the *Philister* is one who is indifferent to all social interests, all public life, as distinguished from selfish and private interests; he has no sympathy with political and social events except as they affect his own comfort and prosperity, as they offer him material for amusement or opportunity for gratifying his vanity.   He has no social or political creed, but is always of the opinion which is most convenient for the moment.   He is always in the majority, and is the main element of unreason and stupidity in the judgment of a "discerning public."   It seems presumptuous to us to dispute Riehl's interpretation of a German word, but we must think that, in literature, the epithet *Philister* has usually a wider meaning than this—includes his definition and something more. We imagine the *Philister* is the personification of the spirit which judges everything from a lower point of view than the subject demands—which judges the affairs of the parish from the egotistic or purely personal point of view—which judges the affairs of the nation from the parochial point of view, and does not hesitate to measure the merits of the universe from the human point of view. At least, this must surely be the spirit to which Goethe alludes in a passage cited by Riehl himself, where he says that the Germans need not be ashamed of erecting a monument to him as well as to Blücher; for if Blücher had freed them from the French, he (Goethe) had freed them from the nets of the *Philister* :—

> "Ihr mögt mir immer ungescheut
> Gleich Blüchern Denkmal setzen !
> Von Franzosen hat er euch befreit,
> Ich von Philister-Netzen."

Goethe could hardly claim to be the apostle of public spirit; but he is eminently the man who helps us to rise to a lofty point of observation, so that we may see things in their relative proportions.

The most interesting chapters in the description of the "Fourth Estate," which concludes the volume, are those on the "Aristocratic Proletariat" and the "Intellectual Proletariat." The Fourth Estate in Germany, says Riehl, has its centre of gravity not, as in England and France, in the day-laborers and factory operatives, and still less in the degenerate peasantry. In Germany, the *educated* proletariat is the leaven that sets the mass in fermentation; the dangerous classes there go about, not in blouses, but in frock-coats; they begin with the impoverished prince and end in the hungriest *littérateur*. The custom that all the sons of a nobleman shall inherit their father's title, necessarily goes on multiplying that class of aristocrats who are not only without function but without adequate provision, and who shrink from entering the ranks of the citizens by adopting some honest calling. The

younger son of a prince, says Riehl, is usually obliged to remain without any vocation; and however zealously he may
study music, painting, literature, or science, he can never be
a regular musician, painter, or man of science; his pursuit
will be called a "passion," not a "calling," and to the end of
his days he remains a *dilettante.* "But the ardent pursuit
of a fixed practical calling can alone satisfy the active man."
Direct legislation cannot remedy this evil. The inheritance
of titles by younger sons is the universal custom, and custom
is stronger than law. But if all Government preference for
the "aristocratic proletariat" were withdrawn, the sensible
men among them would prefer emigration, or the pursuit of
some profession, to the hungry distinction of a title without
rents.

The intellectual proletaires Riehl calls the "church mili-
tant" of the Fourth Estate in Germany. In no other country are they so numerous; in no other country is the trade in
material and industrial capital so far exceeded by the wholesale and retail trade, the traffic and the usury, in the intellectual capital of the nation. *Germany yields more intellectual
produce than it can use and pay for.*

"This over-production, which is not transient but permanent, nay, is
constantly on the increase, evidences a diseased state of the national
industry, a perverted application of industrial powers, and is a far more
pungent satire on the national condition than all the poverty of operatives and peasants. . . . Other nations need not envy us the preponderance of the intellectual proletariat over the proletaires of manual labor.
For man more easily becomes diseased from over-study than from the
labor of the hands; and it is precisely in the intellectual proletariat
that there are the most dangerous seeds of disease. This is the group
in which the opposition between earnings and wants, between the ideal
social position and the real, is the most hopelessly irreconcilable."

We must unwillingly leave our readers to make acquaintance for themselves with the graphic details with which Riehl
follows up this general statement: but before quitting these
admirable volumes, let us say, lest our inevitable omissions
should have left room for a different conclusion, that Riehl's
conservatism is not in the least tinged with the partisanship of
a class, with a poetic fanaticism for the past, or with the prejudice of a mind incapable of discerning the grander evolution

of things to which all social forms are but temporarily subservient. It is the conservatism of a clear-eyed, practical, but withal large-minded man—a little caustic, perhaps, now and then in his epigrams on democratic doctrinaires who have their nostrum for all political and social diseases, and on communistic theories which he regards as "the despair of the individual in his own manhood, reduced to a system," but nevertheless able and willing to do justice to the elements of fact and reason in every shade of opinion and every form of effort. He is as far as possible from the folly of supposing that the sun will go backward on the dial, because we put the hands of our clock backward; he only contends against the opposite folly of decreeing that it shall be mid-day, while in fact the sun is only just touching the mountain-tops, and all along the valley men are stumbling in the twilight.

THREE MONTHS IN WEIMAR.

IT was between three and four o'clock, on a fine morning in August, that, after a ten hours' journey from Frankfort, I awoke at the Weimar station. No tipsiness can be more dead to all appeals than that which comes from fitful draughts of sleep on a railway journey by night. To the disgust of your wakeful companions, you are totally insensible to the existence of your umbrella, and to the fact that your carpet-bag is stowed under your seat, or that you have borrowed books and tucked them behind the cushion. "What's the odds, so long as one can sleep?" is your philosophic formula, and it is not until you have begun to shiver on the platform in the early morning air that you become alive to property and its duties —*i.e.*, to the necessity of keeping a fast grip upon it. Such was my condition when I reached the station at Weimar. The ride to the town thoroughly roused me, all the more because the glimpses I caught from the carriage-window were in startling contrast with my preconceptions. The lines of houses looked rough and straggling, and were often interrupted by trees peeping out from the gardens behind. At last we stopped before the Erbprinz, an inn of long standing in the heart of the town, and were ushered along heavy-looking in-and-out corridors, such as are found only in German inns, into rooms which overlooked a garden just like one you may see at the back of a farmhouse in many an English village.

A walk in the morning in search of lodgings confirmed the impression that Weimar was more like a market-town than the precinct of a Court. "And this is the Athens of the North!" we said. Materially speaking, it is more like Sparta. The blending of rustic and civic life, the indications of a central government in the midst of very primitive-looking objects, has some distant analogy with the condition of old Lacedæmon. The shops are most of them such as you would see in the back streets of an English provincial town, and the commodities on sale are often chalked on the doorposts. A loud rumbling of vehicles may indeed be heard now and then; but the rumbling is loud, not because the vehicles are many, but because the springs are few. The inhabitants seemed to us to have more than the usual heaviness of *Germanity*; even their stare was slow, like that of herbivorous quadrupeds. We set out with the intention of exploring the town, and at every other turn we came into a street which took us *out* of the town, or else into one that led us back to the market from which we set out. One's first feeling was, How could Goethe live here in this dull, lifeless village? The reproaches cast on him for his worldliness and attachment to Court splendor seemed ludicrous enough, and it was inconceivable that the stately Jupiter, in a frock-coat, so familiar to us all through Rauch's statuette, could have habitually walked along these rude streets and among these slouching mortals. Not a picturesque bit of building was to be seen; there was no quaintness, nothing to remind one of historical associations, nothing but the most arid prosaism.

This was the impression produced by a first morning's walk in Weimar—an impression which very imperfectly represents what Weimar is, but which is worth recording, because it is true as a sort of back view. Our ideas were considerably modified when, in the evening, we found our way to the Belvedere *chaussée*, a splendid avenue of chestnut-trees, two miles in length, reaching from the town to the summer residence of Belvedere; when we saw the Schloss, and discovered the labyrinthine beauties of the park; indeed every day opened to us fresh charms in this quiet little valley and its environs. To any one who loves Nature in her gentle aspects, who delights in the checkered shade on a summer morning, and in a walk on the corn-clad upland at sunset, within sight of a little town nestled among the trees below, I say—come to Weimar. And if you are weary of English unrest, of that society of "eels in a jar," where each is trying to get his head above the other, the somewhat stupid well-being of the Weimarians will not be an unwelcome contrast, for a short time at least. If you care nothing about Goethe and Schiller and

Herder and Wieland, why, so much the worse for you—you will miss many interesting thoughts and associations; still, Weimar has a charm independent of these great names.

First among all its attractions is the Park, which would be remarkably beautiful even among English parks, and it has one advantage over all these—namely, that it is without a fence. It runs up to the houses, and far out into the corn-fields and meadows, as if it had a "sweet will" of its own, like a river or a lake, and had not been planned and plant-ed by human will. Through it flows the Ilm,—not a clear stream, it must be confessed, but, like all water, as Novalis says, "an eye to the landscape." Before we came to Weimar we had had dreams of boating on the Ilm, and we were not a little amused at the difference between this vision of our own and the reality. A few water-fowl are the only navigators of the river, and even they seem to confine themselves to one spot, as if they were there purely in the interest of the pic-turesque. The real extent of the park is small, but the walks are so ingeniously arranged, and the trees are so luxuriant and various, that it takes weeks to learn the turnings and wind-ings by heart, so as no longer to have the sense of novelty. In the warm weather our great delight was the walk which follows the course of the Ilm, and is overarched by tall trees with patches of dark moss on their trunks, in rich contrast with the transparent green of the delicate leaves, through which the golden sunlight played, and checkered the walk be-fore us. On one side of this walk the rocky ground rises to the height of twenty feet or more, and is clothed with mosses and rock-plants. On the other side there are, every now and then, openings,—breaks in the continuity of shade, which show you a piece of meadow-land, with fine groups of trees; and at every such opening a seat is placed under the rock, where you may sit and chat away the sunny hours, or listen to those delicate sounds which one might fancy came from tiny bells worn on the garment of Silence to make us aware of her invisible presence. It is along this walk that you come upon a truncated column, with a serpent twined round it, devouring cakes, placed on the column as offerings,—a bit of rude sculp-ture in stone. The inscription—*Genio loci*—enlightens the

learned as to the significance of this symbol, but the people of
Weimar, unedified by classical allusions, have explained the
sculpture by a story which is an excellent example of a modern
myth.   Once on a time, say they, a huge serpent infested the
park, and evaded all attempts to exterminate him, until at
last a cunning baker made some appetizing cakes which contained an effectual poison, and placed them in the serpent's
reach, thus meriting a place with Hercules, Theseus, and other
monster-slayers.   Weimar, in gratitude, erected this column
as a memorial of the baker's feat and its own deliverance.   A
little farther on is the Borkenhaus, where Carl August used to
play the hermit for days together, and from which he used to
telegraph to Goethe in his Gartenhaus.   Sometimes we took
our shady walk in the *Stern*, the oldest part of the park plantations, on the opposite side of the river, lingering on our way
to watch the crystal brook which hurries on, like a foolish
young maiden, to wed itself with the muddy Ilm.   The Stern
(Star), a large circular opening amongst the trees, with walks
radiating from it, has been thought of as the place for the
projected statues of Goethe and Schiller.   In Rauch's model
for these statues the poets are draped in togas, Goethe, who
was considerably the shorter of the two, resting his hand on
Schiller's shoulder; but it has been wisely determined to represent them in their "habit as they lived"; so Rauch's design is rejected.   Against classical idealizing in portrait sculp-
ture, Weimar has already a sufficient warning in the colossal
statue of Goethe, executed after Bettina's design, which the
readers of the "Correspondence with a Child" may see en-
graved as a frontispiece to the second volume.   This statue is
locked up in an odd structure, standing in the park, and looking like a compromise between a church and a summer-house
(Weimar does *not* shine in its buildings!).   How little real
knowledge of Goethe must the mind have that could wish to
see him represented as a naked Apollo, with a Psyche at his
knee!   The execution is as feeble as the sentiment is false;
the Apollo-Goethe is a caricature, and the Psyche is simply
vulgar.   The statue was executed under Bettina's encouragement, in the hope that it would be bought by the King of
Prussia; but a breach having taken place between her and her
12

Royal friend, a purchaser was sought in the Grand Duke of
Weimar, who, after transporting it at enormous expense from
Italy, wisely shut it up where it is seen only by the curious.

As autumn advanced and the sunshine became precious, we
preferred the broad walk on the higher grounds of the park,
where the masses of trees are finely disposed, leaving wide
spaces of meadow which extend on one side to the Belvedere
allée with its avenue of chestnut-trees, and on the other to the
little cliffs which I have already described as forming a wall
by the walk along the Ilm. Exquisitely beautiful were the
graceful forms of the plane-trees, thrown in golden relief on
a background of dark pines. Here we used to turn and turn
again in the autumn afternoons,—at first bright and warm,
then sombre with low-lying purple clouds, and chill with
winds that sent the leaves raining from the branches. The
eye here welcomes, as a contrast, the white façade of a building looking like a small Greek temple, placed on the edge of
the cliff, and you at once conclude it to be a bit of pure ornament,—a device to set off the landscape; but you presently
see a porter seated near the door of the basement story, be-
guiling the *ennui* of his sinecure by a book and a pipe, and
you learn with surprise that this is another retreat for ducal
dignity to unbend and philosophize in. Singularly ill-adapted
to such a purpose it seems to beings not ducal. On the other
side of the Ilm the park is bordered by the road leading to the
little village of Ober Weimar,—another sunny walk which
has the special attraction of taking one by Goethe's Gartenhaus, his first residence at Weimar. Inside, this Gartenhaus
is a homely sort of cottage, such as many an English nobleman's gardener lives in; no furniture is left in it, and the
family wish to sell it. Outside, its aspect became to us like
that of a dear friend, whose irregular features and rusty
clothes have a peculiar charm. It stands, with its bit of
garden and orchard, on a pleasant slope, fronting the west;
before it the park stretches one of its meadowy openings to
the trees which fringe the Ilm, and between this meadow and
the garden hedge lies the said road to Ober Weimar. A grove
of weeping birches sometimes tempted us to turn out of this
road up to the fields at the top of the slope, on which not only

the Gartenhaus but several other modest villas are placed.
From this little height one sees to advantage the plantations
of the park in their autumnal coloring; the town with its steep-
roofed church, and castle clock-tower, painted a gay green;
the bushy line of the Belvedere *chaussée*, and Belvedere itself
peeping on an eminence from its nest of trees. Here, too,
was the place for seeing a lovely sunset,—such a sunset as
September sometimes gives us,—when the western horizon is
like a rippled sea of gold, sending over the whole hemisphere
golden vapors, which, as they near the east, are subdued to a
deep rose-color.

The Schloss is rather a stately, ducal-looking building, forming three sides of a quadrangle. Strangers are admitted to
see a suite of rooms called the Dichter-Zimmer (Poets' Rooms),
dedicated to Goethe, Schiller, and Wieland. The idea of
these rooms is really a pretty one: in each of them there is
a bust of the poet who is its presiding genius, and the walls
of the Schiller and Goethe rooms are covered with frescoes
representing scenes from their works. The Wieland room is
much smaller than the other two, and serves as an ante-chamber to them; it is also decorated more sparingly, but the ara-
besques on the walls are very tastefully designed, and satisfy
one better than the ambitious compositions from Goethe and
Schiller.

A more interesting place to visitors is the library, which
occupies a large building not far from the Schloss. The principal *Saal*, surrounded by a broad gallery, is ornamented with
some very excellent busts and some very bad portraits. Of
the busts, the most remarkable is that of Gluck, by Houdon
—a striking specimen of the *real* in art. The sculptor has
given every scar made by the small-pox; he has left the nose
as pug and insignificant, and the mouth as common, as Nature
made them; but then he has done what, doubtless, Nature
also did—he has spread over those coarsely cut features the
irradiation of genius. A specimen of the opposite style in art
is Trippel's bust of Goethe as the young Apollo, also fine in
its way. It was taken when Goethe was in Italy; and in the
" Italiänische Reise," mentioning the progress of the bust, he
says that he sees little likeness to himself, but is not discon-

tented that he should go forth to the world as such a good-looking fellow—*hübscher Bursch*. This bust, however, is a frank idealization: when an artist tells us that the ideal of a Greek god divides his attention with his immediate subject, we are warned. But one gets rather irritated with idealization in portrait when, as in Dannecker's bust of Schiller, one has been misled into supposing that Schiller's brow was square and massive, while, in fact, it was receding. We say this partly on the evidence of his skull, a cast of which is kept in the library, so that we could place it in juxtaposition with the bust. The story of this skull is curious. When it was determined to disinter Schiller's remains, that they might repose in company with those of Carl August and Goethe, the question of identification was found to be a difficult one, for his bones were mingled with those of ten insignificant fellow-mortals. When, however, the eleven skulls were placed in juxtaposition, a large number of persons who had known Schiller, separately and successively fixed upon the same skull as his, and their evidence was clinched by the discovery that the teeth of this skull corresponded to the statement of Schiller's servant, that his master had lost no teeth, except one, which he specified. Accordingly it was decided that this was Schiller's skull, and the comparative anatomist, Loder, was sent for from Jena to select the bones which completed the skeleton.[1] The evidence certainly leaves room for a doubt; but the receding forehead of the skull agrees with the testimony of persons who knew Schiller, that he had, as Rauch said to us, a "miserable forehead"; it agrees, also, with a beautiful miniature of Schiller, taken when he was about twenty. This miniature is deeply interesting; it shows us a youth whose clearly cut features, with the mingled fire and melancholy of their expression, could hardly have been passed with indifference; it has the *langer Gänsehals* (long goose-neck) which he gives to his Karl Moor; but instead of the black, sparkling eyes, and the gloomy, overhanging, bushy eyebrows he chose

[1] I tell this story from my recollection of Stahr's account in his "Weimar und Jena," an account which was confirmed to me by residents in Weimar; but as I have not the book by me, I cannot test the accuracy of my memory.

for his robber hero, it has the fine wavy, auburn locks, and the light-blue eyes which belong to our idea of pure German race. We may be satisfied that we know at least the *form* of Schiller's features, for in this particular his busts and portraits are in striking accordance; unlike the busts and portraits of Goethe, which are a proof, if any were wanted, how inevitably subjective art is, even when it professes to be purely imitative—how the most active perception gives us rather a reflex of what we think and feel, than the real sum of objects before us. The Goethe of Rauch or of Schwanthaler is widely different in form, as well as expression, from the Goethe of Stieler; and Winterberger, the actor, who knew Goethe intimately, told us that to him not one of all the likenesses, sculptured or painted, seemed to have more than a faint resemblance to their original. There is, indeed, one likeness, taken in his old age, and preserved in the library, which is startling from the conviction it produces of close resemblance, and Winterberger admitted it to be the best he had seen. It is a tiny miniature painted on a small cup, of Dresden china, and is so wonderfully executed, that a magnifying-glass exhibits the perfection of its texture as if it were a flower or a butterfly's wing. It is more like Stieler's portrait than any other; the massive neck, unbent though withered, rises out of his dressing-gown, and supports majestically a head, from which one might imagine (though, alas! it never is so in reality) that the discipline of seventy years had purged away all meaner elements than those of the sage and the poet—a head which might serve as a type of sublime old age. Amongst the collection of toys and trash, melancholy records of the late Grand Duke's eccentricity, which occupy the upper rooms of the library, there are some precious relics hanging together in a glass case, which almost betray one into sympathy with "holy coat" worship. They are—Luther's gown, the coat in which Gustavus Adolphus was shot, and Goethe's Court coat and *Schlafrock*. What a rush of thoughts from the mingled memories of the passionate reformer, the heroic warrior, and the wise singer!

The only one of its great men to whom Weimar has at present erected a statue in the open air is Herder. His statue,

erected in 1850, stands in what is called the Herder Platz,
with its back to the church in which he preached; in the
right hand is a roll bearing his favorite motto—*Licht, Liebe,
Leben* (Light, Love, Life), and on the pedestal is the inscription—*Von Deutschen aller Länder* (from Germans of all lands).
This statue, which is by Schaller of Munich, is very much
admired; but, remembering the immortal description in the
"Dichtung und Wahrheit," of Herder's appearance when
Goethe saw him for the first time at Strasburg, I was disap-
pointed with the parsonic appearance of the statue, as well as
of the bust in the library.   The part of the town which im-
prints itself on the memory, next to the Herder Platz, is the
Markt, a cheerful square, made smart by a new Rath-haus.
Twice a week it is crowded with stalls and country people;
and it is the very pretty custom for the band to play in the
balcony of the Rath-haus about twenty minutes every market-
day to delight the ears of the peasantry.   A head-dress worn
by many of the old women, and here and there by a young
one, is, I think, peculiar to Thuringia.   Let the fair reader
imagine half a dozen of her broadest French sashes dyed
black, and attached as streamers to the back of a stiff black
skull-cap, ornamented in front with a large bow, which stands
out like a pair of donkey's ears; let her further imagine, mingled with the streamers of ribbon, equally broad pendants of
a thick woollen texture, something like the fringe of an urn-
rug,—and she will have an idea of the head-dress in which
I have seen a Thuringian damsel figure on a hot summer's
day.   Two houses in the Markt are pointed out as those from
which Tetzel published his indulgences and Luther thundered
against them; but it is difficult to one's imagination to conjure
up scenes of theological controversy in Weimar, where, from
princes down to pastry-cooks, rationalism is taken as a matter
of course.

Passing along the Schiller-strasse, a broad pleasant street,
one is thrilled by the inscription, *Hier wohnte Schiller*, over the
door of a small house with casts in its bow-window.   Mount
up to the second story and you will see Schiller's study very
nearly as it was when he worked in it.   It is a cheerful room
with three windows, two toward the street and one looking

on a little garden which divides his house from the neighboring one. The writing-table, which he notes as an important purchase in one of his letters to Körner, and in one of the drawers of which he used to keep rotten apples for the sake of their scent, stands near the last-named window, so that its light would fall on his left hand. On another side of the room is his piano, with his guitar lying upon it; and above these hangs an ugly print of an Italian scene, which has a companion equally ugly on another wall. Strange feelings it awakened in me to run my fingers over the keys of the little piano and call forth its tones, now so queer and feeble, like those of an invalided old woman whose voice could once make a heart beat with fond passion or soothe its angry pulses into calm. The bedstead on which Schiller died has been removed into the study, from the small bedroom behind, which is now empty. A little table is placed close to the head of the bed, with his drinking-glass upon it, and on the wall above the bedstead there is a beautiful sketch of him lying dead. He used to occupy the whole of the second floor. It contains, besides the study and bedroom, an ante-chamber, now furnished with casts and prints on sale, in order to remunerate the custodiers of the house, and a *salon* tricked out, since his death, with a symbolical cornice, statues, and a carpet worked by the ladies of Weimar.

Goethe's house is much more important-looking, but, to English eyes, far from being the palatial residence which might be expected, from the descriptions of German writers. The entrance-hall is indeed rather imposing, with its statues in niches, and its broad staircase, but the rest of the house is not proportionately spacious and elegant. The only part of the house open to the public—and this only on a Friday—is the principal suite of rooms which contain his collection of casts, pictures, cameos, etc. This collection is utterly insignificant, except as having belonged to him; and one turns away from bad pictures and familiar casts, to linger over the manuscript of the wonderful "Römische Elegien," written by himself in the Italian character. It is to be regretted that a large sum offered for this house by the German Diet, was refused by the Goethe family, in the hope, it is said, of ob-

taining a still larger sum from that mythical English Crœsus
always ready to turn fabulous sums into dead capital, who
haunts the imagination of Continental people.   One of the
most fitting tributes a nation can pay to its great dead, is to
make their habitation, like their works, a public possession,
a shrine where affectionate reverence may be more vividly
reminded that the being who has bequeathed to us immortal
thoughts or immortal deeds, had to endure the daily struggle
with the petty details, perhaps with the sordid cares of this
working-day world; and it is a sad pity that Goethe's study,
bedroom, and library, so fitted to call up that kind of sympathy, because they are preserved just as he left them, should
be shut out from all but the specially privileged.   We were
happy enough to be amongst these,—to look through the mist
of rising tears at the dull study with its two small windows,
and without a single object chosen for the sake of luxury or
beauty; at the dark little bedroom with the bed on which he
died, and the arm-chair where he took his morning coffee as
he read; at the library with its common deal shelves, and
books containing his own paper marks.   In the presence of
this hardy simplicity, the contrast suggests itself of the study
at Abbotsford with its elegant Gothic fittings, its delicious
easy-chair, and its oratory of painted glass.

We were very much amused at the privacy with which people keep their shops at Weimar.   Some of them have not so
much as their names written up; and there is so much indifference of manner toward customers, that one might suppose
every shopkeeper was a salaried functionary employed by Government.   The distribution of commodities, too, is carried on
according to a peculiar Weimarian logic: we bought our lemons
at a ropemaker's, and should not have felt ourselves very unreasonable if we had asked for shoes at a stationer's.   As to
competition, I should think a clever tradesman or artificer is
almost as free from it at Weimar as Æsculapius or Vulcan in
the days of old Olympus.   Here is an illustration.   Our
landlady's husband was called the "*süsser* Rabenhorst," by
way of distinguishing him from a brother of his who was the
reverse of sweet.   This Rabenhorst, who was not sweet, but
who nevertheless dealt in sweets, for he was a confectioner,

was so utter a rogue that any transaction with him was avoided
almost as much as if he had been the Evil One himself, yet
so clever a rogue that he always managed to keep on the windy
side of the law. Nevertheless, he had so many dainties in
the confectionery line—*so viel Süssigkeiten und Leckerbissen*
—that people bent on giving a fine entertainment were at last
constrained to say, "After all, I must go to Rabenhorst";
and so he got abundant custom, in spite of general detestation.

A very fair dinner is to be had at several *tables d' hôte* in
Weimar for ten or twelve groschen (a shilling or fifteen-
pence). The Germans certainly excel us in their *Mehlspeise*,
or farinaceous puddings, and in their mode of cooking vegetables; they are bolder and more imaginative in their combination of sauces, fruits, and vegetables with animal food, and
they are faithful to at least one principle of dietetics—variety.
The only thing at table we have any pretext for being super-
cilious about is the quality and dressing of animal food. The
meat at a *table d' hôte* in Thuringia, and even Berlin, except
in the very first hotels, bears about the same relation to ours
as horse-flesh probably bears to German beef and mutton;
and an Englishman with a bandage over his eyes would often
be sorely puzzled to guess the kind of flesh he was eating.
For example, the only flavor we could ever discern in hare,
which is a very frequent dish, was that of the more or less
disagreeable fat which predominated in the dressing; and
roast meat seems to be considered an extravagance rarely ad-
missible. A melancholy sight is a flock of Weimarian sheep,
followed or led by their shepherd. They are as dingy as London sheep, and far more skinny; indeed an Englishman who
dined with us said the sight of the sheep had set him against
mutton. Still, the variety of dishes you get for ten groschen
is something marvellous to those who have been accustomed to
English charges, and among the six courses it is not a great
evil to find a dish or two the reverse of appetizing. I suppose, however, that the living at *tables d' hôte* gives one no correct idea of the mode in which the people live at home. The
basis of the national food seems to be raw ham and sausage,
with a copious superstratum of *Blaukraut, Sauerkraut*, and
black bread. Sausage seems to be to the German what pota-

toes were to the Irish — the *sine quâ non* of bodily sustenance. Goethe asks the Frau von Stein to send him *so eine Wurst* when he wants to have a makeshift dinner away from home; and in his letters to Kestner he is enthusiastic about the delights of dining on *Blaukraut* and *Leberwurst* (blue cabbage and liver sausage). If *Kraut* and *Wurst* may be called the solid prose of Thuringian diet, fish and *Kuchen* (generally a heavy kind of fruit tart) are the poetry: the German appetite disports itself with these as the English appetite does with ices and whipped creams.

At the beginning of August, when we arrived in Weimar, almost every one was away—"at the Baths," of course—except the tradespeople. As birds nidify in the spring, so Germans wash themselves in the summer; their *Waschungstrieb* acts strongly only at a particular time of the year; during all the rest, apparently, a decanter and a sugar-basin or pie-dish are an ample toilet-service for them. We were quite contented, however, that it was not yet the Weimar "season," fashionably speaking, since it was the very best time for enjoying something far better than Weimar gayeties—the lovely park and environs. It was pleasant, too, to see the good bovine citizens enjoying life in their quiet fashion. Unlike our English people, they take pleasure into their calculations, and seem regularly to set aside part of their time for recreation. It is understood that something is to be done in life besides business and housewifery: the women take their children and their knitting to the *Erholung*, or walk with their husbands to Belvedere, or in some other direction where a cup of coffee is to be had. The *Erholung*, by the way, is a pretty garden, with shady walks, abundant seats, an orchestra, a ball-room, and a place for refreshments. The higher classes are subscribers and visitors here as well as the *bourgeoisie;* but there are several resorts of a similar kind frequented by the latter exclusively. The reader of Goethe will remember his little poem, "Die Lustigen von Weimar," which still indicates the round of amusements in this simple capital: the walk to Belvedere or Tiefurt; the excursion to Jena, or some other trip, not made expensive by distance; the round game at cards; the dance; the theatre; and so many other enjoyments to be had by a people not bound to give dinner-parties and "keep up a position."

It is charming to see how real an amusement the theatre is to the Weimar people. The greater number of places are occupied by subscribers, and there is no fuss about toilet or escort. The ladies come alone, and slip quietly into their places without need of "protection"—a proof of civilization perhaps more than equivalent to our pre-eminence in patent locks and carriage springs—and after the performance is over, you may see the same ladies following their servants, with lanterns, through streets innocent of gas, in which an oil-lamp, suspended from a rope slung across from house to house, occasionally reveals to you the shafts of a cart or omnibus conveniently placed for you to run upon them.

A yearly autumn festival at Weimar is the *Vogelschiessen*, or Bird-shooting; but the reader must not let his imagination wander at this word into fields and brakes. The bird here concerned is of wood, and the shooters, instead of wandering over breezy down and common, are shut up, day after day, in a room clouded with tobacco-smoke, that they may take their turn at shooting with the rifle from the window of a closet about the size of a sentinel's box. However, this is a mighty enjoyment to the Thuringian yeomanry, and an occasion of profit to our friend Punch, and other itinerant performers; for while the *Vogelschiessen* lasts, a sort of fair is held in the field where the marksmen assemble.

Among the quieter every-day pleasures of the Weimarians, perhaps the most delightful is the stroll on a bright afternoon or evening to the Duke's summer residence of Belvedere, about two miles from Weimar. As I have said, a glorious avenue of chestnut-trees leads all the way from the town to the entrance of the grounds, which are open to all the world as much as to the Duke himself. Close to the palace and its subsidiary buildings there is an inn, for the accommodation of the good people who come to take dinner or any other meal here, by way of holiday-making. A sort of pavilion stands on a spot commanding a lovely view of Weimar and its valley, and here the Weimarians constantly come on summer and autumn evenings to smoke a cigar, or drink a cup of coffee. In one wing of the little palace, which is made smart by wooden cupolas, with gilt pinnacles, there is a saloon, which I recommend to the imitation of tasteful people in their country houses. It has no decoration but that of natural foliage: ivy is trained at regular intervals up the pure white walls, and all round the edge of the ceiling, so as to form pilasters and a cornice; ivy again, trained on trellis-work, forms a blind to the window, which looks toward the entrance court; and beautiful ferns, arranged in tall baskets, are placed here and there against the walls. The furniture is of light cane-work. Another pretty thing here is the Natur-Theater—a theatre constructed with living trees, trimmed into walls and side scenes. We pleased ourselves for a little while with thinking that this was one of the places where Goethe acted in his own dramas, but we afterward learned that it was not made until his acting days were over. The inexhaustible charm of Belvedere, however, is the grounds, which are laid out with a taste worthy of a first-rate landscape-gardener. The tall and graceful limes, plane-trees, and weeping birches, the little basins of water here and there, with fountains playing in the middle of them, and with a fringe of broad-leaved plants, or other tasteful bordering round them, the gradual descent toward the river, and the hill clothed with firs and pines on the opposite side, forming a fine dark background for the various and light foliage of the trees that ornament the gardens—all this we went again and again to enjoy, from the time when everything was of a vivid green until the Virginian creepers which festooned the silver stems of the birches were bright scarlet, and the touch of autumn had turned all the green to gold. One of the spots to linger in is at a semicircular seat against an artificial rock, on which are placed large glass globes of different colors. It is wonderful to see with what minute perfection the scenery around is painted in these globes. Each is like a pre-Raphaelite picture, with every little detail of gravelly walk, mossy bank, and delicately leaved, interlacing boughs, presented in accurate miniature.

In the opposite direction to Belvedere lies Tiefurt, with its small park and tiny château, formerly the residence of the Duchess Amalia, the mother of Carl August, and the friend and patroness of Wieland, but now apparently serving as little else than a receptacle for the late Duke Carl Friederich's rather childish collections. In the second story there is a suite of rooms, so small that the largest of them does not take up as much space as a good dining-table, and each of these doll-house rooms is crowded with prints, old china, and all sorts of knick-knacks and *rococo* wares. The park is a little paradise. The Ilm is seen here to the best advantage: it is clearer than at Weimar, and winds about gracefully between the banks, on one side steep, and curtained with turf and shrubs, or fine trees. It was here, at a point where the bank forms a promontory into the river, that Goethe and his Court friends got up the performance of an operetta, " Die Fischerin," by torchlight. On the way to Tiefurt lies the Webicht, a beautiful wood, through which run excellent carriage-roads and grassy footpaths. It was a rich enjoyment to skirt this wood along the Jena road, and see the sky arching grandly down over the open fields on the other side of us, the evening red flushing the west over the town, and the stars coming out as if to relieve the sun in its watch; or to take the winding road through the wood, under its tall overarching trees, now bending their mossy trunks forward, now standing with the stately erectness of lofty pillars; or to saunter along the grassy footpaths where the sunlight streamed through the fairy-like foliage of the silvery barked birches.

Stout pedestrians who go to Weimar will do well to make a walking excursion, as we did, to Ettersburg, a more distant summer residence of the Grand Duke, interesting to us beforehand as the scene of private theatricals and *sprees* in the Goethe days. We set out on one of the brightest and hottest mornings that August ever bestowed, and it required some resolution to trudge along the shadeless *chaussée*, which formed the first two or three miles of our way. One compensating pleasure was the sight of the beautiful mountain-ash trees in full berry, which, alternately with cherry-trees, border the road for a considerable distance. At last we rested from our broiling walk on the borders of a glorious pine-wood, so extensive that the trees in the distance form a complete wall with their trunks, and so give one a twilight very welcome on a summer's noon. Under these pines you tread on a

carpet of the softest moss, so that you hear no sound of a foot-
step, and all is as solemn and still as in the crypt of a cathe-
dral.   Presently we passed out of the pine-wood into one of
limes, beeches, and other trees of transparent and light foliage,
and from this again we emerged into the open space of the
Ettersburg Park in front of the Schloss, which is finely placed
on an eminence commanding a magnificent view of the far-
reaching woods.   Prince Pückler Muskau has been of service
here by recommending openings to be made in the woods, in
the taste of the English parks.   The Schloss, which is a favorite residence of the Grand Duke, is a house of very moderate size, and no pretension of any kind.   Its stuccoed walls,
and doors long unacquainted with fresh paint, would look dis-
tressingly shabby to the owner of a villa at Richmond or
Twickenham; but much beauty is procured here at slight
expense, by the tasteful disposition of creepers on the ba-
lustrades, and pretty vases full of plants ranged along the
steps, or suspended in the little piazza beneath them.   A walk
through a beech-wood took us to the Mooshütte, in front of
which stands the famous beech from whence Goethe denounced
Jacobi's "Woldemar."   The bark is covered with initials cut
by him and his friends.

People who only allow themselves to be idle under the pretext of hydropathizing, may find all the apparatus necessary to
satisfy their conscience at Bercka, a village seated in a lovely
valley about six miles from Weimar.   Now and then a Weimar family takes lodgings here for the summer, retiring from
the quiet of the capital to the deeper quiet of Bercka; but
generally the place seems not much frequented.   It would be
difficult to imagine a more peace-inspiring scene than this little valley.   The hanging woods—the soft coloring and graceful outline of the uplands—the village, with its roofs and spire
of a reddish-violet hue, muffled in luxuriant trees—the white
Kurhaus glittering on a grassy slope—the avenue of poplars
contrasting its pretty primness with the wild bushy outline of
the wood-covered hill, which rises abruptly from the smooth,
green meadows—the clear winding stream, now sparkling in
the sun, now hiding itself under soft gray willows,—all this
makes an enchanting picture.   The walk to Bercka and back

was a favorite expedition with us and a few Weimar friends,
for the road thither is a pleasant one, leading at first through
open cultivated fields, dotted here and there with villages,
and then through wooded hills—the outskirts of the Thuringian Forest. We used not to despise the fine plums which
hung in tempting abundance by the road-side; but we afterward found that we had been deceived in supposing ourselves
free to pluck them, as if it were the golden age, and that we
were liable to a penalty of ten groschen for our depredations.

But I must not allow myself to be exhaustive on pleasures
which seem monotonous when told, though in enjoying them
one is as far from wishing them to be more various as from
wishing for any change in the sweet sameness of successive
summer days. I will only advise the reader who has yet to
make excursions in Thuringia to visit Jena, less for its traditions than for its fine scenery, which makes it, as Goethe
says, a delicious place, in spite of its dull, ugly streets; and
exhort him, above all, to brave the discomforts of a *Postwagen*
for the sake of getting to Ilmenau. Here he will find the
grandest pine-clad hills, with endless walks under their solemn shades; beech-woods where every tree is a picture; an
air that he will breathe with as conscious a pleasure as if he
were taking iced water on a hot day; baths *ad libitum*, with
a *douche* lofty and tremendous enough to invigorate the giant
Cormoran; and, more than all, one of the most interesting
relics of Goethe, who had a great love for Ilmenau. This is
the small wooden house, on the height called the Kickelhahn,
where he often lived in his long retirements here, and where
you may see written by his own hand, near the window-frame,
those wonderful lines—perhaps the finest expression yet given
to the sense of resignation inspired by the sublime calm of
Nature:—

> " Ueber allen Gipfeln
> Ist Ruh,
> In allen Wipfeln
> Spürest du
> Kaum einen Hauch;
> Die Vögelein schweigen im Walde.
> Warte nur, balde
> Ruhest du auch."

ADDRESS TO WORKING MEN, BY FELIX HOLT.

FELLOW-WORKMEN,—I am not going to take up your time by complimenting you. It has been the fashion to compliment kings and other authorities when they have come into power, and to tell them that, under their wise and beneficent rule, happiness would certainly overflow the land. But the end has not always corresponded to that beginning. If it were true that we who work for wages had more of the wisdom and virtue necessary to the right use of power than has been shown by the aristocratic and mercantile classes, we should not glory much in that fact, or consider that it carried with it any near approach to infallibility.

In my opinion, there has been too much complimenting of that sort; and whenever a speaker, whether he is one of ourselves or not, wastes our time in boasting or flattery, I say, let us hiss him. If we have the beginning of wisdom, which is, to know a little truth about ourselves, we know that as a body we are neither very wise nor very virtuous. And to prove this, I will not point specially to our own habits and doings, but to the general state of the country. Any nation that had within it a majority of men—and we are the majority—possessed of much wisdom and virtue, would not tolerate the bad practices, the commercial lying and swindling, the poisonous adulteration of goods, the retail cheating, and the political bribery, which are carried on boldly in the midst of us. A majority has the power of creating a public opinion. We could groan and hiss before we had the franchise: if we had groaned and hissed in the right place, if we had discerned better between good and evil, if the multitude of us artisans, and factory hands, and miners, and laborers of all sorts, had been skilful, faithful, well-judging, industrious, sober—and I don't see how there can be wisdom and virtue anywhere without those qualities—we should have made an audience that

would have shamed the other classes out of their share in
the national vices. We should have had better members of
Parliament, better religious teachers, honester tradesmen,
fewer foolish demagogues, less impudence in infamous and
brutal men; and we should not have had among us the abomi-
nation of men calling themselves religious while living in
splendor on ill-gotten gains. I say, it is not possible for any
society in which there is a very large body of wise and virtuous men to be as vicious as our society is—to have as low a
standard of right and wrong, to have so much belief in falsehood, or to have so degrading, barbarous a notion of what
pleasure is, or of what justly raises a man above his fellows.
Therefore, let us have done with this nonsense about our being much better than the rest of our countrymen, or the pretence that that was a reason why we ought to have such an
extension of the franchise as has been given to us. The reason for our having the franchise, as I want presently to show,
lies somewhere else than in our personal good qualities, and
does not in the least lie in any high betting chance that a dele-
gate is a better man than a duke, or that a Sheffield grinder
is a better man than any one of the firm he works for.

However, we have got our franchise now. We have been
sarcastically called in the House of Commons the future masters of the country; and if that sarcasm contains any truth,
it seems to me that the first thing we had better think of is,
our heavy responsibility; that is to say, the terrible risk we
run of working mischief and missing good, as others have
done before us. Suppose certain men, discontented with the
irrigation of a country which depended for all its prosperity
on the right direction being given to the waters of a great
river, had got the management of the irrigation before they
were quite sure how exactly it could be altered for the better, or whether they could command the necessary agency
for such an alteration. Those men would have a difficult
and dangerous business on their hands; and the more sense,
feeling, and knowledge they had, the more they would be
likely to tremble rather than to triumph. Our situation is
not altogether unlike theirs. For general prosperity and
well-being is a vast crop, that like the corn in Egypt can

13

be come at, not at all by hurried snatching, but only by a well-judged patient process; and whether our political power will be any good to us now we have got it, must depend entirely on the means and materials—the knowledge, ability, and honesty—we have at command. These three things are the only conditions on which we can get any lasting benefit, as every clever workman among us knows: he knows that for an article to be worth much there must be a good invention or plan to go upon, there must be well-prepared material, and there must be skilful and honest work in carrying out the plan. And by this test we may try those who want to be our leaders. Have they anything to offer us besides indignant talk? When they tell us we ought to have this, that, or the other thing, can they explain to us any reasonable, fair, safe way of getting it? Can they argue in favor of a particular change by showing us pretty closely how the change is likely to work? I don't want to decry a just indignation; on the contrary, I should like it to be more thorough and general. A wise man, more than two thousand years ago, when he was asked what would most tend to lessen injustice in the world, said, "That every bystander should feel as indignant at a wrong as if he himself were the sufferer." Let us cherish such indignation. But the long-growing evils of a great nation are a tangled business, asking for a good deal more than indignation in order to be got rid of. Indignation is a fine war-horse, but the war-horse must be ridden by a man: it must be ridden by rationality, skill, courage, armed with the right weapons, and taking definite aim.

We have reason to be discontented with many things, and, looking back either through the history of England to much earlier generations or to the legislation and administration of later times, we are justified in saying that many of the evils under which our country now suffers are the consequences of folly, ignorance, neglect, or self-seeking in those who, at different times, have wielded the powers of rank, office, and money. But the more bitterly we feel this, the more loudly we utter it, the stronger is the obligation we lay on ourselves to beware lest we also, by a too hasty wresting of measures which seem to promise an immediate partial relief, make a

worse time of it for our own generation, and leave a bad inheritance to our children. The deepest curse of wrong-doing,
whether of the foolish or wicked sort, is that its effects are
difficult to be undone. I suppose there is hardly anything
more to be shuddered at than that part of the history of disease which shows how, when a man injures his constitution by
a life of vicious excess, his children and grandchildren inherit
diseased bodies and minds, and how the effects of that unhappy inheritance continue to spread beyond our calculation.
This is only one example of the law by which human lives
are linked together: another example of what we complain
of when we point to our pauperism, to the brutal ignorance of
multitudes among our fellow-countrymen, to the weight of taxation laid on us by blamable wars, to the wasteful channels
made for the public money, to the expense and trouble of
getting justice, and call these the effects of bad rule. This
is the law that we all bear the yoke of, the law of no man's
making, and which no man can undo. Everybody now sees
an example of it in the case of Ireland. We who are living
now are sufferers by the wrong-doing of those who lived before us; we are sufferers by each other's wrong-doing; and
the children who come after us are and will be sufferers from
the same causes. Will any man say he doesn't care for that
law—it is nothing to him—what he wants is to better himself? With what face then will he complain of any injury?
If he says that in politics or in any sort of social action he
will not care to know what are likely to be the consequences
to others besides himself, he is defending the very worst doings that have brought about his discontent. He might as
well say that there is no better rule needful for men than that
each should tug and rive for what will please him, without caring how that tugging will act on the fine widespread network
of society in which he is fast meshed. If any man taught
that as a doctrine, we should know him for a fool. But
there are men who act upon it: every scoundrel, for example,
whether he is a rich religious scoundrel who lies and cheats
on a large scale, and will perhaps come and ask you to send
him to Parliament, or a poor pocket-picking scoundrel, who
will steal your loose pence while you are listening round the

platform.   None of us are so ignorant as not to know that a
society, a nation, is held together by just the opposite doctrine and action—by the dependence of men on each other and
the sense they have of a common interest in preventing injury.
And we working men are, I think, of all classes the last that
can afford to forget this; for if we did we should be much like
sailors cutting away the timbers of our own ship to warm
our grog with.   For what else is the meaning of our Trades-
unions?   What else is the meaning of every flag we carry,
every procession we make, every crowd we collect for the sake
of making some protest on behalf of our body as receivers of
wages, if not this: that it is our interest to stand by each
other, and that this being the common interest, no one of us
will try to make a good bargain for himself without considering what will be good for his fellows?   And every member of
a union believes that the wider he can spread his union, the
stronger and surer will be the effect of it.   So I think I shall
be borne out in saying that a working man who can put two
and two together, or take three from four and see what will be
the remainder, can understand that a society, to be well off,
must be made up chiefly of men who consider the general good
as well as their own.

Well, but taking the world as it is—and this is one way we
must take it when we want to find out how it can be improved
—no society is made up of a single class: society stands before
us like that wonderful piece of life, the human body, with all
its various parts depending on one another, and with a terrible
liability to get wrong because of that delicate dependence.
We all know how many diseases the human body is apt to
suffer from, and how difficult it is even for the doctors to find
out exactly where the seat or beginning of the disorder is.
That is because the body is made up of so many various parts,
all related to each other, or likely all to feel the effect if any
one of them goes wrong.   It is somewhat the same with our
old nations or societies.   No society ever stood long in the
world without getting to be composed of different classes.
Now, it is all pretence to say that there is no such thing as
Class Interest.   It is clear that if any particular number of
men get a particular benefit from any existing institution,

they are likely to band together, in order to keep up that benefit and increase it, until it is perceived to be unfair and injurious to another large number, who get knowledge and strength
enough to set up a resistance.   And this, again, has been part
of the history of every great society since history began.   But
the simple reason for this being, that any large body of men
is likely to have more of stupidity, narrowness, and greed than
of far-sightedness and generosity, it is plain that the number
who resist unfairness and injury are in danger of becoming
injurious in their turn.   And in this way a justifiable resistance has become a damaging convulsion, making everything
worse instead of better.   This has been seen so often that we
ought to profit a little by the experience.   So long as there is
selfishness in men; so long as they have not found out for
themselves institutions which express and carry into practice
the truth, that the highest interest of mankind must at last be
a common and not a divided interest; so long as the gradual
operation of steady causes has not made that truth a part of
every man's knowledge and feeling, just as we now not only
know that it is good for our health to be cleanly, but feel that
cleanliness is only another word for comfort, which is the
under-side or lining of all pleasure; so long, I say, as men
wink at their own knowingness, or hold their heads high, because they have got an advantage over their fellows; so long
Class Interest will be in danger of making itself felt injuri-
ously.   No set of men will get any sort of power without
being in danger of wanting more than their right share.   But,
on the other hand, it is just as certain that no set of men will
get angry at having less than their right share, and set up a
claim on that ground, without falling into just the same danger of exacting too much, and exacting it in wrong ways.   It's
human nature we have got to work with all round, and nothing else.   That seems like saying something very commonplace—nay, obvious; as if one should say that where there are
hands there are mouths.   Yet, to hear a good deal of the speech-
ifying and to see a good deal of the action that goes forward,
one might suppose it was forgotten.

But I come back to this: that, in our old society, there are
old institutions, and among them the various distinctions and

inherited advantages of classes, which have shaped themselves
along with all the wonderful slow-growing system of things
made up of our laws, our commerce, and our stores of all sorts,
whether in material objects, such as buildings and machinery, or
in knowledge, such as scientific thought and professional skill.
Just as in that case I spoke of before, the irrigation of a country, which must absolutely have its water distributed or it will
bear no crop; there are the old channels, the old banks, and
the old pumps, which must be used as they are until new and
better have been prepared, or the structure of the old has been
gradually altered. But it would be fool's work to batter down
a pump only because a better might be made, when you had
no machinery ready for a new one: it would be wicked work,
if villages lost their crops by it. Now the only safe way by
which society can be steadily improved and our worst evils
reduced, is not by any attempt to do away directly with the
actually existing class distinctions and advantages, as if everybody could have the same sort of work, or lead the same sort
of life (which none of my hearers are stupid enough to suppose), but by the turning of Class Interests into Class Functions or duties. What I mean is, that each class should be
urged by the surrounding conditions to perform its particular
work under the strong pressure of responsibility to the nation
at large; that our public affairs should be got into a state in
which there should be no impunity for foolish or faithless conduct. In this way, the public judgment would sift out inca-
pability and dishonesty from posts of high charge, and even
personal ambition would necessarily become of a worthier sort,
since the desires of the most selfish men must be a good deal
shaped by the opinions of those around them; and for one
person to put on a cap and bells, or to go about dishonest or
paltry ways of getting rich that he may spend a vast sum of
money in having more finery than his neighbors, he must be
pretty sure of a crowd who will applaud him. Now changes
can only be good in proportion as they help to bring about
this sort of result: in proportion as they put knowledge in the
place of ignorance, and fellow-feeling in the place of selfishness. In the course of that substitution class distinctions must
inevitably change their character, and represent the varying

Duties of men, not their varying Interests. But this end will not come by impatience. "Day will not break the sooner because we get up before the twilight." Still less will it come by mere undoing, or change merely as change. And moreover, if we believed that it would be unconditionally hastened by our getting the franchise, we should be what I call superstitious men, believing in magic, or the production of a result by hocus-pocus. Our getting the franchise will greatly hasten that good end in proportion only as every one of us has the knowledge, the foresight, the conscience, that will make him well-judging and scrupulous in the use of it. The nature of things in this world has been determined for us beforehand, and in such a way that no ship can be expected to sail well on a difficult voyage, and reach the right port, unless it is well manned: the nature of the winds and the waves, of the timbers, the sails, and the cordage, will not accommodate itself to drunken, mutinous sailors.

You will not suspect me of wanting to preach any cant to you, or of joining in the pretence that everything is in a fine way, and need not be made better. What I am striving to keep in our minds is the care, the precaution, with which we should go about making things better, so that the public order may not be destroyed, so that no fatal shock may be given to this society of ours, this living body in which our lives are bound up. After the Reform Bill of 1832 I was in an election riot, which showed me clearly, on a small scale, what public disorder must always be; and I have never forgotten that the riot was brought about chiefly by the agency of dishonest men who professed to be on the people's side. Now, the danger hanging over change is great, just in proportion as it tends to produce such disorder by giving any large number of ignorant men, whose notions of what is good are of a low and brutal sort, the belief that they have got power into their hands, and may do pretty much as they like. If any one can look round us and say that he sees no signs of any such danger now, and that our national condition is running along like a clear broadening stream, safe not to get choked with mud, I call him a cheerful man: perhaps he does his own gardening, and seldom takes exercise far away from home. To us

who have no gardens, and often walk abroad, it is plain that
we can never get into a bit of a crowd but we must rub clothes
with a set of Roughs, who have the worst vices of the worst
rich—who are gamblers, sots, libertines, knaves, or else mere
sensual simpletons and victims.   They are the ugly crop that
has sprung up while the stewards have been sleeping; they
are the multiplying brood begotten by parents who have been
left without all teaching save that of a too craving body, without all well-being save the fading delusions of drugged beer
and gin.   They are the hideous margin of society, at one edge
drawing toward it the undesigning ignorant poor, at the other
darkening imperceptibly into the lowest criminal class.   Here
is one of the evils which cannot be got rid of quickly, and
against which any of us who have got sense, decency, and instruction have need to watch.   That these degraded fellow-
men could really get the mastery in a persistent disobedience
to the laws and in a struggle to subvert order, I do not believe; but wretched calamities would come from the very beginning of such a struggle, and the continuance of it would
be a civil war, in which the inspiration on both sides might
soon cease to be even a false notion of good, and might become
the direct savage impulse of ferocity.   We have all to see to
it that we do not help to rouse what I may call the savage
beast in the breasts of our generation—that we do not help to
poison the nation's blood, and make richer provision for bestiality to come.   We know well enough that oppressors have
sinned in this way—that oppression has notoriously made men
mad; and we are determined to resist oppression.   But let us,
if possible, show that we can keep sane in our resistance, and
shape our means more and more reasonably toward the least
harmful, and therefore the speediest, attainment of our end.
Let us, I say, show that our spirits are too strong to be driven
mad, but can keep that sober determination which alone gives
mastery over the adaptation of means.   And a first guaranty
of this sanity will be to act as if we understood that the fundamental duty of a Government is to preserve order, to enforce
obedience of the laws.   It has been held hitherto that a man
can be depended on as a guardian of order only when he has
much money and comfort to lose.   But a better state of things

would be, that men who had little money and not much comfort should still be guardians of order, because they had sense
to see that disorder would do no good, and had a heart of justice, pity, and fortitude, to keep them from making more misery only because they felt some misery themselves.   There are
thousands of artisans who have already shown this fine spirit,
and have endured much with patient heroism.   If such a spirit
spread, and penetrated us all, we should soon become the masters of the country in the best sense and to the best ends.
For, the public order being preserved, there can be no government in future that will not be determined by our insistence
on our fair and practicable demands.   It is only by disorder
that our demands will be choked, that we shall find ourselves
lost amongst a brutal rabble, with all the intelligence of the
country opposed to us, and see government in the shape of
guns that will sweep us down in the ignoble martyrdom of
fools.

It has been a too common notion that to insist much on the
preservation of order is the part of a selfish aristocracy and a
selfish commercial class, because among these, in the nature
of things, have been found the opponents of change.   I am a
Radical; and, what is more, I am not a Radical with a title
or a French cook or even an entrance into fine society.   I
expect great changes, and I desire them.   But I don't expect
them to come in a hurry, by mere inconsiderate sweeping.   A
Hercules with a big besom is a fine thing for a filthy stable,
but not for weeding a seed-bed, where his besom would soon
make a barren floor.

That is old-fashioned talk, some one may say.   We know
all that.

Yes, when things are put in an extreme way, most people
think they know them; but, after all, they are comparatively
few who see the small degrees by which those extremes are
arrived at, or have the resolution and self-control to resist the
little impulses by which they creep on surely toward a fatal
end.   Does anybody set out meaning to ruin himself, or to
drink himself to death, or to waste his life so that he becomes
a despicable old man, a superannuated nuisance, like a fly in
winter?   Yet there are plenty, of whose lot this is the piti-

able story. Well now, supposing us all to have the best intentions, we working men, as a body, run some risk of bringing evil on the nation in that unconscious manner—half-hur-
rying, half-pushed in a jostling march toward an end we are
not thinking of. For just as there are many things which we
know better and feel much more strongly than the richer,
softer-handed classes can know or feel them; so there are
many things—many precious benefits—which we, by the very
fact of our privations, our lack of leisure and instruction, are
not so likely to be aware of and take into our account. Those
precious benefits form a chief part of what I may call the common estate of society: a wealth over and above buildings, machinery, produce, shipping, and so on, though closely connected with these; a wealth of a more delicate kind, that we
may more unconsciously bring into danger, doing harm and
not knowing that we do it. I mean that treasure of knowledge,
science, poetry, refinement of thought, feeling, and manners,
great memories, and the interpretation of great records, which
is carried on from the minds of one generation to the minds
of another. This is something distinct from the indulgences
of luxury and the pursuit of vain finery; and one of the hardships in the lot of working men is that they have been for the
most part shut out from sharing in this treasure. It can make
a man's life very great, very full of delight, though he has no
smart furniture and no horses: it also yields a great deal of
discovery that corrects error, and of invention that lessens
bodily pain, and must at last make life easier for all.

Now the security of this treasure demands, not only the
preservation of order, but a certain patience on our part with
many institutions and facts of various kinds, especially touching the accumulation of wealth, which, from the light we stand
in, we are more likely to discern the evil than the good of. It
is constantly the task of practical wisdom not to say, "This
is good, and I will have it," but to say, "This is the less of
two unavoidable evils, and I will bear it." And this treasure
of knowledge, which consists in the fine activity, the exalted
vision of many minds, is bound up at present with conditions
which have much evil in them. Just as in the case of material wealth and its distribution we are obliged to take the self-

ishness and weaknesses of human nature into account, and,
however we insist that men might act better, are forced, unless we are fanatical simpletons, to consider how they are likely
to act; so in this matter of the wealth that is carried in men's
minds, we have to reflect that the too absolute predominance
of a class whose wants have been of a common sort, who are
chiefly struggling to get better and more food, clothing, shel-
ter, and bodily recreation, may lead to hasty measures for the
sake of having things more fairly shared, which, even if they
did not fail of their object, would at last debase the life of the
nation. Do anything which will throw the classes who hold
the treasures of knowledge—nay, I may say, the treasure of
refined needs—into the background, cause them to withdraw
from public affairs, stop too suddenly any of the sources by
which their leisure and ease are furnished, rob them of the
chances by which they may be influential and pre-eminent,
and you do something as short-sighted as the acts of France
and Spain when in jealousy and wrath, not altogether unpro-
voked, they drove from among them races and classes that
held the traditions of handicraft and agriculture. You injure
your own inheritance and the inheritance of your children.
You may truly say that this which I call the common estate
of society has been anything but common to you; but the same
may be said, by many of us, of the sunlight and the air, of
the sky and the fields, of parks and holiday games. Nevertheless, that these blessings exist makes life worthier to us, and
urges us the more to energetic, likely means of getting our
share in them; and I say, let us watch carefully, lest we do
anything to lessen this treasure which is held in the minds of
men, while we exert ourselves first of all, and to the very utmost, that we and our children may share in all its benefits.
Yes; exert ourselves to the utmost, to break the yoke of ignorance. If we demand more leisure, more ease in our lives, let
us show that we don't deserve the reproach of wanting to
shirk that industry which, in some form or other, every man,
whether rich or poor, shall feel himself as much bound to as
he is bound to decency. Let us show that we want to have
some time and strength left to us, that we may use it, not for
brutal indulgence, but for the rational exercise of the faculties

which make us men. Without this no political measures can
benefit us. No political institution will alter the nature of
Ignorance, or hinder it from producing vice and misery. Let
Ignorance start how it will, it must run the same round of
low appetites, poverty, slavery, and superstition. Some of us
know this well—nay, I will say, feel it; for knowledge of this
kind cuts deep; and to us it is one of the most painful facts
belonging to our condition that there are numbers of our fellow-workmen who are so far from feeling in the same way,
that they never use the imperfect opportunities already offered
them for giving their children some schooling, but turn their
little ones of tender age into bread-winners, often at cruel
tasks, exposed to the horrible infection of childish vice. Of
course, the causes of these hideous things go a long way back.
Parents' misery has made parents' wickedness. But we, who
are still blessed with the hearts of fathers and the consciences
of men—we who have some knowledge of the curse entailed
on broods of creatures in human shape, whose enfeebled bodies
and dull perverted minds are mere centres of uneasiness, in
whom even appetite is feeble, and joy impossible,—I say we
are bound to use all the means at our command to help in putting a stop to this horror. Here, it seems to me, is a way in
which we may use extended co-operation among us to the most
momentous of all purposes, and make conditions of enrolment
that would strengthen all educational measures. It is true
enough that there is a low sense of parental duties in the nation at large, and that numbers who have no excuse in bodily
hardship seem to think it a light thing to beget children,—to
bring human beings, with all their tremendous possibilities,
into this difficult world,—and then take little heed how they
are disciplined and furnished for the perilous journey they
are sent on without any asking of their own. This is a sin
shared in more or less by all classes; but there are sins which,
like taxation, fall the heaviest on the poorest, and none have
such galling reasons as we working men to try and rouse to
the utmost the feeling of responsibility in fathers and mothers.
We have been urged into co-operation by the pressure of common demands. In war men need each other more; and where
a given point has to be defended, fighters inevitably find them-

selves shoulder to shoulder. So fellowship grows; so grow
the rules of fellowship, which gradually shape themselves to
thoroughness as the idea of a common good becomes more
complete. We feel a right to say, If you will be one of us,
you must make such and such a contribution, you must renounce such and such a separate advantage, you must set
your face against such and such an infringement. If we have
any false ideas about our common good, our rules will be
wrong, and we shall be co-operating to damage each other.
But now, here is a part of our good, without which everything
else we strive for will be worthless,—I mean the rescue of our
children. Let us demand from the members of our Unions
that they fulfil their duty as parents in this definite matter,
which rules can reach. Let us demand that they send their
children to school, so as not to go on recklessly breeding a
moral pestilence among us, just as strictly as we demand that
they pay their contributions to a common fund, understood to
be for a common benefit. While we watch our public men,
let us watch one another as to this duty, which is also public,
and more momentous even than obedience to sanitary regulations. While we resolutely declare against the wickedness
in high places, let us set ourselves also against the wickedness in low places; not quarrelling which came first, or which
is the worse of the two,—not trying to settle the miserable
precedence of plague or famine, but insisting unflinchingly on
remedies once ascertained, and summoning those who hold the
treasure of knowledge to remember that they hold it in trust,
and that with them lies the task of searching for new remedies, and finding the right methods of applying them.

To find right remedies and right methods! Here is the
great function of knowledge: here the life of one man may
make a fresh era straight away, in which a sort of suffering
that has existed shall exist no more. For the thousands of
years, down to the middle of the sixteenth century since
Christ, that human limbs had been hacked and amputated,
nobody knew how to stop the bleeding except by searing the
ends of the vessels with red-hot iron. But then came a man
named Ambrose Paré, and said, "Tie up the arteries!" That
was a fine word to utter. It contained the statement of a

method—a plan by which a particular evil was forever assuaged. Let us try to discern the men whose words carry that sort of kernel, and choose such men to be our guides and representatives—not choose platform swaggerers, who bring us nothing but the ocean to make our broth with.

To get the chief power into the hands of the wisest, which means to get our life regulated according to the truest principles mankind is in possession of, is a problem as old as the very notion of wisdom. The solution comes slowly, because men collectively can only be made to embrace principles, and to act on them, by the slow stupendous teaching of the world's events. Men will go on planting potatoes, and nothing else but potatoes, till a potato disease comes and forces them to find out the advantage of a varied crop. Selfishness, stupidity, sloth, persist in trying to adapt the world to their desires, till a time comes when the world manifests itself as too decidedly inconvenient to them. Wisdom stands outside of man and urges itself upon him, like the marks of the changing seasons, before it finds a home within him, directs his actions, and from the precious effects of obedience begets a corresponding love.

But while still outside of us, wisdom often looks terrible, and wears strange forms, wrapped in the changing conditions of a struggling world. It wears now the form of wants and just demands in a great multitude of British men: wants and demands urged into existence by the forces of a maturing world. And it is in virtue of this—in virtue of this presence of wisdom on our side as a mighty fact, physical and moral, which must enter into and shape the thoughts and actions of mankind—that we working men have obtained the suffrage. Not because we are an excellent multitude, but because we are a needy multitude.

But now, for our own part, we have seriously to consider this outside wisdom which lies in the supreme unalterable nature of things, and watch to give it a home within us and obey it. If the claims of the unendowed multitude of working men hold within them principles which must shape the future, it is not less true that the endowed classes, in their inheritance from the past, hold the precious material without which no worthy, noble future can be moulded. Many of the highest uses of life are in their keeping; and if privilege has often been abused, it has also been the nurse of excellence. Here again we have to submit ourselves to the great law of inheritance. If we quarrel with the way in which the labors and earnings of the past have been preserved and handed down, we are just as bigoted, just as narrow, just as wanting in that religion which keeps an open ear and an obedient mind to the teachings of fact, as we accuse those of being who quarrel with the new truths and new needs which are disclosed in the present. The deeper insight we get into the causes of human trouble, and the ways by which men are made better and happier, the less we shall be inclined to the unprofitable spirit and practice of reproaching classes as such in a wholesale fashion. Not all the evils of our condition are such as we can justly blame others for; and, I repeat, many of them are such as no change of institutions can quickly remedy. To discern between the evils that energy can remove and the evils that patience must bear, makes the difference between manliness and childishness, between good sense and folly. And more than that, without such discernment, seeing that we have grave duties toward our own body and the country at large, we can hardly escape acts of fatal rashness and injustice.

I am addressing a mixed assembly of workmen, and some of you may be as well or better fitted than I am to take up this office. But they will not think it amiss in me that I have tried to bring together the considerations most likely to be of service to us in preparing ourselves for the use of our new opportunities. I have avoided touching on special questions. The best help toward judging well on these is to approach them in the right temper, without vain expectation, and with a resolution which is mixed with temperance.

LEAVES FROM A NOTE-BOOK.

To lay down in the shape of practical moral rules courses of conduct only to be made real by the rarest states of motive and disposition, tends not to elevate but to degrade the general standard, by turning that rare **Authorship.** attainment from an object of admiration into an impossible prescription, against which the average nature first rebels and then flings out ridicule. It is for art to present images of a lovelier order than the actual, gently winning the affections, and so determining the taste. But in any rational criticism of the time which is meant to guide a practical reform, it is idle to insist that action ought to be this or that, without considering how far the outward conditions of such change are present, even supposing the inward disposition toward it. Practically, we must be satisfied to aim at something short of perfection—and at something very much further off it in one case than in another. While the fundamental conceptions of morality seem as stationary through ages as the laws of life, so that a moral manual written eighteen centuries ago still admonishes us that we are low in our attainments, it is quite otherwise with the degree to which moral conceptions have penetrated the various forms of social activity, and made what may be called the special conscience of each calling, art, or industry. While on some points of social duty public opinion has reached a tolerably high standard, on others a public opinion is not yet born; and there are even some functions and practices with regard to which men far above the line in honorableness of nature feel hardly any scrupulosity, though their consequent behavior is easily shown to be as injurious as bribery, or any other slowly poisonous procedure which degrades the social vitality.

Among those callings which have not yet acquired anything near a full-grown conscience in the public mind is Authorship. Yet the changes brought about by the spread of instruction and the consequent struggles of an uneasy ambition, are, or at least might well be, forcing on many minds the need of some regulating principle with regard to the publication of intellectual products, which would override the rule of the market: a principle, that is, which should be derived from a fixing of the author's vocation according to those characteristics in which it differs from the other bread-winning professions. Let this be done, if possible, without any cant, which would carry the subject into Utopia away from existing needs. The guidance wanted is a clear notion of what should justify men and women in assuming public authorship, and of the way in which they should be determined by what is usually called success. But the forms of authorship must be distinguished; journalism, for example, carrying a necessity for that continuous production which in other kinds of writing is precisely the evil to be fought against, and judicious careful compilation, which is a great public service, holding in its modest diligence a guaranty against those deductions of vanity and idleness which draw many a young gentleman into reviewing, instead of the sorting and copying which his small talents could not rise to with any vigor and completeness.

A manufacturer goes on producing calicoes as long and as fast as he can find a market for them; and in obeying this indication of demand he gives his factory its utmost usefulness to the world in general and to himself in particular. Another manufacturer buys a new invention of some light kind likely to attract the public fancy, is successful in finding a multitude who will give their testers for the transiently desirable commodity, and before the fashion is out, pockets a considerable sum; the commodity was colored with a green which had arsenic in it that damaged the factory workers and the purchasers. What then? These, he contends (or does not know or care to contend), are superficial effects, which it is folly to dwell upon while we have epidemic diseases and bad government.

The first manufacturer we will suppose blameless. Is an

14

author simply on a par with him, as to the rules of production?

The author's capital is his brain-power—power of invention, power of writing. The manufacturer's capital, in fortunate cases, is being continually reproduced and increased. Here is the first grand difference between the capital which is turned into calico and the brain capital which is turned into literature. The calico scarcely varies in appropriateness of quality, no consumer is in danger of getting too much of it, and neglecting his boots, hats, and flannel-shirts in consequence. That there should be large quantities of the same sort in the calico manufacture is an advantage: the sameness is desirable, and nobody is likely to roll his person in so many folds of calico as to become a mere bale of cotton goods, and nullify his senses of hearing and touch, while his morbid passion for Manchester shirtings makes him still cry "More!" The wise manufacturer gets richer and richer, and the consumers he supplies have their real wants satisfied and no more.

Let it be taken as admitted that all legitimate social activity must be beneficial to others besides the agent. To write prose or verse as a private exercise and satisfaction is not social activity; nobody is culpable for this any more than for learning other people's verse by heart if he does not neglect his proper business in consequence. If the exercise made him sillier or secretly more self-satisfied, that, to be sure, would be a roundabout way of injuring society; for though a certain mixture of silliness may lighten existence, we have at present more than enough.

But man or woman who publishes writings inevitably assumes the office of teacher or influencer of the public mind. Let him protest as he will that he only seeks to amuse, and has no pretension to do more than while away an hour of leisure or weariness—"the idle singer of an empty day"—he can no more escape influencing the moral taste, and with it the action of the intelligence, than a setter of fashions in furniture and dress can fill the shops with his designs and leave the garniture of persons and houses unaffected by his industry.

For a man who has a certain gift of writing to say, "I

will make the most of it while the public likes my wares—as long as the market is open and I am able to supply it at a money profit—such profit being the sign of liking "—he should have a belief that his wares have nothing akin to the arsenic green in them, and also that his continuous supply is secure from a degradation in quality which the habit of consumption encouraged in the buyers may hinder them from marking their sense of by rejection; so that they complain, but pay, and read while they complain. Unless he has that belief, he is on a level with the manufacturer who gets rich by fancy-wares colored with arsenic green. He really cares for nothing but his income. He carries on authorship on the principle of the gin-palace.

And bad literature of the sort called amusing is spiritual gin.

A writer capable of being popular can only escape this social culpability by first of all getting a profound sense that literature is good-for-nothing, if it is not admirably good: he must detest bad literature too heartily to be indifferent about producing it if only other people don't detest it. And if he has this sign of the divine afflatus within him, he must make up his mind that he must not pursue authorship as a vocation with a trading determination to get rich by it. It is in the highest sense lawful for him to get as good a price as he honorably can for the best work he is capable of; but not for him to force or hurry his production, or even do over again what has already been done, either by himself or others, so as to render his work no real contribution, for the sake of bringing up his income to the fancy pitch. An author who would keep a pure and noble conscience, and with that a developing instead of degenerating intellect and taste, must cast out of his aims the aim to be rich. And therefore he must keep his expenditure low—he must make for himself no dire necessity to earn sums in order to pay bills.

In opposition to this, it is common to cite Walter Scott's case, and cry, "Would the world have got as much innocent (and therefore salutary) pleasure out of Scott, if he had not brought himself under the pressure of money-need?" I think it would—and more; but since it is impossible to prove what

would have been, I confine myself to replying that Scott was
not justified in bringing himself into a position where severe
consequences to others depended on his retaining or not retaining his mental competence.   Still less is Scott to be taken as
an example to be followed in this matter, even if it were admitted that money-need served to press at once the best and
the most work out of him; any more than a great navigator
who has brought his ship to port in spite of having taken a
wrong and perilous route, is to be followed as to his route by
navigators who are not yet ascertained to be great.

But after the restraints and rules which must guide the ac-
knowledged author, whose power of making a real contribution is ascertained, comes the consideration, how or on what
principle are we to find a check for that troublesome disposition to authorship arising from the spread of what is called
Education, which turns a growing rush of vanity and ambition into this current?   The well-taught, an increasing number, are almost all able to write essays on given themes, which
demand new periodicals to save them from lying in cold obstruction.   The ill-taught—also an increasing number—read
many books, seem to themselves able to write others surprisingly like what they read, and probably superior, since the
variations are such as please their own fancy, and such as
they would have recommended to their favorite authors : these
ill-taught persons are perhaps idle and want to give themselves "an object"; or they are short of money, and feel disinclined to get it by a commoner kind of work; or they find
a facility in putting sentences together which gives them more
than a suspicion that they have genius, which, if not very cor-
dially believed in by private confidants, will be recognized by
an impartial public; or finally, they observe that writing is
sometimes well paid, and sometimes a ground of fame or distinction, and without any use of punctilious logic, they conclude to become writers themselves.

As to these ill-taught persons, whatever medicines of a
spiritual sort can be found good against mental emptiness and
inflation—such medicines are needful for *them*.   The contempt of the world for their productions only comes after their
disease has wrought its worst effects.   But what is to be said

to the well-taught, who have such an alarming equality in their power of writing "like a scholar and a gentleman"? Perhaps they, too, can only be cured by the medicine of higher ideals in social duty, and by a fuller representation to themselves of the processes by which the general culture is furthered or impeded.

In endeavoring to estimate a remarkable writer who aimed at more than temporary influence, we have first to consider what was his individual contribution to the spiritual wealth of mankind? Had he a new conception? Did he animate long-known but *Judgments on Authors.* neglected truths with new vigor, and cast fresh light on their relation to other admitted truths? Did he impregnate any ideas with a fresh store of emotion, and in this way enlarge the area of moral sentiment? Did he by a wise emphasis here, and a wise disregard there, give a more useful or beautiful proportion to aims or motives? And even where his thinking was most mixed with the sort of mistake which is obvious to the majority, as well as that which can only be discerned by the instructed, or made manifest by the progress of things, has it that salt of a noble enthusiasm which should rebuke our critical discrimination if its correctness is inspired with a less admirable habit of feeling?

This is not the common or easy course to take in estimating a modern writer. It requires considerable knowledge of what he has himself done, as well as of what others had done before him, or what they were doing contemporaneously; it requires deliberate reflection as to the degree in which our own prejudices may hinder us from appreciating the intellectual or moral bearing of what on a first view offends us. An easier course is to notice some salient mistakes, and take them as decisive of the writer's incompetence; or to find out that something apparently much the same as what he has said in some connection not clearly ascertained, had been said by somebody else, though without great effect, until this new effect of discrediting the other's originality had shown itself as an adequate final cause: or to pronounce from the point of view of individual taste that this writer for whom regard is claimed is repulsive, wearisome, not to be borne except by those dull persons who are of a different opinion.

Elder writers who have passed into classics were doubtless treated in this easy way when they were still under the misfortune of being recent—nay, are still dismissed with the same rapidity of judgment by daring ignorance. But people who think that they have a reputation to lose in the matter of knowledge, have looked into cyclopædias and histories of philosophy or literature, and possessed themselves of the duly balanced epithets concerning the immortals. They are not left to their own unguided rashness, or their own unguided pusillanimity. And it is this sheeplike flock who have no direct impressions, no spontaneous delight, no genuine objection or self-confessed neutrality in relation to the writers become classic—it is these who are incapable of passing a genuine judgment on the living. Necessarily. The susceptibility they have kept active is a susceptibility to their own reputation for passing the right judgment, not the susceptibility to qualities in the object of judgment. Who learns to discriminate shades of color by considering what is expected of him? The habit of expressing borrowed judgments stupefies the sensibilities, which are the only foundation of genuine judgments, just as the constant reading and retailing of results from other men's observations through the microscope, without ever looking through the lens one's self, is an instruction in some truths and some prejudices, but is no instruction in observant susceptibility; on the contrary, it breeds a habit of inward seeing according to verbal statement, which dulls the power of outward seeing according to visual evidence.

On this subject, as on so many others, it is difficult to strike the balance between the educational needs of passivity or receptivity, and independent selection. We should learn nothing without the tendency to implicit acceptance; but there must clearly be a limit to such mental submission, else we should come to a stand-still. The human mind would be no better than a dried specimen, representing an unchangeable type. When the assimilation of new matter ceases, decay must begin. In a reasoned self-restraining deference there is as much energy as in rebellion; but among the less capable, one must admit that the superior energy is on the side of the rebels.   And certainly a man who dares to say that he finds an eminent classic feeble here, extravagant there, and in general overrated, may chance to give an opinion which has some genuine discrimination in it concerning a new work or a living thinker—an opinion such as can hardly ever be got from the reputed judge who is a correct echo of the most approved phrases concerning those who have been already canonized.

What is the best way of telling a story?   Since the standard must be the interest of the audience, there must be several or many good ways rather than one best.   **Story Telling.** For we get interested in the stories life presents to us through divers orders and modes of presentation.   Very commonly our first awakening to a desire of knowing a man's past or future comes from our seeing him as a stranger in some unusual or pathetic or humorous situation, or manifesting some remarkable characteristics.   We make inquiries in consequence, or we become observant and attentive whenever opportunities of knowing more may happen to present themselves without our search.   You have seen a refined face among the prisoners picking tow in jail; you afterward see the same unforgetable face in a pulpit: he must be of dull fibre who would not care to know more about a life which showed such contrasts, though he might gather his knowledge in a fragmentary and unchronological way.

Again, we have heard much, or at least something not quite common, about a man whom we have never seen, and hence we look round with curiosity when we are told that he is present; whatever he says or does before us is charged with a meaning due to our previous hearsay knowledge about him, gathered either from dialogue of which he was expressly and emphatically the subject, or from incidental remark, or from general report either in or out of print.

These indirect ways of arriving at knowledge are always the most stirring even in relation to impersonal subjects.   To see a chemical experiment gives an attractiveness to a definition of chemistry, and fills it with a significance which it would never have had without the pleasant shock of an unusual sequence such as the transformation of a solid into gas, and *vice versâ*. To see a word for the first time either as substantive or adjective in a connection where we care about knowing its complete meaning, is the way to vivify its meaning in our recollection. Curiosity becomes the more eager from the incompleteness of the first information. Moreover, it is in this way that memory works in its incidental revival of events: some salient experience appears in inward vision, and in consequence the antecedent facts are retraced from what is regarded as the beginning of the episode in which that experience made a more or less strikingly memorable part. "Ah! I remember addressing the mob from the hustings at Westminster—you wouldn't have thought that I could ever have been in such a position. Well, how I came there was in this way——"; and then follows a retrospective narration.

The modes of telling a story founded on these processes of outward and inward life derive their effectiveness from the superior mastery of images and pictures in grasping the attention—or, one might say with more fundamental accuracy, from the fact that our earliest, strongest impressions, our most intimate convictions, are simply images added to more or less of sensation. These are the primitive instruments of thought. Hence it is not surprising that early poetry took this way—telling a daring deed, a glorious achievement, without caring for what went before. The desire for orderly narration is a later, more reflective birth. The presence of the Jack in the box affects every child: it is the more reflective lad, the miniature philosopher, who wants to know how he got there.

The only stories life presents to us in an orderly way are those of our autobiography, or the career of our companions from our childhood upward, or perhaps of our own children. But it is a great art to make a connected strictly relevant narrative of such careers as we can recount from the beginning. In these cases the sequence of associations is almost sure to overmaster the sense of proportion. Such narratives *ab ovo* are summer's-day stories for happy loungers; not the cup of self-forgetting excitement to the busy who can snatch an hour of entertainment.

But the simple opening of a story with a date and necessary account of places and people, passing on quietly toward the more rousing elements of narrative and dramatic presentation, without need of retrospect, has its advantages which have to be measured by the nature of the story. Spirited narrative, without more than a touch of dialogue here and there, may be made eminently interesting, and is suited to the novelette. Examples of its charm are seen in the short tales in which the French have a mastery never reached by the English, who usually demand coarser flavors than are given by that delightful gayety which is well described by La Fontaine[1] as not anything that provokes fits of laughter, but a certain charm, an agreeable mode of handling which lends attractiveness to all subjects even the most serious. And it is this sort of gayety which plays around the best French novelettes. But the opening chapters of the " Vicar of Wakefield " are as fine as anything that can be done in this way.

Why should a story not be told in the most irregular fashion that an author's idiosyncrasy may prompt, provided that he gives us what we can enjoy? The objections to Sterne's wild way of telling "Tristram Shandy" lie more solidly in the quality of the interrupting matter than in the fact of interruption. The dear public would do well to reflect that they are often bored from the want of flexibility in their own minds. They are like the topers of "one liquor."

The exercise of a veracious imagination in historical picturing seems to be capable of a development that might help the judgment greatly with regard to present and future events. By veracious imagination, **Historic Imagination.** I mean the working out in detail of the various steps by which a political or social change was reached, using all extant evidence and supplying deficiencies by careful ana-

[1] "Je n'appelle pas gayeté ce qui excite le rire, mais un certain charme, un air agréable qu'on peut donner à toutes sortes de sujets, mesme les plus sérieux."—Preface to Fables.

logical creation. How triumphant opinions originally spread
—how institutions arose—what were the conditions of great
inventions, discoveries, or theoretic conceptions—what circumstances affecting individual lots are attendant on the decay
of long-established systems,—all these grand elements of history require the illumination of special imaginative treatment.
But effective truth in this application of art requires freedom
from the vulgar coercion of conventional plot, which is become
hardly of higher influence on imaginative representation than
a detailed "order" for a picture sent by a rich grocer to an
eminent painter—allotting a certain portion of the canvas to
a rural scene, another to a fashionable group, with a request
for a murder in the middle distance, and a little comedy to
relieve it.   A slight approximation to the veracious glimpses
of history artistically presented, which I am indicating, but applied only to an incident of contemporary life, is "Un paquet
de lettres" by Gustave Droz.   For want of such real, minute
vision of how changes come about in the past, we fall into
ridiculously inconsistent estimates of actual movements, con-
demning in the present what we belaud in the past, and pro-
nouncing impossible processes that have been repeated again
and again in the historical preparation of the very system under
which we live.   A false kind of idealization dulls our perception of the meaning in words when they relate to past events
which have had a glorious issue: for lack of comparison no
warning image rises to check scorn of the very phrases which
in other associations are consecrated.

Utopian pictures help the reception of ideas as to construc-
tive results, but hardly so much as a vivid presentation of
how results have been actually brought about, especially in
religious and social change.   And there is the pathos, the
heroism often accompanying the decay and final struggle of
old systems, which has not had its share of tragic commemo-
ration.   What really took place in and around Constantine
before, upon, and immediately after his declared conversion?
Could a momentary flash be thrown on Eusebius in his sayings and doings as an ordinary man in bishop's garments?   Or
on Julian and Libanius?   There has been abundant writing on
such great turning-points, but not such as serves to instruct

the imagination in true comparison. I want something different from the abstract treatment which belongs to grave history from a doctrinal point of view, and something different from the schemed picturesqueness of ordinary historical fiction. I want brief, severely conscientious reproductions, in their concrete incidents, of pregnant movements in the past.

The supremacy given in European cultures to the literatures of Greece and Rome has had an effect almost equal to that of a common religion in binding the Western nations together. It is foolish to be forever complaining of the consequent uniformity, as if there were an endless power of originality in the human mind. Great and precious origination must always be comparatively rare, and can only exist on condition of a wide massive uniformity. When a multitude of men have learned to use the same language in speech and writing, then and then only can the greatest masters of language arise. For in what does their mastery consist? They use words which are already a familiar medium of understanding and sympathy in such a way as greatly to enlarge the understanding and sympathy. Originality of this order changes the wild grasses into world-feeding grain. Idiosyncrasies are pepper and spices of questionable aroma.

Value in Originality.

"Is the time we live in prosaic?"—"That depends: it must certainly be prosaic to one whose mind takes a prosaic stand in contemplating it."—"But it is precisely the most poetic minds that most groan over the vulgarity of the present, its degenerate sensibility to beauty, eagerness for materialistic explanation, noisy triviality."—"Perhaps they would have had the same complaint to make about the age of Elizabeth, if, living then, they had fixed their attention on its more sordid elements, or had been subject to the grating influence of its every-day meannesses, and had sought refuge from them in

To the Prosaic all Things are Prosaic.

the contemplation of whatever suited their taste in a former age."

We get our knowledge of perfect Love by glimpses and in fragments chiefly—the rarest only among us knowing what it is to worship and caress, reverence and cher-**"Dear Relig-ious Love."** ish, divide our bread and mingle our thoughts at one and the same time, under inspiration of the same object. Finest aromas will so often leave the fruits to which they are native and cling elsewhere, leaving the fruit empty of all but its coarser structure!

In the times of national mixture when modern Europe was, as one may say, a-brewing, it was open to a man who did not like to be judged by the Roman law, to choose **We Make our own Precedents.** which of certain other codes he would be tried by. So, in our own times, they who openly adopt a higher rule than their neighbors, do thereby make active choice as to the laws and precedents by which they shall be approved or condemned, and thus it may happen that we see a man morally pilloried for a very customary deed, and yet having no right to complain, inasmuch as in his foregoing deliberative course of life he had referred himself to the tribunal of those higher conceptions, before which such a deed is without question condemnable.

Tolerance first comes through equality of struggle, as in the case of Arianism and Catholicism in the early times—Valens, Eastern and Arian, Valentinian, Western and **Birth of Tolerance.** Catholic, alike publishing edicts of tolerance; or it comes from a common need of relief from an oppressive predominance, as when James II. published his Act of Tolerance toward non-Anglicans, being forced into liberality toward the Dissenters by the need to get it for the Catholics. Community of interest is the root of justice; community of suffering, the root of pity; community of joy, the root of love.

CPSIA information can be obtained
at www.ICGtesting.com
Printed in the USA
BVHW072034210721
612411BV00010B/2849